BY ROYAL DESIGN

History Never Died. It Just Waited to Strike.

NORBERT E. REICH

SWEETSPIRE LITERATURE
MANAGEMENT

To Benjamin: Welcome

TABLE OF CONTENTS

PROLOGUE

Berlin, October 1944

RAINDROPS CLUNG TO THE ATTIC WINDOW PANES of the elegant residence on the Pariser Platz in Berlin. Usually, all the shutters were closed; they had been for many months. However, this morning, the old, bald man had decided to look out of his study again at the square below. He placed the pistol on the card table and walked to the window. It was a windy day, and scattered gray clouds were rapidly moving through the sky, moving with purpose, as if they knew their destination. A light rain was falling, the kind you see in autumn. It would not last, he knew. Although it was only six a.m., the square buzzed with army personnel and vehicles. The red, white, and black swastika flags lined the square waved briskly in the wind. The older man raised a hand and stroked his gray mustache, a gesture and a habit he often used in deep thought. His dark-brown eyes moistened, tears quickly formed, and they found their way down his wrinkled face. Now the older man did not see the tanks, the soldiers, the Nazi flags. He saw a beautiful square lined by lime trees and filled with sunshine. He saw a lively crowd chatting freely, enjoying life. He saw

The Brandenburg Gate with the statue of the goddess Victoria.

The older man was a Jew. He was Joshua Alan Bergman, a German and a Berliner, an artist and a poet of great renown. More German than most Germans, more Berliner than most Berliners. He had lived in this house since birth and would not leave it. His home was located in the heart of Germany's capital and was the meeting place of all of Berlin's political and cultural elite. Everyone enjoyed Josh's company. They respected his directness; they appreciated his Berliner *"Schnauze."* The Berliners adored him, and he loved them. Even the Nazis had to accept him, so great was his popularity.

Then he witnessed the crimes and atrocities committed by the Nazis, and he and his wife, Martha, struggled over the decision to leave the country. In the end, they had decided to stay. Berlin was their home. Germany was their country. But as time passed, he could no longer live with the present and tolerate what he saw. He withdrew. He closed the shutters of his villa and stayed inside. But he knew. Yes, he knew.

For months, he had planned it. He had agonized over it. He had changed his mind often over the months, the last few weeks, and days. But he saw no other solution, no other way to escape. No other way to tell the world, no other way to tell his wife. No other way to tell his unborn child, for his young wife was pregnant with their firstborn. He closed the shutters and pulled the curtains. Then he turned and walked towards the card table. He sat back in the plush leather chair in his study, in the attic of his home. He hesitated but for a moment. He put the muzzle of the 9 mm Luger in his mouth. He pulled the trigger.

Martha Bergman had been admitted to the delivery ward of the Charité Hospital in Berlin as an obstetrical emergency. Dr. Sauerbruch, a family friend and chief of staff, himself had called the hospital needs to arrange for a bed. Martha had gone into premature labor. Only hours before had she learned of her husband's suicide. The delivery went without a complication. Sauerbruch delivered a healthy baby boy.

Martha Bergman had spent the last several weeks of her pregnancy with her mother at their summer home on the Wannsee, one of many lakes in Berlin. Josh had called daily and visited every weekend. She had no idea; he gave her no clue. Why would he do it? But she knew. She knew these past years had changed Berlin, Germany, and her husband. He had become difficult, withdrawn. They no longer enjoyed the lively Berlin, all the parties with all the politicians, artists, and cultural elite of Berlin. It all changed after 1933. The Jews, their friends, were all taken away, away to places unknown. She had heard all the stories. It appeared to be a bad dream, a nightmare. Was it true? Their own lives had not been affected. Josh and she could come and go as they pleased. Yet Josh sensed it; he withdrew. They stayed at Wannsee or at their house in the city. Here, it was the house of a recluse. No visitors, no light. She remembered. He would draw the curtains and close the shutters. He wanted no part of the outside world. It was why she had moved away with her mother to their summer home at Wannsee. She was carrying his first child. She had to take care of it.

She knew Josh was greatly troubled by the conflict. He was a faithful German, a Berliner, and a Jew. His people, his Germans, were killing his blood people, his Jews. It became a conflict too great for him. At first, he tried to ignore it. Ironically, his house was in the center of it all, at the Pariser Platz, right next to the Brandenburg Gate. She knew how much Josh struggled. She knew the depth of his despair. Their child would be born into a world of no hope, a world at war. Yet his suicide had surprised her. It should not have. Josh was an artist, an idealist. He could not deal well with the realities of life, but she had to. She was going to be a mother now. She had obligations and responsibilities, and she had a child to take care of.

Martha Bergman knew that once Josh was gone, the Nazis would show her and her child no mercy. They had tolerated them because Josh's reputation was so excellent. Not only did his Berliners love him, but all Germans and much of the world respected him. The Nazis had no choice but to tolerate him.

Now he is dead. What will happen now, she had thought. I need to protect, to save my child. It will only be days, probably hours, before my child and I will be treated as any other Jews. Deported. We will be taken to a concentration camp, and we will be left to die. I must act, and I must act now. This is what Josh always wanted: to save the Jews. All I can save now is our child.

Martha had a decision and had to make it now, here, at the hospital. This was her only chance. It was the most difficult decision a mother could ever make. She needed support, she needed her husband, and she needed her God.

Her husband was gone, but not his memories, not his dreams. And God was still with her, because she believed deeply in God, in the Jewish faith. She was a Jew first, a German and Berliner second. And she did it. It only took seconds. It happened between the nurses' shifts at eleven p.m. The nurses on the three to eleven shift were about to leave, and the new shift was ready to take over. It was report time. The nurses of the old shift would report to the nurses who had just arrived, what was going on, who did well, who needed what, a routine which never changed. That was her opportunity, fifteen minutes, but she did not need that much time, she only needed seconds. And she did it, urging her sore and weakened body to the task, tearing her priceless child from her. No one would ever know.

CHAPTER I

Napa, California, September

H E LAY CAMOUFLAGED AND MOTIONLESS ON the ground. His face touched the warm, rich soil. He savored the scent of the succulent grapes above, which were hanging heavily on the symmetrical rows of vines. The sun had just disappeared over the mountains to his left. The man was alone. However, he knew others were nearby. At least two of them were standard procedure. He did not know their names or their faces. He wore a dark-green jumpsuit, the kind paratroopers wore. Underneath, he wore an Armani tuxedo and black Gucci shoes. My wedding uniform, he thought with a smile.

It was twilight now. He could hear the festive crowd only two hundred yards ahead. He lifted his head. He had an unobstructed view of the stage where the father would give away the bride. He noticed the many guests beginning to take their seats. With hands covered in latex surgeon's gloves, he removed the small patch of grass that covered the hole he had dug earlier. He pulled out the black, airtight plastic case and removed the components to the Savage-Anschutz .223 sniper rifle. Practiced hands assembled it.

He removed the Leupold optical infrared sight and fitted it. He stroked the cool metal of the barrel. At this time, memories of his father returned to him when he had shown him how to fire a hunting rifle. The same rules applied in this dark trade: one shot, one to kill. He opened the chamber and loaded one bullet. He placed the Savage-Anschutz next to him.

There was almost complete darkness, and he could feel his heart pounding against the soft ground. Adrenaline was kicking in. He lived for these moments. Suddenly, the music began: Wagner's wedding march. He nestled both elbows on the grass between the vines and brought the sniper stock to his cheek. He monitored his breathing. He waited.

Then he saw the couple, at first just their heads because the crowd hid the rest. He watched them, arm-in-arm, approaching the well-lit stage. He would only have a second. Steady fingertips adjusted the scope for windage and elevation. His target moved grotesquely in the infrared glow.

The father of the bride did the expected and stopped at the center of the elevated stage, which was lavishly decorated with red roses. And when he did, three shots almost simultaneously thundered through the calm valley, blowing the head from the Arab's torso, whirling it through the still night air, and landing it four feet in front of the stunned bridesmaids. Blood, bone, skin, and brain fragments spattered the expensive designer gown of the dead man's daughter. The torso was lying prone in a pool of blood amidst the many rose petals spread over the stage. But the body did not lie still. It twitched. It lasted a second, maybe two.

The three assassins had not used silencers. On the contrary, they wanted noise. They wanted pandemonium, confusion, hysteria, and chaos to make their escape easy. But at first there was only an echoing silence. The music had stopped. The crowd was stunned. The silence lasted for a breath. Then what the assassins had expected set in, all hell broke loose, screaming, crying, calls for help, and blind running to get away. Women kicked off their shoes to run faster. Men grasped their children. All seemed to be heading to their cars in the parking lot. Then one of the killers pulled the main switch of the electric box. The vineyard was engulfed in darkness.

The camouflaged figure slowly got to his knees, placing the gun and scope into the plastic case and the hole. As he stood, he removed his jumpsuit and put it in the hole. Finally, he removed the powdered surgeon gloves and tossed them in with the weapon. Then he replaced the square of grass. He gently stepped on the patch to pad it down. He did not have to mark the spot. He would remember, and when the time was right, he would return to retrieve the gear.

Dressed in his black tuxedo, he strolled toward the wedding grounds through the rows of vines. He stopped for a second, picked a grape, and tasted it. Yes, he thought, California would have another good year of Cabernets. When he reached the scene of chaos and confusion, he joined the rest of the crowd and ran to the parking lot to retrieve the car that had been left there for him.

He drove directly to the San Francisco airport. Before reaching the Golden Gate Bridge, he pulled off the highway into a gas station to use the men's room. Here, the young, athletic man removed his tuxedo and put on his favorite attire: loose khaki pants, brown sandals, and a blue, short-sleeved Bahamian shirt. He could not wait to return home to Miami Beach, to his comfortable apartment on South Beach.

Innsbruck, Austria, September

He stood by the floor-to-ceiling window of his office on the fifth floor of the two-hundred-year-old fieldstone building. Statues of Austrian royalty buttressed large arched windows and portals. He often sought solitude and privacy in his office. Today was no exception.

Bright sunshine filled the room and illuminated the portrait prominently adorned on one of the wood-paneled walls. It was a seventeenth-century painting of the man he had been named after, Emperor Maximillian I. Max looked pensively out at the street scene below. In the distance, the rugged Alps were blending with the sky. A smile drifted across his lips.

He walked across the worn, antique red carpet covering the old wooden floor. When he reached his desk, he looked once more at the portrait on the wall. Some of the bright hues of oil had faded since the seventeenth century. He noticed the firmness of his ancestor's mouth, the eyes piercing like a hawk's. That chin could lead crusades. Today, the portrait was different; it appeared to come to life.

The emperor seemed proud, more intense, as if he was assured that destiny was yet to come. Then their eyes met. Max did not look away. He was communicating with his forefather, and Max felt a chill. He felt the sunlit nod of approval. Max was never superstitious or believed in seances, so this was a strange exchange. He sat in the chair and leaned back. He touched the large ring on his index finger. It was the ring all his forefathers had worn. It was the ring of the Habsburg dynasty. It bore his family's crest.

Max placed his hands behind his neck and stretched. Then he closed his eyes and let out a deep sigh. When it was time, he picked up the telephone and made the call. The familiar voice answered.

"William," he said, "old friend, how are you? I may have good news for you. I think I have found him, finally the man we have been looking for."

He braced for the staccato of questions he knew would come. They spun down the wires from Berlin.

"You have? I cannot believe it. Are you certain? Who is he? Where is he? You need to tell me all about him. We need to be sure. We cannot make a mistake."

"William, I agree, but all in due time. You know I can't talk about him to you now, over the telephone. Next week, on Wednesday, I will be in Berlin. We will have dinner then. How about eight o'clock at your favorite restaurant?"

"Yes, of course. Max, you are right as always. I will see you then. *Auf Wiedersehen.*"

The call ended. Maximillian von Habsburg put down the telephone receiver and looked out of his office window in the Altstadt of Innsbruck. He looked at the mountains in the distance. Now he again had a smile on his face. From this city, five hundred years ago, the Germanic people had ruled much of Europe. Over seventy years ago, they could have ruled the world from Berlin. This time, maybe, just maybe. Sunlight slanted across the seventeenth-century portrait, then moved on.

Boston, September

As a rule, Peter Schneider had no trouble sleeping. He routinely worked a long day, leaving the house at six a.m. and returning in time for supper. This was always served promptly at seven p.m. His days were structured, planned well in advance, and run efficiently. Every minute was accounted for. That was the way it had to be. There was never enough time. He had learned that long ago, when he first started medical school.

Schneider had slept poorly last night. He had tossed and turned for hours until he finally decided to move to the guest bedroom to allow his wife Katie some rest. Schneider had much on his mind these days, and the fact that it was the second Wednesday of the month, the day of the monthly Executive Committee meeting at the hospital, had not helped.

Schneider showered and quickly dressed in a dark-blue blazer, light-gray slacks, a white button-down shirt, a red and blue striped tie, and dark-brown loafers. He then walked to the kitchen of his colonial-style home and poured himself a cup of decaffeinated coffee.

At 6:35 a.m., the black BMW sedan pulled into the parking space marked "Chief of Staff" at the large teaching hospital in Boston. Peter Schneider reached for his leather briefcase in the passenger seat. The case had been a gift from his wife upon completing his cardiology fellowship at the Mayo Clinic more than thirty years ago. He stepped out of the car, pushed the remote control to lock it, and walked briskly to the door marked "Doctors' Entrance."

Innsbruck, Austria, September

At the exact moment, almost four thousand miles to the east, the well-dressed, distinguished-looking gentleman was finishing his lunch at the Goldener Adler restaurant in the Altstadt of Innsbruck.

He loved to eat out and always dressed for the occasion. Today he wore his favorite suit was traditional Tyrolean clothing: a deep green Loden jacket with a brown suede-trimmed collar. The pants were dark-brown knickers. The knee socks were hunter green, and the shoes were nut brown.

Although Maximillian von Habsburg had finished his favorite dish of roast saddle of venison with red wine sauce, potato dumplings, and red cabbage with apples, he was already thinking about dinner with his friend William tonight. What would he order, the trout or the calf's liver? He knew he would have plenty of time to think about it on his drive to Berlin. Max settled the bill with cash and left the customary small tip. He left the crowded restaurant, strolling, studying his surroundings. As he entered the hotel's small lobby, he smiled at the young blonde receptionist, tipped his Tyrolean hat, and stepped onto the cobblestone street. Max crossed the narrow, busy Herzog Friedrichstrasse and entered the building directly opposite. He took the elevator to his office on the fifth floor. Max never took the stairs.

Max had returned to his office to prepare for his Berlin drive and dinner with William. His butler had already packed his suitcase and placed it in the trunk of his car. However, Max had to change his clothing because he knew his Tyrolean attire was inappropriate for his visit to Berlin.

Max left his office and walked to the parking garage outside the pedestrian-only Altstadt. He passed many of the buildings his forefathers had built, which was why he loved this town. From here and from Vienna, his family ruled much of Europe and parts of the world. Today, he felt sure that the Habsburgs would rule again. This time, it would not be Europe. This time, it would be the world. That was the Habsburg destiny. That was God's will.

When Max reached the garage on Maria-Theresienstrasse and his car on the second floor, he pushed the remote control to open the locks and lower the top of his brand new Porsche Carrera. It was a beautiful day, and he intended to enjoy it.

He removed his suit jacket, fitted himself behind the wheel, and carefully placed his coat in the seat next to him. He turned the key and listened with satisfaction to the insistent hum of the turbo engine. The drive to Berlin was long, but Max loved to drive.

He left the city of Innsbruck and merged onto the highway. Munich was less than 50 miles away, and Berlin was another 360 miles. He should be able to do the entire trip in seven hours, traffic permitting, or maybe six hours. After all, he was driving a Porsche. He pulled his new car into the passing lane and sped for Berlin.

Miami Beach, September

It was only seven a.m., but he could feel the humidity since it was Miami Beach in September. Dressed in shorts and black running shoes, he glided down the long driveway of Portofino Towers, his fashionable apartment building on South Beach, and headed out for his daily run. He began at a slow trot but rapidly lengthened his steps. By the time he reached the park, he was cruising at his pace.

His stride was that of an athlete, a true runner. His deeply tanned chest glistened with perspiration, yet his breathing was slow and controlled. He ran past Government Cut, the narrow waterway that led to Miami's harbor. Here, fashion models were already posing for photo shoots. He was oblivious. He had a single purpose: to prepare for a marathon.

He crossed the boardwalk and reached the beach. Now he was in full stride. His breathing was controlled, just as his father had taught him: breathe in through the nose, out through the mouth. Neophytes spend all their energy breathing. Experts control it. His eyes were focused ten yards ahead, as his father had taught him. When he was young, they often ran together. They were not joggers. They were runners. His father had said there is a difference; you can tell by the breathing, by the stride.

Other people were jogging on the beach this morning, as they were every morning. There were the beach volleyball courts, planes overhead advertising restaurants, bars, and shows, and beautiful women spread on the sand, some topless. He never noticed. However, they noticed him. He was six feet two inches and weighed 180 pounds. The shape of a true athlete is muscular, not overbuilt. He was in full stride, a sight to see.

He stopped to adjust his shoelaces when he reached the halfway mark, four miles from home. As he did, someone stood over him. She said, "Tired already?"

He smiled and looked up. This woman was beautiful, slim, and toned. He stood up, wiping the perspiration from his face.

She looked at him and smiled. "If you can keep up, follow me."

She bolted. He followed, at first several paces behind, using the distance to admire her lean body, her long legs. Sorry, Dad, he thought, I lost my focus. Won't let it happen again. I promise. As they reached the volleyball courts, he pulled even with her. He glanced at her. She was breathing in through her nose, out of her mouth. Controlled, a true runner, he thought. They ran off the beach and onto the boardwalk at Government Cut. When they reached Smith and Wollensky's Steak House, her pace eased. She was walking when they entered the park in front of his apartment building. At the third bench, she stopped and turned to face him. She had long black hair in a ponytail, blue-green eyes, full lips, and a beautiful smile.

"That was fun. You really kept up." He smiled, still breathing hard. "Yeah," he said. "That was fun. We'll have to do it again. I really enjoyed the run with you. What's your name anyhow? You're a real runner."

"Thanks, I guess that's a compliment," she laughed. "I'm Nicole. But before we run again, you need more training and serious coaching. Next time I don't want you to breathe so hard," she said, smiling.

"That's a deal. I'm always willing to learn, so let's not waste time and begin today. How about discussing your training techniques at lunch? Damn, I can't. I plain forgot. My company wants me to go to Europe this afternoon. It's a short trip, just a few days. I'll be back on Tuesday. Let's have lunch then."

She thought momentarily, hesitating as if checking her schedule in her head.

"Sure," she said, flashing another smile. How about around one? You pick the place, and since you're the student and I'm the teacher, I'll buy a deal?"

"Fine, let's meet at 'Prime Fish' on Collins." "And you are?" Her blue-green eyes sparkled. "Adam."

"Okay, Adam. See you on Tuesday, at one."

Nicole Amy Jefferson left Adam Bergman in the park, where he went through his routine post-run stretch exercises. She entered the lobby of the South Pointe apartment building, the older apartment tower that shared its grounds and amenities with the newer Portofino Tower.

"Bonjour, Pierre," she said to the guard behind the desk in the airy lobby of the building.

"Bonjour, Nicole." He went back to his newspaper.

Nicole entered the elevator. The door closed, and Nicole leaned against the glass wall and closed her eyes. Finally, she had done it; she had met him. In a few days, she would have lunch with him.

For weeks, she had watched him in the parking garage, Marina, and Neam's market. But never an opportunity, never a chance. Was he blind? They were at the pool together. He never noticed. He came, read his books, listened to music, and talked on his cell phone, never looking or glancing. Now she'd gotten his attention. What had happened? She had made the first move. She thought there was nothing wrong with being aggressive, not if you really want it.

She entered her sparse but well-decorated apartment. She went first to the bathroom, removed her sports bra, shoes, and shorts, and stepped into the shower. She let the hot water stream over her exhausted body. She had run hard to impress him, and she felt it now. She got out and dried herself. What to wear? I want this man; I want to excite him. Should I be subtle, should I be suggestive? She decided understated elegance would be the way to go and chose a Prada shift. The dress, she knew, accentuated every line of her body. No makeup, natural beauty, that's what his kind of man appreciates. She put the dress aside, chose her shoes, a bracelet, and a purse. She could not wait until next Tuesday. She wanted to be ready now; she had waited too long. She was like a young schoolgirl anticipating her first date. Now she picked up her Gucci purse and put it on her dresser with the other items she had chosen for her special date. The NAA Guardian .32 caliber pocket pistol was an uncompromising presence, a reminder of her work as a CIA case officer. She pulled it out of her bag, then hesitated. Lethal force protocols required her to go armed at all times, a thigh holster on an evening dress, perhaps. But with him? She placed the handgun into the top drawer of her nightstand adjacent to her four-poster bed. This job would not require violence. It was a routine assignment. After all, she smiled, I am not involved in a plot to change the world. She laughed out loud at the thought.

CHAPTER II

Berlin, September

OH, THIS IS A FLOWER, HE thought, leaning to smell the fragrance of the deep-pink rose. He had spilled a bit of his wine as he bent over. Damn. He didn't like to waste things, although he could afford to buy the vineyard if he chose. He was Crown Prince William Frederick von Hohenzollern, the present head of the house of the Hohenzollerns, the great-grandson of Emperor William II, the last Emperor of the Holy Roman Empire of German States. He straightened and continued his stroll through the rose garden of his expansive estate in the Grunewald in Berlin. His family had owned this property in what was now the most fashionable suburb of Berlin for generations, ever since one of his forefathers, the Elector Joachim II, had pronounced Berlin a Lutheran city and promptly confiscated all of the Catholic Church's property, including its vast land holdings. Joachim had then built himself a royal hunting lodge, the Jagdschloss Grunewald, located not far from where William was walking.

"The year was 1542, I think," he mused, "a long time ago."

He had finished lunch, a freshly caught trout fried in butter and garnished with cucumbers, served as always by his butler Heinrich on the veranda of the palace. Although it was a weekday, William was at home, as he was every day. William did not work. Actually, William never had to work. His family was enormously wealthy. To keep himself occupied, he had appointed himself chairman and trustee of the large charity his mother had founded just after the war. However, over the last several months, he had begun to find his responsibilities and handed his position to his younger sister, Charlotte. And he had more important work to do now.

Though he would be fifty-nine years old next month, he looked much younger. He had complete, curly black hair and brown-green eyes. He stood six feet and had a slim, carefully nourished body. William had never married but was very active socially, and many Berlin newspapers had proclaimed him Berlin's, if not Germany's, most eligible bachelor. William was an amateur athlete and worked out regularly. He rose at seven-thirty each morning, had a cup of decaffeinated coffee, and immediately proceeded to the gym in the basement of the palace for a ninety-minute weight-lifting session with his personal trainer.

William believed in physical fitness. Unlike most of his forefathers, he had an athletic build. He worked at it, chest and triceps one day, biceps and back muscles the next. The third day was a shoulder workout, but abdomen exercises and stretching were a daily routine. He did not take a day off. Every day, he also ran for four miles along the beautiful paths of the Grunewald. He loved to run through the woods and often extended his runs to five or six miles.

William was again thinking of last week's phone call with his friend Max. He took another sip from his wineglass. He could not wait to meet with his friend. William was an impatient man. He hated to wait.

He continued slowly through his manicured rose garden. He insisted that his staff cut fresh roses each morning and place them on his breakfast table. He took great pride in his roses. Although the gardeners cared for the estate, William liked to help cultivate the roses. He would take a glass of white wine each afternoon and walk through his garden. He would always carry a pair of shears to trim his favorite blooms. It was a time to be alone, reflect, and admire his estate's beauty. It was located right within the Grunewald itself, a large expanse of woodlands and lakes.

The Hohenzollern estate was situated on thirty-five acres. It had a large heated swimming pool, two tennis courts, one lit, stables, and the palace. It was a forty-room home built in the eighteen hundreds of stone and marble. It was furnished with precious antiques and extensive artwork, which many of Berlin's famous museums often asked to exhibit. William was always happy to accommodate them.

As he was growing up after the war, he had experienced none of the hardships that most Berliners had to endure. In the early postwar years, his mother took him and his sister to Seefeld, a small Austrian town at the German border. They lived there until the children became of school age, and then the family moved back to the estate in the Grunewald.

William had fond memories of Seefeld, and he often returned. It was one of his favorite winter resorts. His best friend, Max, lived only fifteen minutes away in Innsbruck. Although they were born only a couple of months apart, Max had become like a brother to him, like an older brother. This was because Max always knew what to do. Even as children, William had followed him unthinkingly.

Whenever William went to Seefeld, Max would join him, and they would stay at their favorite hotel, the Klosterhof, in the center of town. William booked the same suite, the Kirche Suite, which had been part of the old monastery adjacent to the medieval church.

He strolled through his garden, sipping his white wine, and wondered what the man Max had chosen was like. William knew that this man had to be just right and have all the qualities he and the other nobles had decided this man had to possess for their mission to succeed. Ultimately, everyone would have to agree on this, all the others, not just the nobles. But that was Max's job; he was the matchmaker. After all, the Habsburgs have always been known to prefer marriages to war as a means of expanding their empire. *Bella gerant alii, tu, felix Austria, nube.* "Let others wage war, you happy Austria, marry." That was the Habsburg motto.

They were so different, the Hohenzollerns and the Habsburgs: the latter preferred weddings, the former wars. The Hohenzollerns had fought wars since the very beginning of their empire, when Emperor Sigismund gave them the Mark Brandenburg, a 10,000-square-mile wilderness of sand and scrub, forest and swamp in the farthest corner of the Holy Roman Empire, at the beginning of the 15th century. And they continued to fight for almost 500 years when their reign over Germany and parts of Europe finally ended with their defeat in World War I, and when William's great-grandfather abdicated the throne and fled to Holland. However, this time they would not fight a war. William would let Max do it the Habsburg way this time, at least for a while.

Boston, September

Dr. Peter Schneider entered the building and quickly walked toward the staircase. Though his office was on the sixth floor, he always took the stairs. This was particularly important this morning, because he'd missed his early morning run. The day wasn't beginning the way he wanted. Worst of all, there was the meeting of the Medical Executive Committee. Schneider loathed those meetings. The committee comprised all the chairpersons of each hospital department, the hospital's chief executive, the chief of staff, and the medical director. They all saw the monthly meeting as an opportunity to tell everyone how clever, skillful, and wonderful they were. Ten egos, each bigger than the next.

Schneider entered his office on the sixth floor of the hospital. Because of low occupancy rates, some hospital rooms had been converted into administrative offices three years ago. Not much work had been done for the conversion; very little money had been spent. Schneider's office was a hospital room. It was white, it was sterile. The bed had been removed, and a Formica desk had replaced it. The oxygen wall outlets and the suction device were still in place, as was the curtain doctors drew when they examined their patients. Peter had never bothered to decorate. A purple, five foot partition separated him from his secretary, Mary Ann.

Mary Ann was an attractive redhead in her early forties. She smiled at Peter and handed him the day's itinerary. It routinely included the names and room numbers of the hospitalized patients he needed to see and the many administrative meetings he had to attend. But today, as on every second Wednesday of the month, his itinerary was short. One of the other cardiologists would attend to his patients, and Schneider never scheduled more than three meetings on these Wednesdays. He reached into his briefcase and removed the agenda for today's Medical Executive Committee meeting and last month's meeting minutes. Then he left his office to head for the meeting in Conference Room C on the third floor of the large physician's office building that abutted the hospital.

The physicians referred to the third floor, somewhat resentfully, as "mahogany row." There was plush carpeting, expensive, heavy wood furniture, and large offices with bay windows for the administrative staff. There were secretaries, administrative assistants, VPs of this, and VPs of that.

Navigating the deeply carpeted hall toward Conference Room C, he glanced at the day's agenda. It was mercifully short. It usually was this time of the year. He leaned on the heavy door to the conference room and noticed that all the seats were filled but for his at the head of the long table.

The meeting began. Voices droned about this study and that budget, and Schneider's thoughts quickly drifted and focused once more on the changes he wanted to make in his career.

Though distracted, Schneider managed to get through the agenda in less than forty-five minutes. It is evident that everyone was anxious to leave, attend to their patients, and take the afternoon off. No office hours today for most of the committee members, it was Wednesday. It was a beautiful September morning, and many had tee times to get to. They had reviewed and approved the minutes of the previous month's meeting. Each department head had given his report. The chairmen of the Utilization Committee and the Quality Assurance Committee had also reported briefly. Since no new business was on the agenda, Schneider was about to call for adjournment.

Just then, Dr. Paul Gallagher, chief of surgery, interrupted. In his usual curt and aloof manner, Gallagher again began to complain about the availability of the operating rooms, as he did at every meeting. Gallagher liked operating first thing in the morning, as did most other surgeons. Since only a limited number of rooms, OR nurses, and anesthesiologists were available, not everyone could begin surgery at seven a.m. The scheduling of operating rooms had been an item of contention, and more often of heated discussion, for as long as Schneider could remember. Gallagher had always favored the seniority system, where the most senior surgeons had first pick. He did so because no other staff surgeon enjoyed the tenure he did. But when Schneider took over the post of chief of staff, he instituted a system based on rotation. That's when Schneider became Gallagher's enemy.

Today, Gallagher was irate. Soon, civil conversation turned to heated discussion, anger, and finally a shouting match. Ignoring everyone else in the room, Gallagher, at the top of his lungs, called for a change in the hospital's leadership and the medical staff. He demanded the resignations of the CEO, Tom Peterson, and Schneider. Everyone fell silent.

The strained silence was cut short by the musical sound of Gallagher's beeper. He picked up a telephone on a side table and listened for a second or two.

"They need me in the O.R., stat. A ruptured abdominal aortic aneurysm was just admitted from the ER. I've got to go."

"That damned Gallagher," Tom Peterson shouted after the surgeon had left. "We're all getting sick and tired of his tricks." Schneider decided to end the meeting. He inquired whether there was any new business to discuss. There was none. The meeting adjourned, and everyone left the conference room in haste. But they all knew that it would all happen again, at the next monthly meeting of the Medical Executive Committee, hospital leaders, the decision-makers, the cream of the crop of the medical staff.

This was not Peter Schneider's day—no run in the morning, then the infighting at the meeting. A colleague asks him to resign, and doctors are turning against doctors. Now he had seen it all. This is he thought, "The time has come, maybe now I should get out. They have won. The government and the other third-party payers, the insurance companies, have succeeded. They have pitted one physician against the next. They have divided and conquered. They have succeeded in their policy of not paying for and not delivering necessary healthcare, care that the people needed and had paid for.

He needed to clear his head and go for a run. He returned to his office and instructed Mary Ann to cancel all his meetings. He took the stairs to the parking lot, got into his car, and drove home to retrieve his running gear.

It was close to noon as he ran along the Charles River. Now, he could relax, think, and certainly retire. He would turn fifty-nine years of age soon. He had invested wisely. His children were on their own, and he and Katie could move to that cabin in Vermont, which they had owned for years. They could live in comfort, visit the kids, and enjoy life.

Yet, there was a voice that said no. As he ran, it became clearer with each step: he needed time, time to think, time to talk to Katie, time to speak to the children, time to speak to himself, so he decided. He was going to take a leave of absence. He had been invited to Berlin to lecture at the World Congress on Health and Education. He would go to Berlin, and that's where he would decide.

CHAPTER III

Innsbruck - Berlin, September

THE RED PORSCHE HAD REACHED THE stretch of the Autobahn south of Potsdam where there was no speed limit. Max applied firm pressure to the accelerator, moved into the far-left lane of the eight-lane highway, and watched the speedometer climb to 200 kilometers per hour. Though the day was bright, he switched on the high beams and settled into his seat.

Along much of the drive from Innsbruck, Max had thought about William. They had first met in 1950 in Kitzbuehel, one of Austria's finest ski resorts. They had met in ski school over the Christmas holidays. William's mother, Sophia, had enrolled her son in the same class Max's mother, Theresa, had placed Max. They were only six then, and over the ten-day holiday, they quickly became friends, as only children can do. Max's mother and William's mother also grew close. Both of them were widows. Both had lost their husbands in the war. Their backgrounds were also remarkably similar. Theresa was of direct Lorraine descent and had married into the Habsburg family, who were former rulers of Austria and much of Europe and parts of the world. Her husband had been the grandson of Emperor Franz Joseph, the last Habsburg emperor. Sophia also was of royal descent.

Her parents had come to Berlin from Königsberg, the former capital of East Prussia. Her son William was heir to the Hohenzollern Empire.

After meeting in Kitzbuehel, the two boys remained close friends and visited each other often. When college arrived, both decided to study together. First, they went to Heidelberg. They then spent two semesters at Oxford, until William decided to return to Berlin to finish his studies there. Max stayed at Oxford, but they would still see each other at every opportunity.

Max's Porsche was now entering that portion of Autobahn 115 that leads right through the splendid Grunewald forest. This stretch of highway is straight; in the past, it had been part of an automobile racing circuit. To Berliners, the road here was known simply as the Avus. Max was just minutes from his destination, the restaurant Schildkroete on the Uhlandstrasse. He had made good time and still had an hour before his dinner date with William. He parked his Porsche along the central strip of Berlin's fashionable avenue, the Kudamm, and headed towards one of the cafes along the boulevard. It was a beautiful, warm summer evening, and he sat at one of the many tables along the sidewalk.

Berlin, September

William finished his Pinot Grigio glass and returned through the rose garden to the house. He instructed the butler to prepare one of the many guestrooms for Prince Maximillian von Habsburg, who would be spending the night. He then climbed the stairs to his bedroom suite to take his customary after-lunch nap, a luxury he had instituted since his retirement from the family charity. Precisely two hours later, at four-thirty p.m., he rose, showered, and dressed in a double-breasted blue blazer adorned with the crest of Brandenburg, a light blue Armani shirt, no tie, khaki pants, and dark brown Gucci loafers. Although the Schildkroete is quite a casual restaurant, many Germans still find it proper to wear a jacket for dinner, and William was no exception.

He called Heinrich and instructed him to have the chauffeur bring the Mercedes limousine to the front of the palace, for he would not be driving himself tonight. William drove only his Ferrari. He knew tonight would be an occasion for celebration, and he and Max enjoyed their liquor.

Though the drive from the estate would take less than thirty minutes, William planned to leave early. He had a stop to make and wanted to be the first at the restaurant to greet his old friend.

Stepping into the limousine, he asked the chauffeur to stop at the small tobacco store near the Gendarmenmarkt. Though neither he nor Max smoked as a habit, both enjoyed a cigar on special occasions. Both could afford the best Cuban, yet they preferred the Padrón, a cigar they had seen years ago while vacationing together in Miami, Florida. Driving from the Miami airport to Miami Beach, where William kept an apartment, they'd gotten lost in the Cuban section and had stopped at a small cigar shop. Both had a Cuban coffee and a Padrón there. Ever since, this had been their cigar. When William returned to Berlin, he asked the tobacco store owner near the Gendarmenmarkt to keep Padrons on hand. William did not want them at home. That was too tempting.

The proprietor of the Schildkroete knew William well. He greeted William warmly and showed him to his table in the back. The place was crowded. The decor was heavy wooden tables and chairs, with no tablecloths. Three well-dressed men were having a glass of beer at the small bar. They were engaged in an animated discussion, but one recognized William.

"Prince, Prince, what do you think about this female candidate for the U.S. presidency? She kept all of America's secrets on her private server for all to see."

The man was obviously quite drunk, but William stopped to answer him anyway. He loved interacting with his people, his Berliners.

"I must confess that I don't know all the facts."

"Well, that's okay, Prince, no one does. The lady herself does not remember what was classified, secret information. Not remembering, I guess, makes it all okay. Not only okay. She might be the next President! Just think, if they'd ever caught Hitler, he'd have to say he didn't remember, and he'd have been off the hook."

He laughed and turned to his companions, who raised their glasses in approval.

William continued to his table. He thought that was typical "Berliner Schnauze," or Berliner big mouth. His Berliners were famous for it; they always told it how it was. They didn't care. They rolled with the punches. That's what made them unique, that's what made them survivors. He remembered an old Berlin song, just a line: *"Du, mein Berlin, du wirst nicht untergehen."* "You, my Berlin, will not cease to exist." Indeed, William thought his Berliners had proved that true.

William sat at his table, ordered a Santa Margherita Pinot Grigio glass, and waited for Max.

Maximillian von Habsburg walked in. He wore a tan suit, a light blue shirt, and a yellow tie. He stood about five feet and eleven inches, of stocky build, and his impeccable suit could not hide the slight paunch, he fondly attributed to the good Bavarian beer he loved so much. His hair was dark blond and receding above his tanned face and engaging smile. He spotted his friend at his customary table. William jumped to his feet, and the two friends embraced.

"Max, good to see you. I hope your drive was not too long. But then, what takes everyone else six hours you do in three."

"And you do it in two," Max replied with a smile. "I guess it's that Ferrari. Well, William, I know this is a time for celebration, and since I know we can't get any good champagne in this place, I brought my own."

He produced a bottle of Cristal champagne and placed it on the table. Then he reached into his suit's coat pockets and pulled out two champagne glasses.

"Max, you think of everything. You are as thorough as any German I know."

"I am Austrian, you are German."

Max now placed the glasses next to the bottle.

"You know we're all the same," William laughed. "Please, now you must tell me about our man. I have waited all week; I can't wait any longer. Please start from the beginning. I want to hear it all, all the details, every conversation. Do not leave anything out-name, age, background, the color of his eyes, the number of his toes, all of it."

"Hmm, number of toes," Max said, sitting down and feigning a reflection. "That is a detail I have overlooked. But let us assume there are ten, okay?"

"Max, get to it."

"Well, let me see. Where should I start? Let's start with the requirements, the criteria, and the characteristics we all agreed upon that this man needs for our mission. By the way, you are the first one to know, naturally. I have not told others, but I called them and arranged visits. Tomorrow I'll begin, and by the end of the week, everyone will be informed. Then we must vote to agree that he is the right man and how to proceed. All right?"

"Yes," William said. "Absolutely."

Max slowly raised his champagne glass, which the waiter had filled while the two princes ordered dinner. Both ordered the calf's liver prepared Berlin style. The liver was served with onions, bacon, and apples, all fried in butter and placed on a bed of mashed potatoes.

"Well, back to the requirements," Max began. "Most important, we have decided that this man must be very un-German, yet he must be very German indeed. At first, I thought this would be very difficult to accomplish, if not impossible. How can you be green but not green at all? Difficult, no? As it turns out, it is not so difficult, not for Germans. There are many Germans who don't want the world to know they're Germans, while inside they are still very much Germans; they love their country. I suppose it is guilt over the war, shame over the crimes. I don't know. What do you think?"

William twisted the wine glass stem between his fingers as he responded.

"Max, that is a difficult question. Both of us were born near the end of the war, so it is easy for us to say that we had nothing to do with it. I think that this is right. Yet, I sometimes also feel that these were our people, and therefore I feel a sense of responsibility."

As he spoke, William noticed an older man sitting at the following table and wondered about his service during the war.

"Although the German people are not the only ones who committed crimes," he continued, "their guilt seems greater, probably because their crimes were also greater. Yet, if I kill one hundred instead of one, how can I feel more guilt? You should feel all the guilt there is, all the shame, after you kill one. I don't know. It never seems to stop. No one ever seems to learn. Look at the Koreans and the

Vietnamese killed by the Americans. Americans, of all people! The pillars of democracy, freedom, and liberty. I don't have the answer." Both men were leaning over the table and speaking in hushed tones. "You and I, as much as we would like to, will never find these answers. But back to our man, our requirements. As I said, to find an un-German German was not as difficult as I had thought. I began my search here in Germany. Soon, I realized that the German we wanted would be much more un-German if he no longer lived here. That would be better if he lived in another country, far from Germany. However, it would be better only if he were still German. William, you understand where I am going?"

"I do, I do. Go on." Max leaned forward and touched William's glass with his. Both men were silent. Both men smiled and took a sip of the sparkling white wine.

"Well," Max continued. "You have already said it. What country is better to become less German than in the country of liberty and justice for all? I decided the United States was the perfect place to look for our man. I wanted a born German who emigrated to the United States early on in his life. Not too early, you understand, because he still has to be very much German, but early enough to become as much un-German as he needs to be. That was the most basic criterion for our man. The other requirements were not as essential, but each did help to complete the picture. As you recall, he should be at least bilingual, certainly fluent in German and in his adopted country's tongue, preferably, as I pointed out, American. He needs to be of high intellect. He needs to be a teacher, a leader, and a motivator. He needs to be a person who can assume and manage a role of great authority and responsibility."

"And you did it?" William asked. "You found this man?"

"Yes, my friend, I did. Call it luck. Call it fate. I think I found him. His name is Peter Schneider. He is a doctor in Boston."

"Have you spoken to him?"

"No, I saw him only once, briefly and from a distance."

"Where?" William asked. "Tell me more."

The waiter interrupted the conversation as he placed two large plates filled with liver, mashed potatoes, bacon, onions, and apples on the wooden table.

"I will, I will. Now I am hungry. Let's eat some, and then I will continue. You always tell me that the calf's liver is delicious here. So let's enjoy it."

"Yes, of course."

William felt uneasy. The older man he had noticed earlier at the table next to them seemed too interested in their conversation. Several times, he appeared to lean over to hear more. Then he had gone to the public telephone twice and spoken emphatically, yet he had never taken his eyes off the princes' table.

"Max," William said. "Let's have dessert and our favorite cigar at a quaint bar I know not far from here. That's where we can continue our conversation."

"Sure. That sounds fine with me."

William called for the waiter and settled the bill. Both princes left the restaurant. As they did, William turned and noticed that the older man was once more on the telephone. And once more, he was watching the princes.

They did not call for a taxi but walked briskly up the street. William turned to see if they were being followed. He saw no sign of the man in the restaurant. They reached the small cigar bar and took a table at the window. William wanted to be sure they were not being followed. The street was empty. Both men ordered a cognac and lit their favorite cigar.

"Now, Max, you must continue. When can I meet him?"

"Soon. As a matter of fact, later this month, at the Berlin marathon."

"At the marathon? Is he a runner?"

"Yes, he is. Unlike you, this will not be his first marathon. He has run in many. Now he wants to do Berlin, and intends to set a personal best."

"Well, he picked the right city. The course is entirely flat. It is one of the fastest sports. But Max, something troubles me. There is one requirement you did not address. Remember, you and I talked about it. Does he understand? Does he have a grasp of the future?"

"He does. Believe me, there is no one better."

William turned to be sure no one was listening. The bar was almost empty. A young couple sitting at the other end of the small bar was deeply involved in a conversation.

"No, Max, I am not talking about being a leader, running the world. Does he understand that everything will be different after September 11? Does he know how to fight our new wars?"

"Please, William, relax. He is the expert. He wrote the book on the subject."

"Are you sure? Why? How does he know so much about it?"

Max lifted his cognac glass and took a large drink. He carefully placed the glass on the round table where they sat. Then he continued explaining to his friend how Schneider had been asked to be a physician for the U.S. Olympic team while doing his cardiology training at the Mayo Clinic. In 1972, he went with the team to Munich for the Olympics. He took his wife and six-year-old son. Over there, he became good friends with one of the Israeli wrestlers. His young son adored the guy and spent as much time with him as possible. When the massacre happened, the young boy was in the dormitory room with him. He was killed. That is how Schneider learned about terrorism. Schneider learned a long time ago, long before 9-11. Moreover, Schneider learned the hard way; he lost his firstborn. He realized then what all of us know now. He knew the free world was facing a new enemy, a new kind of warfare." "Is our choice equipped to handle the New World, the new warfare?"

William wanted to know. Again, he looked up the dimly lit street. "William. I told you he meets all the criteria. Let me finish. When his son was killed in Munich, he realized then the U.S., the world, was facing a new kind of enemy, an enemy without a face, an enemy who could strike at any time, anywhere. Schneider realized we, the free world, were defenseless against such strikes. After all, his son was a victim. He was innocent, six years old, in the wrong place. But do these terrorists care? They do not. They are fanatics. They will be very difficult to fight."

"I know, I know," William said. "But why is he up to leading the new European Union? Is he qualified to cope with this new type of warfare, with these fanatics?"

He said it in a hushed voice and nervously looked about him. "When his son died," Max replied solemnly, "Schneider decided to become an expert on antiterrorism. And he did. He wrote a book about it. Actually, it is sort of the bible on the topic. I have a copy in my car. Please read it. In the book, he actually predicts the strikes some of the terrorist groups, including Al Qaeda, had planned for New York, Washington, Brussels, Paris, and Tokyo. That is only the beginning. It is the way war will be waged in the future. Not just by Islamic fundamentalists, but by others as well. Everyone will be vulnerable, no one will be safe."

"It's incredible, Max. How do we safeguard against it? How do we protect ourselves and preserve our countries, our democracies, our families, yours and mine?"

"Our current system, our democracy, has to change. Our system is too vulnerable. We are too liberal, and other groups will take advantage of our freedoms; they already have. Just look at the United States. They were our leaders, pillars of democracy and freedom of choice and speech. Look at what happened to them. They could not protect themselves. Things have changed. We need a new form of government, a new leader, new guidelines, and new rules. Everything is different now."

William's face was dark with skepticism. He took a large mouthful of the cognac and swooshed it before he swallowed it.

"Please tell me how we can create a union, a nation, a world that can be safe, not afraid of all these terrorists' attacks."

"Very well, let me talk to you as straight as possible. Let me pose a question. I know it will shock you. But please think about it, and then let me explain." William watched him, his eyes fixed on his friend. "Yes, of course, I have always trusted your judgment."

"I know that neither you nor I, nor all the royals ever wanted it to happen, but think about it, if Adolf Hitler had succeeded, do you think we would be fighting this new kind of war now?"

He said it in a hushed voice, leaning closely towards his friend. "No," William answered without hesitation. "No, it would be impossible. The state would control everything. There would be no liberties. There would be a complete police state. No freedoms, none of the rights we are all accustomed to."

"Well, William, there you have it! Now you understand. The quest for a new European leader was much more than anticipated at first. We, Europe, need to replace the United States of America as the leader of world democracy. The United States, in its fight against terrorism, will become a police state, as you just described. There will be no different from Nazi Germany. They have no choice. There is no other way they can win this war. They will begin by limiting their citizens' travel rights, speaking freely, and finally voting. Officials will no longer be elected; they will be appointed. Already, their president has appointed a director of homeland security. Homeland, William! How often did our people hear this? Then they proposed to set up a propaganda ministry to spread false information about governments that didn't go along with the U.S. It all sounds like Nazi Germany. Did you hear his comments on their TV during the Olympic Games at Salt Lake City? You talk about nationalism. The handwriting is on the wall. Soon, their president will be self-appointed. He will make all the laws; he has already written all these executive orders to bypass Congress. He will prove to be no different from all the other demagogues. Remember, history always repeats itself."

Again, William turned around and saw only the couple still engulfed deeply in a conversation. Two lovers, no doubt, he thought. Then he once more checked the street. Empty.

"But Max, our plan will make the difference and change the world!"

"William, my family, and your families have always changed the world. Only we know how to do it. The people will realize it; they will come to us. We will become the new United States of America, the United States of Europe. And when the USA has finished fighting their new war, when their resources are depleted, their people are in despair, that's when we take over, that's when we become the United States of the World. Remember, William, it is our families' destiny. It has always been God's will."

CHAPTER IV

Basel, Switzerland, September

THE MAN FROM THE MIDDLE EAST had no chance. He struggled; he fought for his life. He did not want to die. He had too much to live for. He had a beautiful young wife and two lovely children, the center of his universe. But the grip would not let go. Two strong hands prevented his breathing, obstructing his trachea. The hands felt different, he thought; there was no feeling, no warmth. They felt sterile. Then there was the scent, the odor of powder.

Only minutes ago, he had left the restaurant; his spirits had been high, no doubt helped by the cocktails and wine his dinner companions had urged on him. He did not mind. It was a time to celebrate. His mission had been successful. He had negotiated long and hard. He was sober then. He was always sober, he reminded himself, for his religion did not allow alcohol. However, there were always exceptions. Tonight was one of them. After all, he had helped the cause, the mission. It did not just help; he had done more, and he had done it all. He had purchased the missiles they needed, their favorite weapon, the Strellas. And all had agreed that they would be kept in the camp in Bosnia, the camp they had such easy access to.

When he left the Bel Etage restaurant in Basel, Switzerland, he decided to walk and catch some fresh air. He had to rid himself of the demons that the alcohol had let surface. He did not hail a cab; he decided to walk along the bank of the beautiful Rhine River.

And now his feet were kicking violently, to no avail. The man behind him was too strong; he would not let go. He was an expert, a professional, a trained assassin. Then he saw all his hopes and dreams pass away. At first, he felt only light-headed, almost a good feeling, delirious, then he saw the end, the darkness, and no longer could he kick. The man behind him did not let go. Not until the limbs hung lifeless, the heart had stopped, the breathing had ceased. Then the man dropped the body abruptly, only a yard from where he had first put his hands on it. He did not bother to hide it, but he threw the Middle Eastern man into the river. No need. No one would ever know. He walked up to the bank of the Rhine River and picked up a rock the size of his fist. He stripped off his powdered surgeon's gloves, stretched them over the stone, and tossed it into the water.

Then he strolled along the flowing water and headed back to his hotel.

Berlin, September

The Mercedes crunched to a stop along the fine gravel drive in front of the Grunewald palace. William and Maximillian got out, and Heinrich the butler accompanied them to the study to serve cognac. He left, closing the door behind him, and William and Max sat down to sip their drinks in two deep leather chairs facing a massive floor-to-ceiling stone fireplace. The crest of Brandenburg was prominently carved into the stone above the fireplace. Pictures of many of the Hohenzollern kings and princes, as well as William as a child and young adult, covered the walls. In many ways, Max was part of it.

It was a warm September evening, but Heinrich had prepared a fire. He knew his master enjoyed having his cognac and favorite cigar before a roaring fire. William handed Max one of the Padrón cigars they both cherished. They lit them and inhaled.

"Well, William, it has been a while since I have been here. This is still my favorite room. It brings back so many fond memories."

"This is where I retreat to relax, remember, and think of the future. It is all here, right in this room."

"I agree. I, too, love this library. It is full of history and memory. And your cognac beats the one we had earlier at the cigar bar." William nodded and smiled.

"Thanks, Max. Now you must tell me more about our man."

"Very well, as I told you, he is German. He was born in Berlin at the end of the war. His parents were Prussian. His father came from a small town near Königsberg before the war. He actually is, or was, I should say, for he died during the war, of distant Hohenzollern descent. I don't know the exact lineage, but I am now looking into it. He was a businessman who never had to join the army or the party. He was in the wholesale food business, and the Nazis deemed him and his business to be essential to the German economy and the war effort. Near the end of the war, he went back to Königsberg. He never returned. The family suspected that he was shot by the Russians, who by then had advanced well into Prussia."

Max exited his chair, took his cigar and cognac, and slowly walked towards the fireplace. Heinrich had placed large logs on the wrought iron grates, which caused a roaring fire to brighten the dark study. Max leaned against the mantel and drew on his Padrón. He loved to play the game with William. He loved to make him wait and let him know who was in charge. He had done it all his life. It was in his genes. The Habsburgs knew how to manipulate; they were the best at it. Now he slowly swirled the cognac glass. He was in no hurry, but he knew William was anxious. Warriors always were. They have no patience. They need immediate results. And he knew William had the warrior genes, the Hohenzollern genes.

"Please, Max, continue, and tell me the rest of it. I want to know it all," William demanded.

Max sniffed his cognac. Again, he had won; again, he had predicted it. It was so easy.

"All right, my friend," he smiled. "The mother took care of him-he was the only child. It was difficult, but she made ends meet. Actually, with the help of relatives, she did pretty well. They moved to Dahlem, a fashionable suburb, around 1950. He attended grammar school and high school at the Arndt Gymnasium. He did not finish here because his mother decided that they should move to the United States. He was about fifteen then. They moved to Brooklyn, New York, where he attended public school. He became quite an athlete, a runner. He won the New York State championship in the mile in high school. Then he went to college in upstate New York, on athletic and scholastic scholarships. He also ran there, I believe, but he did far better in the classroom. He went on to medical school at the University of Pennsylvania, did his residency and fellowship at the Mayo Clinic, and is now a professor at Harvard. He is also married to-guess who? a former president's daughter. Katie is her name, and she has two kids. One is a lawyer in Miami, the other is married in California. He has written numerous papers and books and lectured worldwide, including in Germany. Recently, he has become very disillusioned with medicine. He decided to change the system from within, and

I don't think it works. I think he is getting discouraged and fed up, ready for a change, for a challenge. He has taken trips back to Berlin, not so much to visit family, which he does have here. I think he feels his roots are still here. Yet, he is totally American. Just what we need: un-German yet very German."

"He certainly sounds like our man. But will he do it?"

"Now, there, I have no idea," Max said. "That is the second phase. That will happen during the marathon at the end of the month."

"Very well," William said. "I think it's time to tell the others and to vote. Let's hope this year's Berlin Marathon will go down in history."

He raised his glass of Remy Martin and said, *"Prost,* my friend."

William reflected as he settled back in his bed. Well, not really nine months ago. It had started for the first time 1200 years ago, then again 130 years ago, and the last time less than seventy years ago.

William stretched and smiled into the darkness. He had often wondered what it was like to be the first Germanic emperor, 801 Charles I, Charlemagne, as he was known. He did it; he created a true empire, the First Reich. Yet it did not last. Not his fault, William allowed. A thousand years later, the fighting among his descendants destroyed his dream. The Hanovers, the Saxons, the Bourbons, the Lorraines, and the Hohenzollerns could rule the world now if they had ceased their bickering.

Of course, they had tried again. Last time it was his family's turn. In 1871, his great-great-grandfather, William I, ascended to the throne. However, the Second German Reich tumbled far more quickly than the first. William's grandson was forced to abdicate the throne and leave his country. Then the Third Reich: Adolf Hitler. He was not one of us, William thought. First, he was Austrian; second, he was a commoner, not nobility. Not part of the family. Not a Hohenzollern, or even a Habsburg. He had to fail.

Now it would be different, William thought. Now we all agree, all the families that count. Now we can do what had not been done for more than 1200 years. It had started nine months ago. Max had called, knowing William would drive from Berlin for his annual ski vacation. This time, he had chosen Tyrol, in northern Italy. Well, Austria, really. It had belonged to Austria until the Allies, in their wisdom, took these Germanic people who loved Austria, took them against their will, and made their country part of Italy. This is the wisdom that starts wars. It is not the people. They only suffer the consequences.

William sat up in his bed and looked out of the large bay window of his bedroom. The full moon shone on his estate; it was a clear night. He looked at the moon and smiled, knowing God was with him and his family's destiny would be fulfilled.

Then he leaned back on the plush pillows. He tried to recall all the events. He tried to remember. Remember what actually happened. He recalled he had grown tired of the fashionable ski resorts: St. Moritz, Kitzbuehel, Gstaad; he had been to them all. This time he wanted a different environment. No five-star hotel. He wanted to be part of a village, to live the way the people lived. In the morning, he goes to the bakery, buys bread for breakfast, and eats at home, in his apartment. He needed a change.

Max had called just days before he left. He wanted to meet. They decided on lunch at the Hotel Post in Mittenwald, in Austria. The border is not far from Innsbruck. It was near William's way to northern Italy, close enough for Max. Max arrived precisely on time, as always. They embraced, sat, and ordered. As soon as the waiter had gone, Max said it. No buildup, no preamble, he just said it.

"William, we, and I will explain 'we' momentarily; we need to rule Europe."

William just laughed. "Rule Europe? What do you mean, we need to rule Europe?" William stroked the large ring on his left index finger bearing his family's crest.

"Well," Max continued, "you know that our families have been destined to lead Europe. Only petty family rivalries prevented us from doing so. Why?"

"Max, you said it already. Our families could not get along. We each wanted it all, and never trusted each other. God, we did not trust our brothers, fathers, or even mothers. How could it ever have worked?"

"It can work, though, if we learn from our history."

William again rubbed the ring of his ancestors bearing the crest of the Mark Brandenburg.

"The Third Reich was doomed to failure. Do you know why? Our families did not rule it. Europe and the world can only be ruled by us, our families, and William. This is destiny; what God has always wanted!"

"Max, I don't know what to say. I expected just a peaceful lunch between two old friends."

The waiter approached and placed a glass of the white wine they had ordered on the wooden table before them. It was approximately one o'clock in the afternoon, and the quaint and popular restaurant was beginning to fill. Max looked out of the window and noticed it had begun to snow. Large flakes floated lazily through the air before reaching the ground to join others and create a white, glistening carpet on old, gray brick.

"I apologize," Max continued as his attention returned to William. "In about a year, the European Union will elect a new president, its first real president. He will be powerful, the office will rival the presidency of the United States. This new president must be one of us. It is what my family, your family, and the royal families have always worked for. We have had our differences in the past, but now all the important European aristocratic families are in harmony. Do you understand the enormous significance of this? Do you, my friend?" William was stunned. He could not believe what Max was suggesting. He had no reason to question the validity of such a plan, yet he had not been prepared to hear it. There had been no warning.

Yet, this was typical Max, typical of the Germanic approach, straight to the facts, no emotions, and no second thoughts.

"Why didn't I hear about this before, Max? All the others already know, but I don't even know who the others are."

"Yes, you were the last to be told. However, let me explain, please. My idea was to elect a president of Europe whom we chose and controlled. I'll take the credit, or the blame. Nevertheless, you must be in charge of the mission. And that's why you were the last to know. I had to convince all the other princes before I approached you. It is not only my love for you that makes me insist on this. There are many practical reasons why only you can lead this operation. Don't get me wrong. You can't be the president of Europe. You already know this. You are all that Europe fears, aristocrat, German, Prussian, Hohenzollern."

"So why me?" William interrupted. "Why not one of the other European houses, the French, the English? Why not you?"

"I thought about all of them. But it has to be you. You are a German, and no German today will accept anything else. Berlin will be Europe's capital, Germany its backbone. We all know it. It is not Austria, though I wish it were. It is not France, Italy, or Great Britain.

It is Germany. We have decided on you because you are German. Only you can head our committee."

Max stopped and took a sip of his wine to clear his throat.

"We need support from all avenues. The industrialists, the politicians, the members of the European Union, newspapers, bankers, everyone must be won over. So, William, do not say no. I need you, the princes need you, and our new Europe needs you."

William listened to every word. It made sense, he thought, one president, a German president, a united Europe, controlled by all the aristocratic families, and my family, the Hohenzollerns, finally, and again, in control. My forefathers would have wanted it; it was their wish, the people's wish, God's wish. And now the time has come.

William took a deep breath. He wanted time to think, but that was not his nature. He was a warrior; he had those genes; he was impatient. Instinct, his genes, told him to go for the kill. What Max had outlined was his destiny, and he would grasp it.

"You have convinced me," he said. "This is the path that Europe must take. I have thought of it many times before. However, never as thoroughly as you have, Max. You are a political genius. Too bad you can't be the leader. But I see your reasons. Tell me, how do we proceed?" "The committee and I have developed a detailed plan. Of course, since you are now our leader, you need to approve it. First, we must find a man who can win the European presidency. Once you approve, he will be presented to the other princes, the politicians, and the industrialists we have recruited. But you will control him; he will be your man."

William leaned back in his chair and looked out the window at the snow. He could not contain his excitement. This is what he had waited for. He knew one day there would be a mission to serve the fatherland.

"Max," he said abruptly. "A toast."

They both smiled and called for the waiter. Max's smile lasted longer. He had done it again. His family had a heritage of expert manipulation. They were the consummate diplomats, and in the end, they always held the real power. Of course, William is my friend, Max thought, but he is not a Habsburg, only a Hohenzollern, a Prussian. Only Habsburgs can rule the world. History has shown it. Besides, it has always been God's wish.

CHAPTER V

Saxony, September

THE RED PORSCHE HEADED SOUTH FAST on the Autobahn E55. It was a beautiful September morning. Prince Maximillian von Habsburg had just left his friend William's estate in the Grunewald. Everything had gone according to plan. William was all the way in. He could not resist the idea of his family being in power again. Max never doubted William would go along. The Hohenzollerns were easily manipulated. They had no skill in diplomacy; they did not know how to negotiate. All the Prussians ever knew was how to fight wars. But that, Max thought, is not the way to control the European Union. To do that, you need diplomacy, to know how to shape events, and to be a Habsburg. Max smiled and pressed a little harder on the accelerator. Yes, a Habsburg. He would ultimately control it all.

In an hour or so, Max would be at his next stop. It was in Dresden, home of the descendants of the Saxon Empire. Max had debated for a long time on whom to include in his plan to take over the European Union. Though the Habsburgs would be in charge, some other European royal families had to be included. The front man would have to be a German, and that would be William.

Max had considered including the British royal family, but dismissed the idea. They may be family, but this part of the family he wanted no part of. The British could not be trusted; they even spied on their allies. Besides, they are not European. They can never decide if they belong to Europe or America. Let them be Americans, he thought with a smile. They deserve each other. The French are different. The French are true Europeans. They would have to be offered a role. After all, they had started the move toward a united Europe. Undoubtedly, they had their own reasons for doing so, but that's part of the game.

The Saxons are not very important, Max reminded himself. However, Albrecht, grandson of King Frederick Augustus III of Saxony, had a score to settle. Max relished this game and particularly enjoyed revenge, even if it took centuries to get it. That was the Habsburg way. Albrecht's enmity could be put to practical use in forming the new EU. He was well respected as a businessman throughout Germany and had the ear of most of the German industrial giants.

Max thought about Albrecht's grievance. What a catastrophe. Dresden was once called the Florence of the North, Florence on the River Elbe. It was one of Germany's most beautiful cities, the Saxon kingdom's capital and the royal family's seat. Then, on February 13, 1945, Churchill destroyed it. At 10:15 p.m., 244 Lancaster bombers dropped incendiary bombs, and three hours later, twice as many planes struck again. Most of them were British, but seventy-seven were Canadian. The next day, American B-17s dropped incendiaries shortly after noon.

The bombs created a firestorm. Dresden burned for seven days, and the city was reduced to a wasteland of rubble and smoldering corpses. No one knows precisely how many people died. Estimates run as high as 100,000. There was no strategic reason for the attack.

The war was virtually over. There was no industry in Dresden, and the town at the time had been filled with women, children, and refugees fleeing the Eastern Front. It was Churchill's way of shattering any possible civilian resistance. No wonder, Max thought, that Albrecht did not want the British to be part of the alliance. He had even opposed Britain's presence in the EU, and he had not been alone there. Twice, de DeGaulle had vetoed the United Kingdom's application. Only after Pompidou replaced DeGaulle as president of France did the UK gain admission to the European Union.

Max understood Albrecht's anger, but Max was not an emotional man. He was practical; he was a politician. He wanted Albrecht's support for two reasons. One, Albrecht's friends among the German industrialists were crucial for Max's plan to succeed; and two, Albrecht would help keep England out of the geopolitics. Max had never felt comfortable dealing with the British, nor had his forefathers. Granted, their royal family was Germanic, and some of their kings had spoken only German. But the British had their own agenda. So Max would use Albrecht, heir to the throne of Saxony, to keep the Brits out. A Habsburg would never stoop to such dirty work.

Max reduced his speed as he entered the city of Dresden. What a sight—so much construction. More than 12,000 buildings had been destroyed in the bomb attack. However, Germany had made a commitment to rebuilding its city, to restore it to its place as one of Germany's most beautiful places, and they were well on their way.

Max steered toward the Altstadt, the site of most of Dresden's best architecture. He would stay at the Kempinski Hotel in the historic Taschenberg Palace, the former residence of the Saxon Crown Princes. Destroyed during the war, the palace had been rebuilt as the Kempinski. But Max would not have much time to enjoy his accommodation. He had a busy agenda. He was to lunch with Albrecht at the Carousel Restaurant in the Buelow Residenz, a baroque palace built in 1730.

After lunch, there would be several meetings with prominent German industrialists. Albrecht had made the arrangements. In the evening, he, Albrecht, and some of the businessmen would be at the famous Semper Opera House. Max enjoyed opera.

Now Max drove along the beautiful Elbe River. The city sparkled in the sunlight. Much rebuilding had been done, and once more the town showed its splendor of the past. After Dresden, Max had three more stops to make. First was France, where he would meet with Prince Jerome Bonaparte, descendant of Napoleon Bonaparte's youngest brother, whose name was also Jerome, and Catherine of Württemberg. Jerome Bonaparte had been king of Westphalia and had married Catherine bigamously. Like many of the European royal families, Prince Jerome was important to Max's plan. After all, it was the destiny of the Royals to rule Europe. This was God's wish. But beyond that, Max was a practical man. He knew he needed the support of others.

He needed the industrialists, the politicians, particularly the heads of state of France and Germany, and the ministers of the critical European Union departments. Indeed, they all have their own agendas, he thought, but so do I. Max had made promises, told stories, and told each what they wanted to hear to accomplish his agenda. This is my strength, Max thought. It's in the genes, the Habsburg genes. Max drove past the famous and beautiful Semper Opera house and noticed the many tourists sightseeing the city. Dresden once more had become one of Germany's favorite tourist destinations.

After he visits with Jerome, Max would go to Brussels, home to most of the essential departments of the European Union. In

Brussels, Max would have final meetings with ministers who had been recruited to his cause. He would also meet with members of the European Council, the heads of state of the member countries. These meetings were crucial. With the help of the German and French heads of state, Max had already convinced many members of the European Council to go along with his plan.

Max's plan was quite simple. Europe needed to be one nation; it required one government and one president. That president needed to be strong, with powers similar to those of the president of the United States. However, unlike the U.S. president, the people would not elect the EU president; those best informed, those best qualified to choose, would nominate him. Those clearly were the Royals, his princes. But he would tell all the others, the ministers and industrialists, they would choose. He urged everyone that the European Union needed to avoid the dirty politics now every day in the U.S.— prevent corruption, enormous spending, and most importantly, electing the wrong man. In the end, they had agreed: only those qualified should choose. It was an easy decision, for who was more qualified than they were? Who stood to benefit more than they did? A united Europe speaking as one would be a new superpower, strong economically, strong militarily.

Of course, Max did not reveal everything. He did not say that he would decide on the man who would be president of the EU.

Max's last stop before returning to Berlin would be Frankfurt, the business capital of Germany and Europe. There, he would meet again with the European industrialists whom he and the other princes had chosen, for they too needed to be kept abreast of developments. Max knew that their support was ultimately the most important of all because, in the end, power flows from money.

Slowly, he made the left-hand turn to pull his Porsche into the entrance of his elegant hotel. He left the car running as he stepped out of the car and walked up the stairs to enter the lobby of the magnificent Taschenberg Palace.

Max knew he had succeeded because of his method of recruitment, the same method employed by leaders throughout history. It worked with business people, it worked with politicians. It worked because it was based on two emotions that all people respond to: greed and fear. Very clearly, he had explained to all that a united Europe would be the strongest economic power in the world, and that not everyone could or would be included. He told his recruits they had been carefully selected, and they would lead the new Europe to unprecedented economic heights and get very rich in the process.

Greed and fear, they never failed.

CHAPTER VI

Tel Aviv, Israel, September

HE LIT ANOTHER CIGARETTE. THE LAST one was still burning in the ashtray on his desk in the small, plainly furnished office on the fifth floor of the Hadar Dafna building. His blue polo shirt was unbuttoned, revealing his hairy chest. He had gone immediately to the office after his long overseas flight. No time to go home to change. Besides, he always kept a change of clothing in the office. He had to. He had to be ready, be available at all times, because he was the protector of the state of Israel. He was Maza Sharef, the head of the Mossad, Israel's renowned intelligence agency.

"What a trip," he mumbled, deeply inhaling the smoke of his Marlboro cigarette. You win some and you lose some. He removed his shirt, revealing his trim and muscular upper body. He was proud of his build. He worked hard at it. Not a bad body for a fifty-nine-year-old. He stepped in front of the mirror in the small bathroom of his office. He splashed cold water on his face. He had just returned from meeting the president of the United States, a meeting that had changed his world. His world had changed before. It always did. There are always new intrigues, new players, new plots. The trick is to turn them to meet your ends and make sure the world does don't change too much. And he, Maza Sharef, was the best at it. His meeting with the president had been a surprise, but he had already made new plans. He knew what to do.

He stepped into the shower, recalling the events of the day. Maza had not waited long. That had surprised him. Fifteen minutes after his arrival, he was escorted into the Oval Office.

While he waited, Sharef again wondered if he was doing the right thing. It was a most difficult decision.

The office was empty. He considered the two chairs facing the large desk and the two couches facing each other in the middle of the room. As he stood, he observed. He looked at the desk of the president of the United States. A grin entered his intelligent face. So this is the famous desk, the one President Kennedy allegedly had sex under. What a tough job, the presidency of the United States.

He continued to observe. This is what he had been trained to do. He noticed the presidential seal on the rich blue carpet and the matching seal on the ceiling. The office was actually relatively small, but comfortable. Behind the desk were two flags, the American flag and the presidential flag. Someone had left the office in a hurry. Papers were scattered on the desk. A fountain pen, undoubtedly used for signatures, lay uncapped. He had gone only seconds ago. A drop of water ran slowly down the side of a glass.

A large, sixtyish man hurried into the room through the French doors that led to the rose garden.

"Hello, Maza," said the president, taking Sharef's hand briskly. "Sorry I made you wait, but I had an emergency. Moses wanted out. The older he gets, the less he can hold it. He's out there now, fertilizing the roses."

"Hello, Mr. President," Sharef smiled. "How are you?"

"Fine, fine. How's Hershey?"

"She's fine, about to have puppies."

"Maza, if it were up to me, I'd take one. That's the most beautiful chocolate setter I've ever seen. But Catherine won't let me have more than one dog in the house."

The president turned serious. He walked behind his desk.

"Sit down, Maza," he said, gesturing toward one of the two chairs beside his desk.

Sharef had met President Allan Levenson twice before, the first time in Tel Aviv when Levenson was vice president. The prime minister of Israel, Oren Peres, had asked Sharef to join them in a discussion of Israeli security. The second time, Sharef traveled with the prime minister to Washington to meet with Levenson and his staff about forming closer relations between the two countries' intelligence agencies.

Sharef and the president liked each other. Despite their differences, they had a few fundamentals in common. They were of similar age. Both were devout Jews. Both were devoted to their chocolate Irish setters. They respected each other, and both men spoke their minds, at least in private.

"Well," the president said as he placed both hands on the desk, "your call certainly surprised me, Maza. I can't wait to hear what brought you all this way. Why couldn't we discuss this over the phone?"

"It is a most delicate matter, Mr. President. I know telephone lines can be secured, but someone is always listening. I could not afford to take a chance. But most importantly, I wanted to look you in the eye when I tell you this."

"I'm listening."

Sharef nodded. "My country, your country, not all countries can and will be affected. Before I go on, you must give me your word that for now, you will not share with anyone what I tell you today. I mean, no one. It is that important."

The president picked up the fountain pen and rotated it in his fingers, "Maza, as I told you on the telephone, you have the word of the president of the United States. I don't have to tell you what that means."

Sharef wondered what it meant, but he had no choice but to say what he had come to say.

"Mr. President, few people know what I am about to tell you, very few. My boss, the prime minister of Israel, does not know. He does not know I am here. I am putting myself at great risk, but I know I am doing the right thing for us."

The pen stilled. "Explain to us.'"

"You know that without your financial aid, your political support, your military support, Israel cannot exist. My country's interests and yours are the same. Since you entered politics, you have been one of my nation's strongest supporters. You know what I am talking about."

The president smiled. Years ago, when he ran for the congressional seat in his district, the Jewish vote got him to Capitol Hill, the Senate, the vice presidency, and the White House. He had taken office only nine months ago, when the elected president, Mrs. Barbara Rutherford, had died in a freak skiing accident. Nonetheless, the Jewish support had gotten him where he was today. He had taken many trips to Israel as a congressman and senator. He had supported Israel on the hill; he knew who his constituents were. He was a politician. Unfortunately, the man across his desk was an idealist, unusual for an intelligence officer. And he believed in causes.

"Maza, Israel is important to my country, and Israel is important to me. I will always do what needs to be done to assure its safety and independence."

"That is why I am here today. I believe that our safety is threatened. Not just the safety of my country, but possibly the safety of yours, the safety of the world."

"Hold on now," the president said, raising a hand and smiling. "Isn't this all a little melodramatic?"

"No." Sharef suppressed his impatience. "As you well know, in about twelve months, the European nations will appoint a president and form a new European Union, more like a European empire."

"A European empire!" The pen disappeared into his fist.

"Come on, now, Maza. I know you have your perspective, but you're starting to sound paranoid."

"Mr. President, please. Hear what I have to say. You and your government have worked hard to prevent the European states from uniting. So have we. So has Britain, so has Russia, all to no avail. A united Europe will change the balance of power; it will be a threat, as you will see. We lost, they won. They will have their united Europe. We cannot change this. But there is a way we can control it, to make sure Europe's interests are our interests."

"Let's say handle, Maza. I don't like to use the word 'control' in politics."

"Fine, Mr. President, you can play word games, but I will get right to the point. We know, and I know you know, that this new European Union will not be controlled by the European people, but by the Ring?"

"The Ring," the president said. "What the hell is the Ring?"

"Mr. President, we agreed to be straight."

Maza pushed the boundary line, relying on earlier goodwill. He reminded the president of how the Mossad had shared with the CIA the information on how several houses of European nobility intended to control the new European Union. How they had decided that once Europe is united, the aristocracy again will rule it, specifically the descendants of the Habsburgs and Hohenzollerns. They had included a handful of other European houses to increase the basis of their support. But they thought they could control it. After centuries, they had made peace and formed a union. The Mossad called it the Ring. The chairman of the Ring, the Mossad knew, was a Prussian, a Hohenzollern descendant. However, the Royals had realized that he could never be elected to the European presidency; there was too much history there. Therefore, they had handpicked a candidate. He was one of them, though his bloodline was perhaps remote. And yet he was unlike them, a paradox they could exploit. The man they had picked was an American, Dr. Peter Schneider. He had not yet been confirmed by everyone involved; the man himself knew nothing about it. Soon, he would be introduced to all the right people. The plan was up and running.

"But what they do not know, what you do not know, what the CIA does not know, what only two people know, is that the Ring made a significant mistake when they picked Dr. Schneider," Sharef continued, unable to hide the pleasure and satisfaction of possessing more information than the most powerful person in the world.

The president, who until now had been listening attentively, tossed his pen down in agitation.

"How come I don't know about this mistake? Why didn't the CIA tell me?"

"I have told you, the CIA does not know. The Mossad uncovered this information. I guess we got lucky again. But we have not told anyone. Only I know. Even the prime minister of Israel does not know. He can't. However, I have decided you should know, because we need your help. It's the only way we can control, I'm sorry, handle the new European Union."

"Okay, tell me. What was this mistake?"

"Dr. Peter Schneider is a Jew."

"A Jew?" the president snorted. "The German nobility sought out a Jew? That's impossible." Now Maza Sharef was on his own turf. When it came to obtaining and controlling information, no one was better. Not even the president of the United States and Sharif enjoyed making no bones about it.

"Let me explain. Years ago, during the war, there was a German poet named Joshua Bergman.

He lived in Berlin and was born there. He was a Jew. He was so well-loved that even the Nazis could not touch him. When the Holocaust began, he turned into a recluse and barricaded himself in his house. However, near the war's end, his wife became pregnant with their first child. Just before she was to give birth, he could take it no more. He committed suicide, shot himself in the head. They say the shot was heard clear across the Pariser Platz. Shortly thereafter, his wife, much younger than him, gave birth to a son at the Charité Hospital in Stadtmitte of Berlin. She panicked. She thought that with her husband dead, the Nazis would send her and her child straight to a concentration camp. She had volunteered at this hospital in the obstetrical ward for years because she loved children. She knew the routine. Three other boys were born on the day her boy was born, October 15, 1944. To save her child from the Nazis, she switched babies."

"Switched babies?" the president interrupted. "What mother would do such a thing?"

"Mr. President, this woman was desperate. She took her child, put him in a different crib, took the child from that crib, and put him in her own. She removed the identification bracelets from all the babies and threw them on the floor of the nursery. When they left the hospital, she thought the Nazis would send them off to a camp. Not so. She asked to emigrate to the United States, and guess what? The Nazis obliged. They were happy to get rid of her. She went to Le Havre in France, boarded a freighter, and sailed to New York."

"I don't want to guess what happened to her son, do I?"

Sharef smiled. "Her son grew up to be an American, father of two children, a devout Catholic, and married the daughter of a former president. He is Dr. Peter Schneider, the future president of Europe. His new family had emigrated to the United States as well. Not until he was fifteen or so. He did the rest of his schooling here, finished high school, college, and medical school."

The president watched him, his eyes cold. "What about the mother? What about the other child, the one she brought with her?"

"Mrs. Bergman is still alive, though she's rather old now. She lives near her grandson, or perhaps, adopted grandson, in Miami Beach. Her adopted son and his wife died in an accident thirteen years ago.

She and the grandson are very close, inseparable. I guess she is making up for what she did. This relationship with her grandson helps with all the guilt."

The president leaned back in his chair.

"Incredible. The new president of Europe will be a Jew, selected and installed by the German aristocracy. Perhaps there is justice after all."

"Mr. President," Maza put in quickly. "No one knows that Peter Schneider is a Jew, the Ring does not, he himself does not. Only I know. Martha Bergman had shared her secret only with her rabbi. A few weeks ago, before he died, he told me the story. The rabbi was my cousin. And now you know Martha's secret. But we need to keep it that way until the time comes."

"Until what time comes?" the president said, growing irritated. "Spit it out. What are you talking about?"

"I believe that at the right time, not now but soon, Schneider will become one of us. I will have to go to him and explain, but all in due time."

"You keep saying 'us.' I don't know what that means. Who's 'us'? Can we cut the cloak-and-dagger crap?"

"As I said earlier, we, you, the United States, you personally need to control the European Union. With my help, and the Mossad's help. Once Schneider is appointed, I will go to him, explain who he is, explain who we are, and you, Mr. President, can then sit down with him and form a union of Europe and the United States. Moreover, you will be the leader. The United States already leads the world so that it will be official. Think of it, us, the chosen people, leading the world."

Levenson's face darkened with blood. "Are you telling me that we are to manipulate an election, elect me as president of whatever in the world you call it, without the consent of the people? Who do you think I am? My country is a democracy. The people elect us. 'For the people, by the people,' remember. We do not rig elections. I don't want to hear any more." He stood up behind his desk. He tried hard to control his anger.

"The whole idea is incredible; it is a fantasy. I think you need a reality check. Please excuse me now. I have to get back to what is happening in this world. Do have a safe trip back home."

Sharef was stunned. He had made a mistake, an enormous mistake. He had misjudged. He sat frozen in his chair, his mind racing through his options.

"Thank you for coming, Maza, but now you must get out."

Sharef got to his feet. He did not look at the president and did not say goodbye as he left the Oval Office. By the time his limousine left via the west gate of the White House, he knew he had to come. He came up with a new plan. He wanted the Americans included because they could have helped win Schneider over. Of course, he had never intended to let the president run the operation, and now, the president could not be permitted to wreck it.

Sharef had traveled to Washington in secret. Not even his wife and children knew where he had gone. They would not know; he would return to Tel Aviv within hours. By the time his flight began to taxi for takeoff, a plan had started to take shape in his mind. The Mossad knew the U.S. president would soon visit Berlin to attend an international congress. Sharef would assemble three teams, perhaps three Mossad men in each. The teams would go to Berlin, and they would terminate the president. He now knew too much. He could ruin it all. He could jeopardize the children of Israel. The teams would act in sequence. If the first saw no viable chance of success, it would shut down its mission, go home, and the second would set its plan in motion. Maza had not concluded where exactly he would deploy his men. Still, his preliminary choices were the airport at Tegel, where the president would arrive, and Schloss Bellevue, official residence of the president of Germany, where President Levenson would spend his two nights in Berlin. Sharef's preliminary intelligence indicated Schloss Bellevue would be the optimal target. Park and woods surrounded the Schloss, and the interior layout was well known. When the president of Germany was not in residence, the grounds were open to the public. He was also considering the Reichstag, where President Levenson was scheduled to give a speech the day of his arrival, and the State Opera House, where he was expected to see a performance on the evening of that same day.

The president would be well guarded, but presidents had been shot before. And Sharef had to try, Israel, the children of Israel, had to be protected, Sharef's third team would be an immediate reaction force, ready to seize its opportunity. He knew that to win in his business, you had to expect the unexpected, that the unexpected could be your trump card, because surprise meant confusion, events unplanned, and a breakdown in protection.

Sharef had already decided on the name for his third team: Allah 1. It would consist of three of his best men. He knew they would not fail. The president of the United States would never foil his plan; he would not reveal the true identity of Peter Schneider, future president of Europe, future agent of the Mossad.

CHAPTER VII

Miami Beach, September

HE WOULD BE EARLY. TEN MINUTES early. It was only a short stroll from his apartment to his favorite place for lunch on the beach. He knew she would be late, women always are, gorgeous women like Nicole. They expect you to wait for them because they are worth waiting for.

He looked up as he crossed the street and approached the restaurant. Only two of the sidewalk tables were taken. At the corner table sat Nicole, studying the menu, a glass of white wine in front of her. Her jet-black hair was pulled back in a ponytail; she wore black-metal sunglasses and no makeup. Her plain beige shift accentuated her figure. She was one beautiful woman.

"Hello," Adam said, pulling up a chair at the table. "Sorry, I'm late."

"You're not late, you're early," Nicole Jefferson greeted him with a smile, extending her hand.

He took her hand and noticed the firmness of her touch. He also noticed she let it linger longer than a casual acquaintance might. And as she withdrew her hand, she caressed his. It was a subtle gesture. He found it much more exciting than aggressiveness. She removed her sunglasses and looked him straight in the eye, smiling, challenging. Suddenly, he felt uncomfortable, not in control of the situation.

"Have you eaten here before?" she asked. "Tell me what I should order."

"Sure," he said, "I always come here. My grandmother brought me here when first opened a few years ago. Then it was called "Nemos", now it has changed ownership and is called "Prime Fish." I always have the same dish for lunch, as does my grandma."

"It must be pretty good. What is it?"

"Hang on," he said, and motioned for the waitress. He ordered the Sword Fish Schnitzel, a large bottle of mineral water, and a glass of Pinot Grigio for himself. He felt at ease now. The moment of uncertainty had passed. He wouldn't let her derail him again.

"Nicole, I can't help but think, and I don't want to sound conceited or anything, but somehow I get the feeling that our meeting on the beach last week wasn't all accidental."

He took off his sunglasses and slid them into the breast pocket of his light-blue Bahamian shirt. He liked to dress casually. Brown sandals, loose khaki pants, and a Bahamian shirt were his favorite ensemble, not just in the afternoon but also in the evenings. There was no need to get dressed up in a beach town.

"Caught on, did you?" she replied broadly. "I worked long and hard at this. You're not that easy to get to know. I tried everything to get your attention. Once in the garage, I even pretended my car wouldn't start. You walked past me, put on your helmet, and jumped on your motorcycle. Off you went. I swear you must wear blinders. Do you ever notice anything around you?"

"Wow, now I really am flattered," he responded, laughing nervously. "I hope I'm worth all the effort."

"I'll be the judge of that," she said, as the waitress placed their dishes on the table.

"Hey, that does look delicious," she exclaimed. "Tastes as good as it looks," he said. "Dig in."

First, she raised her glass. "Let's have a toast. Let's drink to my not being disappointed."

They laughed, touched glasses, and drank. For several moments, they did not speak, concentrating on their food. Then, a cell phone rang, and Nicole reached for her purse. She pressed a button, held it to her ear, and briefly listened.

"Just a second," she said into the telephone. "Adam, I'm sorry, but I must take this privately. I'll be right back, okay?"

"Sure," he said. "No problem. I've got all day."

She stood up and went inside, speaking just out of his hearing. He turned and watched her go, admiring her legs and her tight, firm butt. She's a handful, he thought. When she returned, her attitude had changed. She seemed preoccupied.

"I'm sorry," she said, "but I had to take that. It was my boss. There's a sales meeting, last-minute, and he said I have to be there. I am sorry, but I promise to make it up to you. Call me later. I will be home by four. Promise?" She wrote her number on a napkin, then said, "There's my cab. I've got to go."

She stood up, leaned over, and kissed him lightly. It surprised him. Then she was gone. As the cab drove away, he watched her, but she didn't look back.

He put his elbows on the table and took another drink of wine, not knowing what to make of her. He wondered if she was playing a game. He motioned for the waitress and asked for the bill, but she told him the lady had already paid.

Making his way back to his apartment, he thought back over the day they first met, the encounter on the beach, the quick date for lunch. What did she know about him? He stopped walking. Use your training. A beautiful woman picks you up on the beach and makes no bones about wanting to get to know you. He needed to be more careful. He had been careless once before with another beautiful woman, on the job, on assignment in South America. Then it almost cost him dearly. But he always had difficulty with beautiful women, always too accepting. Yet he should know better; he had been trained by the best.

Three yellow cabs were parked along the sidewalk on Collins Avenue, the usual queue outside Joe's Stone Crab Restaurant. As he neared the last cab in the line, the driver got out and said to him in a loud voice clearly intended for the other cabbies to hear.

"Sorry, I can't take you to the airport. You have to take the first cab in line."

Adam's response was quick.

"No, I want you to drive me," he said, opening the back door and sliding into the man's cab.

"Get in! I'm in a hurry."

The driver mumbled some words in Spanish and climbed behind the wheel, shrugging his shoulders elaborately at the other two drivers. He pulled onto South Pointe Drive to head toward the airport. He didn't start the meter. He glanced in the mirror and nodded at his passenger. The Mossad had called, Adam Bergman had responded.

"Adam, you're cutting in and out. I can't hear you."

"Hang on, Grandma," he said loudly. "I'm on my cell. It'll be better in a second."

"Where are you?" she said. "Are you far away?"

"I'm on my way to the airport."

"The airport?" she asked, disappointment in her voice. "Where are you going?"

"That's why I'm calling. I have to break our dinner date tonight. The company wants me to go to Rio right away. An important client got nervous about some of our investments, about the stock market in general, I guess. I have to go and see him, do some hand holding."

"That's a long way to go to hold a man's hand."

"It's a lot of money, Grandma. I may have to spend a few days there. If it's okay with you I'll go straight to Berlin from Rio and we can meet at the hotel. Will you be all right traveling on your own?"

"Adam, darling, stop treating me like an old lady. I can manage quite well by myself. You just take care of yourself and we will meet at the hotel. If you are delayed, I can visit some of my old friends."

Adam felt a lump forming in his throat. He loved his grandmother. She was a remarkable woman. Almost ninety and she looked and acted twenty years younger. Her mind was as sharp as ever, she had none of the memory loss some of her Miami friends were suffering. Although her hair had turned gray many years ago, she was still a handsome woman. Physically active, must be where he got his genes. Not for the first time he listed for himself all the hardships his grandmother had endured. She truly was a survivor. She lived through the war; she witnessed all the atrocities against her people, and how traumatic it must have been to learn of her husband's suicide only weeks before she was to give birth to her first child. He couldn't imagine how she had done it. Then she had to leave Germany, her place of birth, her home. A strong woman. He remembered again the story she had told him so often when he was a boy. Her flight from Berlin during the war, finding her way onto a freighter in France, carrying only a small suitcase and making the voyage to the U.S. Fortunately, she had friends here, friends of her husband, friends who had helped.

At first, she had taken a job in a bank. But with her passion and talent for painting, it had not taken long to make a go of it. Her art allowed her to stay home with her son and paint in their small flat. After a couple of years, she started a midtown Manhattan gallery. She became quite successful, and soon she and Adam's father had moved into a townhouse on East 51st Street. She had always wanted to be in the Village, where her friends lived, but she didn't feel it was a proper place to raise a child. She was very protective of her son, Daniel, and proud. After public grammar school and high school in New York City, he'd earned an academic scholarship to New York University, where he majored in history.

Ever since he'd been old enough to understand what had happened to his father, Daniel had been interested in history. His grandmother had told Adam how, even as a child, Daniel wanted to know why some of his father's fellow citizens hated their family, hated their people. Why did they want to kill them? He often asked. They spoke the same language, ate the same food. Your father never did understand, Adam's grandmother used to tell him, not as a child, not even as an adult.

Adam's grandmother was also very proud of her son Daniel's career as a history professor. He was an authority on Germanic history and had published many books and articles on the subject. Daniel had been a prolific writer, a gift Adam's grandmother always told him he had inherited from his father, Joshua Bergman. Like his father, Daniel loved to entertain, particularly his intellectual friends. There were frequent parties at the Bergman flat in Manhattan, and they always reminded Adam's grandmother of the parties in Berlin before the war. Like his grandfather, Adam's grandmother often told him, his father continued cultivating his people, the Jewish community. Most of his friends were of the Jewish faith, and Daniel was a devout Jew, raised that way, Adam's grandmother used to say.

Then Martha Bergman left New York and moved to Miami. Adam was fourteen then, and his father had just been asked to take the chair of history at Stanford University. It was a position he'd longed for and worked toward for years. That was when his grandmother informed the family she would not be going with them to California. She said she had always wanted to live in Miami Beach, and this was the perfect opportunity to make the move. Her most profound regret, she told Adam, was leaving him behind. She made him promise to visit her often, and he did, spending most of his school holidays in Miami. When both of Adam's parents died in a tragic accident, he moved to Florida to live with his grandmother.

The taxi pulled up next to the curb right under the sign of Varig Airlines.

"*Baruch hashem*, blessed be God, and don't worry, no one followed. I made sure."

The cab driver did not smile. Adam left the taxi to head towards the check-in counter at Miami International Airport.

CHAPTER VIII

Miami – Rio de Janeiro, September

THE FIRST-CLASS CABIN OF THE FLIGHT from Miami to Rio de Janeiro was almost empty. Adam Bergman eased his long frame into his seat adjacent to the aisle. No one was sitting next to him, and in that seat he placed the briefcase the driver had handed over when he got out of the cab at the airport and paid the set $35 fare. No discounts for Mossad agents. He would bring it up with Maza.

Adam reached for the Diet Coke the flight attendant had placed on the tray table. He drained the plastic cup, rattled the ice, slid a piece into his mouth, and put his briefcase in his lap. Inside was a single manila envelope he had opened earlier in the terminal. Now he opened it again and went through the contents more carefully. Ice melted away as he checked: an itinerary, plane tickets, passports, cash. Maza had been thorough, as usual. He indicated a destination, Berlin, but as usual, he had given no hint of the mission. This information was delivered only when an agent was in place.

The 747 climbed. As soon as the flight attendant announced that electronic devices could be used, Adam remembered. He pulled the telephone from the seatback in front of him, swiped his credit card, and dialed. He let it ring many times before he slowly replaced the phone. The call heightened his suspicion. The ice cube slowly melted in his mouth.

Adam tilted his seat back and closed his eyes. He took the warm towel the flight attendant had just handed him and laid it over his forehead and eyes. The events of the day again flashed through his head: his lunch with Nicole, the contact by the Mossad. Had he made all the necessary calls? He wondered. He had called his grandmother from the cab, and he had called Maria, his Cuban housekeeper. He chewed slowly on more ice. He had called his office on the way to the airport. This was mainly a courtesy call, since Adam had a lot of flexibility in his work hours. He generally worked on the road, visiting clients and stopping at the office only twice, maybe three times a week. There were stretches when he wouldn't go in for two or three weeks at a time. He thought he had landed the best job in the world. The 747 banked slightly onto a new heading. Sunlight cascaded through the small window.

While at Harvard, Adam had seriously considered attending medical school to become a physician like Dr. Allan Bernstein, his family doctor and a close friend of his father. He admired and respected Bernstein, and it was Bernstein who had talked him out of medical school. Paper pushers had disillusioned Bernstein with the practice of medicine; he often spoke bitterly about the interference in the healthcare system by the government, insurance agencies, and, more recently, managed care organizations. The physician no longer practiced medicine, Bernstein said. Care was no longer dictated by what was best for the patient. The physician, the patient's true advocate, had lost control. To Bernstein, medicine was a simple equation: medicine equals doctor plus patient, nothing else. But the dollar and Wall Street had taken over. Wall Street, Bernstein told Adam, that's where you should be. Because in the end, it's the almighty dollar that plays the tune.

Adam reached for the small canvas bag that the airlines supply on long-distance flights. He removed his sandals, retrieved the stockings from the bag, and put them on his feet. He also removed the blinders and put them next to him. He intended to catch a nap on the flight.

As he shut his eyes, he recalled Bernstein's advice. This and a couple of undergraduate business courses he had taken convinced Adam to earn an MBA at Harvard Business School. The summer after his first year, he interned at the investment bank of Goldman Sachs in Manhattan. The hours were long, but he loved every minute of it. In his final year at Harvard, almost every banking firm on Wall Street recruited him. It was not only his grades, which were top of his class, but also his charisma, he was a leader, he had looks and presence. He was also multilingual, raised by his parents and grandmother to be fluent in German. He had learned Spanish in high school and in college had spent a year in Spain as an exchange student. He also spoke Hebrew.

Adam's thoughts were interrupted by the pretty brunette airline attendant. She handed him the menu and asked if he wanted another beverage. He asked for a glass of red wine. Adam reclined his seat, put the white pillow behind his head and continued to recall the events which had brought him here.

Adam was deciding whether to go with Goldman Sachs or Morgan Stanley, the other Wall Street giant, when one day he got a call from a boutique bank on Wall Street, specializing in private wealth management. He would have dismissed the offer, but the same day his grandmother mentioned the firm during their daily phone conversation. Apparently, she knew the bank's owner, a Jewish man by the name of Morris Ross. Ross and Adam's father had been friends for many years; he was part of that circle that Daniel Bergman had cultivated. Adam didn't remember ever meeting Ross, although his grandmother assured him that he had. Therefore, as a favor to her, and a courtesy to Mr. Ross, Adam had agreed to interview with the Ross Bank. He flew to New York and met with Ross in his boardroom on Wall Street. It was an impressive place, antique furniture, Persian rugs, an atmosphere of wealth and elegance, an air of relaxation, a feeling of security, a sense of accomplishment.

Adam waited only briefly in the reception area before a gentleman in his early sixties, dressed in a charcoal pinstripe suit, white shirt and maroon tie, greeted him. This was Mr. Ross. In the boardroom another man was waiting, a much younger man, about Adam's own age. He was introduced as Mathew, Ross' son. After the usual pleasantries, Morris Ross explained the background of his business. Years ago he had worked at one of the large investment houses on Wall Street. He had been very successful and had built a stable of wealthy and influential clients. Many of them wanted more personalized services than the firm could provide, so Ross decided to strike out on his own. He started Ross Bank, specializing in wealth management, or "wealth maintenance," as he liked to call it. The Ross Bank handled clients' every need, investments, taxes, bills, budgets, everything.

Before long, Ross decided to expand to Asia and South America. His son, Mathew, had a business degree from Dartmouth and a master's in Cantonese from Harvard, and he took charge of the Ross Bank's Asian interests. In the past three years, this section had accounted for almost 20 percent of the Ross Bank's revenues. A cousin of Mathew had likewise expertly developed the South American market. The cousin had done even better, a full 33 percent of the Ross Bank's revenues were emanating from South America. and the future was even brighter. Then Mathew's cousin had died in a private plane crash just three weeks ago. The bank needed a new point man in South America, and they wanted that man to be Adam. Adam stopped his reminiscing. He rubbed his eyes and looked about him. He was surprised to see that the cabin was almost empty. He exited his seat to stretch his legs and go to the bathroom. The pretty airline attendant smiled at him as he went to the lavatory.

When Adam returned to his seat, he recalled how overwhelmed he had been by the offer of the Ross bank. He remembered that the salary was $400,000 and bonuses could easily exceed the $1 million mark. Eventually, he would receive a full partnership. Yes, there would be a lot of travel involved, but to Adam's mind, this was an attraction. He was single, no ties, and he liked to travel. He could not believe his good fortune. At twenty five he'd be making more money than his father ever had, and he'd practically be his own boss. He felt he should agree immediately. He liked everything about the job and everyone he had met. Yet, on a general principle, he said he would have to think about his answer. He waited just twenty-four hours.

Best decision I ever made, Adam thought now, removing the lukewarm towel from his forehead and tossing it onto the blue tray the flight attendant had presented him. He reclined his seat further. It was a long flight to Rio. Once there, he would buy new clothes, a suitcase, and other essentials. In addition, he would prepare for the circuitous route to his final destination, Rio to Paris to Frankfurt. No plane from Frankfurt, Maza's instructions had read. He would be taking the train to Berlin.

Boston, September

"That was a wonderful party," Katie Schneider told her husband, Peter.

They had just closed the front gate to Dean O'Reilly's house. It was Friday, a beautiful late-summer night, and they were walking back to their house, only three blocks away.

"Very thoughtful of him to give us a going-away party for the Berlin Marathon," she continued. "And then the gifts, that box of Band-Aids to put on your tits so they won't bleed in the marathon. Now that was funny."

"How about the Vaseline for my armpits?" Peter replied. "How did he put it? To help grease the twenty-six miles? He really is a good friend. I wish he were coming along with us. But I guess some of us have to make a living."

Katie caught a hint of regret in her husband's voice. After all, it was only a six-month sabbatical. Still, it had taken him some time to decide to go. He had spoken to several of his closest colleagues, including Dean O'Reilly. They had often discussed it between themselves and their two kids.

At first, Peter had wavered. He stated a compelling argument to stay one day, to leave the next. He wanted to stay because he had long ago committed to working from within and helping reverse the trend toward health care as a big business. Leaving now meant failure. Then again, maybe he wasn't the right man for the job. Or perhaps nobody could reverse this trend, and why should he spend his career trying to stave off the inevitable? Katie had often made this point: one man couldn't do it alone. He'd agree, but in the next breath, he'd remark that someone had to lead, someone had to set an example.

In the end, though, the other voice inside him prevailed. It urged him to take time off to think, to explore other options. It was a heart-rending decision. Long ago, he had dedicated his life to caring for others. He remembered the moment he had made the decision. He was sitting in an office at a hospital. Across the desk from him was a dour-faced old nun, chief administrator of the Catholic hospital. He was a senior in high school, and it was just weeks before prom night. Less than an hour earlier, the police had come to his house and told him of the accident. Peter's parents and his sister, his only sibling, had been on their way home when a truck ran a red light and hit their car. They had brought Peter directly to the hospital administrator's office. That is where he had heard the news. Both his parents were declared dead on arrival; his sister was in critical condition in the ICU. However, there was not much hope; she had suffered severe head trauma. Peter sat in the nun's bleakly furnished office, helpless, while his sister struggled for her life. He desperately wanted to do something, to make a difference. He decided then he would never let himself be in that position again.

Then the nun's telephone rang. The nun picked it up, listened, put it down, and looked at Peter. "I'm sorry," she said. Your sister is gone." At that moment, the idea crystallized: He would be a doctor. He would be a man with the power to act, save, and contribute.

At first, all had gone according to plan. He loved his work. But in the past few years, he had grown bored with the medical routine. At first, he had assigned his waning interest to the frustrations of modern-day medicine, the government regulations, insurance companies' unwillingness to pay, HMOs, paperwork, and bureaucracy. Indeed, that was a big part of it, Katie recalled, as they walked hand in hand toward their quiet and comfortable suburban home, but not all of it. Ultimately, it wasn't medicine that was the problem; it was Peter. He had the "seven-year career itch," as he would say. She had laughed at that. "More of a thirty-year itch," she had said. However, she'd added that it was never too late, and he had agreed.

Schneider had made his final decision just a few days ago. Naturally, his colleagues at the medical school and the hospital tried to change his mind, except for his long-time rival, the vascular surgeon, Dr. Gallagher. Gallagher was elated and did not even have the good manners to conceal his delight. He had called Schneider at home one evening, wishing him good luck, telling him not to worry about affairs at the hospital and the medical school. He had reassured Schneider that his posts as assistant dean of the medical school, chief of staff, and board member at the hospital would be in good hands. "In confident, experienced, professional hands," that was how he had put it. Gallagher left no doubt whose hands he was referring to. Everyone knew, Gallagher had said, that he was the right man for the position.

Katie recalled how her husband had related the conversation to her. He had smiled. How typical of our profession, he had said. We were always fighting each other. There was the infighting, the disagreement, the condescension verging on arrogance. No, he had corrected himself, not verging on arrogance, more like outright arrogance.

"Just think," Schneider said to his wife as they walked up the path to their front door. "Two days from now, we'll be in Berlin. I'm so looking forward to being there again. Much of the reconstruction will be done by now. And this time we won't have to rush home; we'll have time to explore. Oh, by the way, did I tell you about the strange invitation I got at the office the other day?"

"No, no, you didn't," Katie answered. "What kind of invitation?"

"It came in the mail the other day. It was weird. At first, I figured they had mailed it to the wrong address. But it was my name on the envelope."

"Well, what'd it say?"

"It was an invitation," he said, pausing on their front doorstep, "to a party. But it was more like a letter. It started 'Dear Peter,' as if it was from someone who knows me. The person who wrote it knew we're going to be in Berlin, knew I was going to run in the marathon from one of the organizers of the race, apparently a close friend of his. What really surprised me is that our host, if we accept this invitation, claims to be a member of my family. He said we're related. He didn't say how, exactly. 'Distant relative,' he called it."

Peter reached into his right trouser pocket and retrieved the house key. Then he continued.

"At first I thought it was a joke. I called my friend Otto. You remember, the editor of the Berliner Zeitung, the newspaper. Well, to my complete surprise, Otto knew this fellow right away. Apparently, he's very well known, not just in Berlin but all over Germany. So, anyway, we're invited to this fancy party, some kind of post-marathon party at some posh place in Berlin, hosted by some very old, established German family. Otto said their parties are the social events of the year in Berlin. He told me we'd meet everyone. Certainly the mayor of Berlin, maybe even some celebrities, movie actors, CEOs, all sorts of artists. Otto told me he wouldn't be surprised if the chancellor and the president of Germany would attend. What do you think?"

"I can't believe you didn't tell me right away, is what I think, Peter," Katie said. "But tell me more about our host, who is he?"

Schneider began to open the front door.

"Oh, just some cousin or other," he said. "You had no idea I came from such a fine family, did you?"

"Peter, stop joking. I want to know who he is. I just wonder why you never heard from that part of your family before."

"I'm curious about that myself," he admitted. "So let's go find out."

"What is his name, anyway?"

"All I can tell you is how he signed the invitation: 'Your cousin William.' And what was on the letterhead."

"It's like pulling teeth getting anything out of you. For God's sake, what did it say?"

"It said Crown Prince William Frederick von Hohenzollern. Apparently he's a direct descendent of the imperial family of the Holy Roman Empire of German States."

CHAPTER IX

Frankfurt – Berlin, September

"**M**AY, I SEE YOUR TICKET, PLEASE?" The conductor asked politely in German. Adam Bergman was the only occupant in his first-class compartment on the Frankfurt-to-Berlin high-speed train.

"Of course," Adam replied in English, reaching for his ticket. "What a beautiful day to travel. I love traveling by train. It relaxes me."

"Sorry," the man replied in German. "I do not understand. I only speak German."

"That's all right," Adam responded in fluent German and repeated his remark.

"I agree," the man said. "That's why I took the job. Have a nice day and a pleasant trip."

The conductor closed the door behind him. Adam got to his feet and opened the door of his compartment. He looked down the compartment way of the train. It was empty. Perhaps the man had already entered another cabin to check on his passengers. Adam felt uneasy. The conductor had spoken German to him. But he had a slight accent. Not out of the ordinary these days in Germany. Much of Germany's workforce was foreign. But the accent got Adam's attention. It was British, very unusual, he thought. And he denied speaking any English. Adam had to ensure he was not being followed. Maza had planned this circuitous route. Now it was up to him. He closed his compartment door and took a seat on the comfortable bench. He needed to be careful, and he had to follow up on the conductor. He knew he had time. It was a long train ride to Berlin. He unbuttoned his shirt and kicked off his sandals. In about four hours, he would be there. The Intercity Express was scheduled to arrive at Bahnhof Zoo, Berlin's central railroad station, at 7:19 p.m. What a curious route, he thought. But Maza Sharef, he knew, was always cautious, and he was usually right. It's much easier to enter one European country from another. Never enter your target directly, Maza had taught him. The Mossad knew.

Ha Mossad-le Modiin ule-Tatkidim Meyuhadim, they call it in Israel: the Institute for Intelligence and Special Operations. The motto is, "By way of deception thou shalt do war." David Ben-Gurion, Israel's first prime minister and minister of defense, had created the agency in 1951 to be an intelligence organization independent of Israel's ministry of foreign affairs. Officially, the institute did not exist; the name of its leader was never made public until 1996.

Usually, the Mossad acts on its own. Often, even the Israeli government and the prime minister do not know the Mossad's agenda; frequently, they do not want to know. Unlike other intelligence agencies, the FSB, the CIA, and the Mossad employ few case officers, or *"katzas."* The entire personnel in the Mossad is estimated to be 1200. The CIA and the FSB have many thousands. Yet the Mossad is as good as intelligence agencies get. It relies on the loyalty of the Jews. Mossad officers are never afraid to approach a Jew to ask for help, because they know, although help may be denied, Jews will not tell, they will not inform on the Mossad. And usually they do agree to help because they believe Israel is in constant danger, they pull together no matter what their differences to protect themselves from their enemies. The Mossad's helpers are numerous and are located all over the world. It's said that there are more than 2,000 helpers in London alone. The helpers are called *"sayanim,"* and are always one hundred percent Jewish. They are not agents; they are volunteers. If one owns a car rental agency, when the Mossad calls for a car, it will be supplied immediately, free.

Adam decided it was time to make sure about the conductor. He left his compartment and walked to the front of the train in the direction the man had headed. It was also where the dining car was located. He walked through the narrow companionway and watched the beautiful early fall landscape rush past him. He entered the dining car, surprised to see it empty. He continued his way forward. He was about to leave the dining car when he saw the conductor on the platform leading to the next vehicle. He was speaking into a cell phone. He was speaking in perfect English. Adam knew there was no time to ask questions. No time to make sure. It only took a few seconds, not much longer, a quick snuffing out. As soon as he spotted the man, he had put on his favorite gloves minutes before.

Adam strolled leisurely back to his train compartment, drinking from a bottle of Evian placed on the tables in the dining room car. He entered his compartment, took a seat, stretched, and continued to reminisce. He had already forgotten about the man.

Adam was not a volunteer, a *sayan*. He was an agent. He had been recruited by the TSOMET, Mossad's recruiting department. He was approached shortly after he had joined the Ross Bank. The overture seemed innocent at the time; one of his co-workers at the bank had invited him over for dinner. As the evening wore on, they began discussing their backgrounds, their families. When Adam's co-worker Efram, Effy for short, found out he was the grandson of Joshua Bergman, and he expressed amazement. What a coincidence, or so it seemed. Effy had studied literature and poetry in college, and Josh Bergman was his favorite poet. It did not take long to get from there to the tragedy of Joshua Bergman's death, the tragedy of the Second World War, and the many tragedies throughout the history of the Jewish people. Adam had heard it all before. But Effy appeared to know more about his grandfather than most people.

That evening, Effy had convinced Josh Bergman's grandson that a bill was to be paid for his grandfather's death. What made him believable was his directness, his cards-on-the-table appeal. As the train sped through the German countryside, what a way to recruit an agent, Adam thought. He knew that agents in the intelligence business can be recruited by several "hooks," as they call them. The main ones were money, sex, and emotion. Indeed, in his case, money and sex would not have worked; he had plenty of both. It had to be emotion, ideology, and revenge. Effy was very clever and he played on both. By the end of the evening, Effy had been sure that he'd won over a new agent, an agent, he thought, who would prove a very valuable asset to the Mossad.

However, there was another aspect of the spy business that appealed to Adam, the challenge. You always had to be at the top of your game. It was like a race, and if you won, it was more exhilarating, more satisfying than any other feeling. Indeed, the cause could justify many things, but Adam wasn't really in it for the cause. He just loved the race.

Technically, he was not even part of the Mossad, the Institute, as it is known. The agency did not directly employ him, though they had offered to pay $3,000 monthly plus bonuses. Adam had declined. He was not in it for the money, he told his *katza,* Effy. He'd convinced him he was doing the job for his grandfather.

Adam's thoughts were interrupted by a knock on his door. He got out of his seat and inched the door open. The left hand held the door; the right was poised to strike. A freckled-faced teenager blushed and ran down the compartment way without saying a word. Adam returned to his seat and his thoughts.

The Institute wanted Adam Bergman. They wanted his life, his heart and his soul. They had plans for him. They wanted him to enroll in their program and become a *katza*. They would even make an exception for him. The Mossad had never before let anyone become a *katza* unless they were Jewish and Israeli. For Adam they would bend the rules. They knew how valuable he could be, and they knew his family, knew his grandfather, and knew his grandmother, a devout Jew loyal to Israel. They knew Adam had been raised a Zionist, spoke Hebrew, loved his grandmother, and they knew he could be won over to do his grandfather's work, to save the children of Israel.

The Institute planned to groom Adam as a special *katza,* one of only a few based in the United States. Legally, the agency is not supposed to be spying in the United States, Israel's most loyal ally, and Israel always denies any Mossad presence in the U.S. In fact, it has a strong American presence, particularly in New York and in Washington. It employs about two dozen veteran field personnel, led by two or three *katzas.* Only the most experienced, the best *katzas,* get their station in the U.S., and they take it at great risk. Officially they do not work for the Israeli embassy, and are not protected by diplomatic immunity. If caught in the U.S. they can be tried as spies; if found guilty they can be executed. In any other nation they work under diplomatic immunity; there their worst punishment is extradition.

In the end, Adam declined the position of *katza.* Instead he joined the AI, a top-secret division within the Mossad. He became a member of the most clandestine unit in all of the Mossad, a unit in which you did not even know your partner's name. It was called the *Kidon,* or Bayonet. It was the Mossad's assassination unit.

Adam Bergman was hungry. He got out of his seat, straightened his pants, and buttoned his shirt. He slid open the door of his compartment and made his way toward the dining car. When he arrived he noticed that it was almost filled now. He found an unoccupied table near the rear of the car. He didn't bother to look at the menu. The waiter approached and he ordered a Wiener schnitzel with pommes frits and a glass of Pinot Grigio.

He checked his watch. Ninety minutes until the train pulled into Bahnhof Zoo. Adam was now in Europe. Mossad rules dictated that his U.S. *katza* Effy was no longer in charge. Since he'd joined the AI, all his communications from the field were directly with Tel Aviv, either by telephone, telex or the Internet. All were coded Urgent-Tiger-Black. This meant they were seen only by his boss, Maza Sharef, head of the Mossad.

As he ate he recalled that whenever the Mossad called, he went. He had no trouble taking leaves of absence from the Ross Bank. Mr. Ross was always very accommodating. At first, Adam had made excuses for why he needed six weeks off, then another month or two. Mr. Ross would have none of it.

"Adam," he used to say, "Adam, if you need time off, take it. Ultimately I know we, the bank, will benefit. You are a true asset to this firm, and I want you to be your own man. That's when people work at their best, when they're most productive. Every time you come back from one of your trips, you seem to be a better man. I don't know where you go, I don't care. All I know is that you keep getting better in this business, you're adding valuable clients and improving our bottom line. So why should I interfere?"

The Institute first sent Adam to Kfar Sirhin, a former British air force base just east of Tel Aviv. It is used mainly to train foreign agents; the Mossad will train anyone who pays the fee there. Clients have included the German antiterrorist group Grenzschutzeinheit, Taiwanese agents, SWAT teams from India, as well as Tamils and Sinhalalese from Sri Lanka; people from both those warring factions were on the training grounds at the same time. The Mossad did not care. They needed the money to finance their operations. That's why the Institute is also deeply involved in the drug business and illegal arms sales, anything for a profit, a profit to help protect the children of Israel. The Mossad sells weapons to anyone who will pay for them. That's part of the program: come to Israel to train and train with Israeli weapons. Then, of course, you have to buy them, because your trainees perform best with the weapons they've trained on. It does not matter to the Mossad if they're training their own enemies or enemies of the United States. The U.S. sends over seven million dollars a day in foreign aid to Israel, but the Institute has a higher obligation. And remember, Adam recalled Maza Sharef telling him, remember the Institute's motto: "By way of deception thou shalt do war."

Although Adam had spent only six weeks at Kfar Sirhin, he had proved very adept at learning weaponry. As a child and teenager, he often hunted with his father, and another of their favorite pastimes was skeet shooting. Adam was a superb shot. He'd won his club's championship at age eleven, and by age sixteen, he'd won the U.S. National Clay Shooting Championship. He knew how to squeeze a trigger and hit a target.

Adam took another bite of the Wiener schnitzel. It was excellent. Cut thin, just the way his grandma prepared it.

The Institute quickly recognized his talent. His next extended trip from the Ross Bank sent him to Midrasha in Tel Aviv. He'd been surprised when he received the instructions from his katza, Effy. Everyone knows the Midrasha is the summer residence of the Prime Minister of Israel. What Adam did not realize at the time was that this was also the Institute's training academy.

He had thought he would be a guest of the prime minister. Instead, he'd been taught everything someone could learn about the spy business, Mossad style, in twelve weeks. The course was intensive. Adam was an outsider; only political katzas are usually trained at Midrasha. How difficult it was to be a *katza*, Adam thought at the time. Thousands are interviewed, and only twelve to fifteen are admitted to the course. Sometimes all would complete it, sometimes none. The Institute did not care; it wanted, it needed the correct type of people. The course was extensive; it took three years.

Adam's own training had been rigorous. He'd learned about safe houses, or "operational departments," as the Mossad calls them. When anyone asks, he'd learned about the "office," which is what Katzas works for. In fact, they all are defense department employees, but the "office" is as much as they'll say.

Then there were the exercises: how to tail your target, especially in "fast areas," which means busy streets where agents need to follow more closely, and how to write reports in Mossad's own language, the NAKA, its code.

He learned how to carry a gun. A .22-caliber Beretta is standard issue. It is kept inside the pants, right on the hip. Although some *katzas* wear holsters, most do not. The Institute likes the Beretta because it is small. To facilitate access to their guns, most agents sew a few small, flat lead weights are inside their jacket hem lining. The extra weight allows the flap of the jacket to swing away more easily when agents reach for their guns. Adam was taught to fire as many bullets as possible at the target; once the target is down, fire four more times from close range. Insurance. The bullets used were hollow points, designed to expand and do maximum damage.

He learned about the passports. All kinds of passports, all of varying quality: top, second, field operation, and throwaway. He never used throwaways, passports that were found or stolen. These are used only in situations where they can be flashed and will not be closely inspected; they are not used for identification. A special department's job is to gather information from still subjects to conduct break-ins or surveillance. They carry throwaways. Field operation passports are for work in foreign countries. Usually, this involved work done very quickly; field operation passports are never used to cross borders. Second and top passports are perfect.

The Mossad has a small factory where they are produced, a small chemistry laboratory in the academy's basement. Here, chemists analyze and duplicate the papers in passports from all over the world. The papers are then stored at just the proper humidity and temperature. Never does an operation go sour due to a bad Mossad document.

Adam was always issued a top passport. Although a second-class passport is perfect in quality, it is built on a case agent's or Katza's cover story; there is no backup or real person behind it. A top-level passport is different; there is a real person behind its photograph.

When Adam had completed his training, the Institute assigned him to Al. Al is Hebrew for "top" or "above." Members of the Mossad have no access to its computer files; they don't even know what Al does. It employs only twenty-five or thirty agents, only two or three active *katzas*. The Al Katzas are the best and most experienced in the Mossad. Effy was one of them, and Effy was one of the best. Adam's Mossad officer knew his business.

Adam finished his dinner, stretched out in his seat, and considered his life. It was exciting and challenging, and it would likely get even more so. He did not know the goal of his present mission. His only instructions were to go to Berlin, to the Hotel Adlon on the Pariser Platz, where a suite had been reserved for him. He knew that this mission had to be out of the ordinary. Maza himself had taken charge. What would happen next, Adam had no idea.

He knew that his unit was special. The Al is so well insulated from the Mossad that it reports directly to the head of the Institute. Unlike other Mossad sections, it does not work out of Israeli embassies but only out of operational apartments. The Al *katzas* have no diplomatic immunity; if caught they will likely be tried as spies. Allegedly, their role is to gather information on the Arab world. According to the Institute, the Al operates in the U.S. only for that purpose; it claims to have no interest or involvement in the affairs of the United States. Adam smiled at the thought.

The Mossad is no different than all its rivals. It's involved in an old and dirty game and it plays by old and dirty rules. During World War II the British tapped the United States' transatlantic cable, then fed the U.S. misinformation to indicate that Hitler was poised to invade the United States. They did it not to help the United States but to help the United Kingdom. What a world, Adam thought. Can we ever put aside our differences, our religions, our nationalism, and our colors? That's what my grandfather had always wanted to do, what he had written about. That was more than sixty years ago. Has anything changed?

The waiter returned and asked if Adam desired dessert. He ordered a double espresso. The next few days would be the kind of excitement he had always wanted. He had no morals about his mission. When they told him he'd be part of the Kidon, the assassination unit, they had assured him the Mossad never executed anyone unless he had blood on his hands, or unless he was pointing a gun at the children of Israel. Yet, now he felt uneasy. He watched as his wine shifted gently in its glass to the sway of the train. He could not explain the feeling, but he suspected his unease was due to his grandfather. It had to do with his family.

CHAPTER X

Berlin, September

THE HIGH-SPEED TRAIN FROM FRANKFURT PULLED into Berlin's main railroad station, the Bahnhof Zoo, within one minute of its scheduled arrival. Adam Bergman stepped onto the platform and through the crowds of travelers to the Hardenbergstrasse exit. He hailed one of Berlin's beige Mercedes cabs and asked the driver to take him to the Hotel Adlon on the Pariser Platz. The driver had at first looked skeptically at Adam's casual dress, but his demeanor changed perceptibly when Adam mentioned the Adlon, one of Berlin's oldest and most luxurious hotels. It is located on the famous Unter den Linden thoroughfare on the Pariser Platz, just next to the Brandenburg Gate. Adam thought his grandfather had lived and died here on the opposite side of the plaza.

Adam went straight through Adlon's crowded lobby to the registration desk. He took a brief note of the large lobby's decor. The walls were of cream-colored Jurassic stone, and the ceilings were vaulted. In the center was a large mosaic glass dome of gold and blue. The entire space was open and bright.

Again, his polo shirt and sandals attracted mild attention. He had bought a suitcase and some clothes on his layover in Rio de Janeiro but he must add a local flavor to his dress to avoid standing out. First, there were the basics to attend to—basics he had learned in spy school, as he liked to call his training with the Mossad. "May I help you, sir?" the registration clerk asked politely in English.

"Yes. I'm checking in. My name is Adam Bergman."

"One moment, please." The clerk tapped at his computer and peered at the screen. "Ah, yes, you will stay with us for fourteen days. You are in the Presidential Suite, our best. Here is your key. Do you need more than one?"

"No. One is fine, thank you."

"Help with your luggage?"

"No thanks. I travel light," he responded, continuing in English. He knew that Germans enjoyed practicing foreign languages and did not want to deny the desk clerk this opportunity. Adam did not need to brush up on his German; his grandmother always took care of that by speaking only in German.

"Very well. If there is anything you need, please don't hesitate to ask. Welcome to Berlin and enjoy your stay. Walter will show you to your suite. Your car is parked in the garage. Here is your ticket. Just call from your room when you need it. And here is your ticket for the performance tonight of the Berlin Philharmonic."

Adam was surprised, though he did not show it. He had known nothing about a car or a concert that night—typical Mossad. They took a need-to-know basis to an extreme.

The suite was magnificent, with a beautiful view of the Brandenburg Gate. It was furnished in the German style of the early twentieth century. There was a large fireplace, a piano, a sauna, and a whirlpool. All of it was in keeping with his cover of a successful investment banker. He tipped Walter generously, then closed and locked his door.

Immediately, he went to locate the slicks. There would be two of them. The instruction package he had received from the Miami The Cab driver said so. It also said where they would be. Slicks are hiding places where the Mossad can leave instructions, weapons, and other mission-critical items. Mossad helpers, probably maids, Adam suspected, would have been here before he checked in. They would have swept the suite for surveillance, then installed the two slicks. He opened the bathroom door and slowly ran his hand along the top of the door frame. The door consisted of two plywood panels, mostly hollow in the center. He felt it, the hole, and the string when he reached the halfway mark. Gradually, he pulled the string out. At the end of the string was a hook. It was empty. This was where the Mossad would leave him messages or tools he might need as the mission moved forward. He dropped the string back in place.

Usually, when an agent enters a target country, he communicates directly with the Institute's headquarters in Tel Aviv. Adam knew this mission would be different. The operation was too large, too essential. It was beyond the means of the *Yarid,* the Mossad's department for European security. The Yarid consists of three teams of five to seven members each. Usually, only one at a time is deployed in Europe, while the other two train in Israel, but Sharef had decided to put two teams in Berlin. He had also put on jumpers, *katzas* usually stationed in Israel and used elsewhere as needed. This was an *air force* mission, a no-miss operation.

Adam went to the closet in the suite's large bedroom and removed the clothes rod. He turned it on its end and squinted inside by the gleam of his small flashlight. Empty. They would probably make contact at the concert tonight.

Since there was nothing else to do, he decided to jog. He needed to do it anyway. He was scheduled for a tapering run to prepare for the upcoming Berlin Marathon. He put on his shorts, a T-shirt, and his running shoes. He strapped his heart monitor around his chest. Finally, he added a new item, something he had picked up during his layover in Rio. It was a plain tan cap, which he folded and tucked inside the waistband of his running shorts. He had to carry the cap every day while he was in Berlin. It was a Mossad signal.

He hoped he would never have to put the cap on his head because once he did it meant his mission over, time to go home. He had been carefully trained to detect tails. The Institute's instructions were clear. If you believe someone is following you, do not lose them. Verify that you are being followed. When you are certain you have a tail, put on your cap. Any other Mossad people in the area will then know you are being followed and will stay away. Then walk to a phone, dial the number, identify yourself, and say you are being followed. Now you are done. Go to a movie, go to dinner or just go home. You are out of the mission. If a *katza* is followed, his entire station will be closed down, maybe for months. The Mossad takes no chances. They know the game, they are the best.

It was just minutes before the concert by the Berlin Philharmonic, one of the best orchestras in the world. The members of the orchestra had taken their seats at the front of the beautiful Konzerthaus, the former Schauspielhaus on the Gendarmenmarkt. As the members of the orchestra tuned their instruments and awaited the entrance of their conductor, Adam noticed that every seat was taken, almost every seat. The chair to his right was still empty.

Adam had arrived only a short while ago. By the time he got back to the hotel after his run, he was already late. He took a quick shower and called room service for a snack. He had a craving for

American food, so he ordered a hamburger and a diet Coke. He planned to eat late, after the concert, he asked the concierge to make a reservation at Borchardt's at the Gendarmenmarkt, one of Berlin's best restaurants. After his shower he put on the dark blue Armani suit he had bought in Rio. When he dressed formally, he only wore Armani. He rose with the rest of the audience to applaud as the conductor made his entrance. The applause lasted several minutes, and as it subsided Adam noticed the woman standing next to him. Many people had noticed. She was dressed in a low-cut black evening gown. She had long blond hair, blue eyes, and full lips. She was beautiful. But more than that, she was exciting. Adam could feel it, he sensed it, and there was an air about her. He turned to address her as the applause subsided. He tried to say hello, but the words never materialized because Kirill Petrenko, the conductor, was tapping the lectern, ready to start the concert. Adam took his seat again, looking at the woman, trying to make eye contact. Either she did not notice or she was ignoring him. He wondered if she might be his Mossad contact. Could he be so lucky? At his first opportunity he would try to confirm his suspicion. And if he was right, he would need to remember to thank Sharef for sending him such an attractive partner.

The concert began and it was magnificent, drawing Adam in. When intermission came he turned to speak to the woman, but she had left her seat. She was moving toward the aisle which led to the lobby. Adam joined the rest of the audience as they made their way through the doors on their way to the bar. He joined the line at the bar. It was a long line, but he had the urge to drink a glass of champagne. As he stood waiting he felt a tap on his right shoulder and a glass of champagne was placed gently into his hand. He turned. There she was. She smiled and ushered him out of the line.

"I thought you might need this," she said. She also had a glass of champagne.

"You read my mind," he answered. "Thanks."

"You must be American," she said. Her English was excellent, but he caught the faint German accent.

"How did you figure that out?"

"Your cologne," she said. "Americans always use plenty." She smiled confidently.

"Sorry if it offends you."

"Not at all," she said quickly. "It's not offensive, just different.

European men don't use much cologne. In fact, I rather like it. It's different. *Vive la difference!*" she added. "I like Americans. They're so pure, so…. naive."

By this time, the crowd at the bar was standing shoulder to shoulder, and the two of them were pressed close together. She touched Adam's right arm and asked him to step outside onto the square. As they walked, she put her arm into his and gently brushed her breast against his chest. A wave of excitement passed through him. They stepped outside into the warm Berlin night. Damn, he thought. Get control of yourself, and do it right away. I always fall for this. Then he noticed the large diamond on her left ring finger. His look did not escape her.

"You did buy me the most beautiful diamond for our engagement." She stopped, pulled him close, and kissed him.

"I have a wonderful idea," she said, squeezing his arm. "Let's enjoy the rest of the concert and then have dinner together."

"Sorry," he said. "I'm afraid I've got other plans."

"Oh," she said, "maybe some other time."

Then she pulled him close, very close. Her lips touched his right ear, and she whispered slowly and clearly.

"Borchardt's Restaurant," she told him, her tone changing from seductive to professional, "right after the concert, lovebird."

The Berlin Philharmonic received a standing ovation. The applause lasted ten minutes or more. Adam clapped vigorously. He did not want to leave. He enjoyed the music, the surroundings, the people, and the atmosphere. Then he felt the expected tug on his right arm. Time to get back to work. Sure, she was beautiful, but she was Mossad. She would be watching him. Time to play the game he had been trained for. Adam looked at her and smiled. "What's your name?" he said above the applause.

She leaned into him and gave him a quick kiss on the lips, the kind of kiss you give to your date to say thank you, thanks for the concert. She was good, he thought. She should be; she was one of Sharef's people.

"I'm Lisa," she said as she straightened. "I'm your fiancee."

She led him through the crowds, out of the concert hall, and onto the plaza of the Gendarmenmarkt. It was a beautiful evening. There was a full moon, and he was walking with one of the most beautiful women he had ever met, his fiancee. Now they were holding hands like lovers. She knows her part, he thought, and I'm no slouch either. This is part of the job. I'll have to do it, he thought with a grin.

They crossed the square and went to the restaurant. It was packed, as Borchardt's usually is. The maitre d immediately recognized Lisa, a sayan, Adam thought. The man led them to a table set for four people and occupied by another diner.

"Miss Schroeder," the maitre d' addressed Adam's companion, "if this table is not private enough, please let me know. We can make other arrangements."

"No, thank you," she replied. "This is perfect." It was the most secluded table in the restaurant.

The maitre d' left, and they sat down. There were no introductions. Everyone made believe that they were old friends. So they looked at the menu. Adam asked for the wine list. While he waited, he studied the third person at the table. He was older, in his forties. He was in excellent physical shape. Although he had not stood up when they approached the table, good friends usually don't, Adam could see he was tall, six-foot-two or three.

"Jacob, how are you? Good to see you again," said Adam's date.

"Yes," he replied kindly, leaning forward and kissing her. "Ever since you two lovebirds got engaged, we don't see you much anymore."

Lovebirds, that was the code word. These would be the two other members of Sharef's roving team. They were also part of AI and were here for one purpose. This was Maza Sharef's assassination team.

CHAPTER XI

Berlin, September

AIR FORCE ONE, UNDER THE COMMAND OF Colonel Harold Peterson, United States Air Force Academy graduate and former Vietnam squadron leader, touched. German soil at Tegel Airport in Berlin, seven hours and ten minutes after departing Washington. It was a beautiful morning, and the sun was already shining in a clear sky.

The German government had prepared a hangar at the north end of the field to receive the passengers, and as the plane taxied toward it, President Allan Levenson loosened his seat belt, stretched his legs, and smoothed his pants. Before landing, he had showered and changed into a fresh blue pinstriped suit. Those who knew him well thought him a rather vain man, but Levenson considered bright dress an essential part of his image. It simply would not do for the leader of the free world to appear in public in wrinkled trousers.

The plane was still moving down the runway at a good pace when the unforeseen, the improbable happened. Having just reminded his passengers to remain seated, Captain Peterson looked out the windshield and was horrified to see a Learjet crossing the tarmac directly in front of him. Collision, no way to avoid it. He did the only thing he could. He stood on the brakes, reversed thrust, and throttled full. And he prayed that the Lear jet pilot would be a professional and see the same chance Peterson saw and take it. Luckily he did. The small jet accelerated. The two men never communicated, there wasn't time. There were only two professionals and their shared instinct. Captain Peterson fought as the brakes screamed and the engines roared. The plane shuddered violently as it decelerated. Passengers were tossed in their seats, first forward, then sharply back.

Half out of his seat, Levenson was slammed even more violently forward, then back, and immediately he felt a sharp pang in his chest. Up in the cockpit, Captain Peterson watched the Lear jet pass just fifty yards in front of him; sweat appeared as he slumped in his seat. Sweat was also forming on the forehead of the president. He was in severe pain and had difficulty breathing.

"Chief!" said Brad Hamilton, the president's press secretary, who was sitting across the aisle. "Chief, are you okay?"

"I don't know. I don't think so," Levenson answered. "My chest. Get the doc."

The president's personal physician, Dr. Nathan Cole, was sitting only two rows behind Levenson. Cole had attended Yale Medical School, trained at Hopkins and had run a successful private practice before joining the staff at Columbia University in New York City, as Chief of Internal Medicine. His wife, Sarah, and the president's wife, had met years ago when the president was still a New York senator. The two women had done charity work together and had become close friends.

As Cole approached the president, he knew right away there was trouble. Levenson was breathing rapidly, holding his chest. Cole immediately called for the gurney, which was standard equipment on Air Force One. He took the president's blood pressure, 180 over

102. Elevated. His pulse was racing, 120 beats per minute. Levenson complained of chest pain, and pain in his back, between his shoulder blades, describing it as severe, a tearing pain. A heart attack, Cole thought at first.

He opened the president's shirt and fastened the electrodes of the EKG machine to his chest and limbs. The electrocardiogram showed nothing but sinus tachycardia, a rapid heartbeat. No sign of acute myocardial infarction. Cole listened to the president's heart through his stethoscope, no heart murmur, no rub. His lungs were clear as well. He checked Levenson's pulses, the radial pulses in the wrists, both carotid pulses in the neck and the femoral pulses in the president's groin. They were strong and equal. Or were the femoral pulses slightly weaker? He was not sure.

If not a heart attack, then what? Cole thought. He ran through the symptoms again in his head and arrived at a different diagnosis. The sudden stop of the plane, the lurching, led him to suspect the worst: acute aortic dissection, a tear in the president's aorta, the primary blood vessel in the body. The chances of survival in such cases were not good. He had to get the president to a hospital. He needed a CT, a MRI and perhaps an aortogram; he needed a cardiovascular surgeon. Cole started an intravenous line and gave the president a narcotic analgesic to manage the pain. Cole also had to control the pulsatile load. This had to be done by controlling the velocity of the blood ejected from the president's heart and reducing his systolic blood pressure. Keeping the blood pressure down was vital to prevent further dissection. He added an antihypertensive and a beta- blocker to the I.V. Cole remained calm. He had been trained for these situations; he experienced them all the time. He had to stabilize his patient and then get him to a hospital. But Cole was the only there was a passenger on board who remained calm. There was pandemonium on the plane, with people crying, screaming, and confusion everywhere.

"We need to get the president to a hospital as fast as possible," Cole told Brad Hamilton, who was hovering over him.

"Call an ambulance and have the cardiovascular team stand by when we arrive. And, their best cardiovascular surgeon, if we're going to save the president's life."

"Charitee Hospital," said a member of the president's staff.

"That's Berlin's best. Their cardiovascular surgeon trained back in the United States."

"No," said Hamilton, the press secretary. "Baker. Charles Baker. He's the best cardiac surgeon in the world. And he's here, in Berlin, to give a lecture. I read the conference lineup this morning."

Levenson, now sedated, was breathing less rapidly.

"All right," said the president's chief of staff, speaking for the first time. "All right, everyone, calm down. Somebody call the vice president, tell him what's going on, and tell him to get his ass to the White House, just in case. And somebody get this Baker guy. Now! Get going!"

Charles Baker hurried through the revolving door into the Regent Hotel at the Gendarmenmarkt at a quarter past noon. He had just taken the quick Berlin tour. He had arrived in Berlin at eight a.m. and had some time to kill. Take a city bus, had said a friend who had visited Berlin several times. Take Bus 100. So he did. He got on at the Opernplatz and went up to the second level of the yellow double-decker. He spotted an empty seat in the front row and sat down. The locals, the commuters, stayed at the bottom; they wanted to get on and off as quickly as they could.

The bus rolled up Unter den Linden past the famous Humboldt University and through the Brandenburg Gate. Charlotte, the wife of King Frederick I, originally laid out Unter den Linden in 1642. The queen wanted a fashionable avenue, so she planted lime trees on either side of the broad street. Since German unification, this has again been one of Berlin's most popular thoroughfares.

The 100 bus passed many of Berlin's best-known places: the Zoo, the Brandenburg Gate, the Reichstag, the Pariser Platz, and the Opernplatz, built by Frederick the Great and his royal architect, Knoblauch. It also passed Museum Island, where some of Berlin's top cultural institutions are located.

As a museum fanatic, Baker decided to visit Museum Island on foot the next day and study the museum exhibits. So when his bus reached Alexanderplatz, he climbed off and hailed a cab back to his hotel.

Riding back to the Gendarmenmarkt, he felt the jet lag set in. But he knew from years of traveling that an afternoon nap was the worst remedy. Not that he could afford to take a nap anyway. He had a lecture at the Congress on Health and Education at the Messegelaende near the Funkturm. He wanted to be there early and see the opening address by President Levenson.

As the cab neared the Regent Hotel, Baker asked the driver to stop near the side of Gendarmenmarkt Square where the French dome stands. Baker wanted to cross the magnificent square on foot. He crossed the plaza and admired the domed towers of the French and German Domes, the two Protestant churches that face each other across the square. In the center of the square was the Konzerthaus, a neoclassical masterpiece. There, Leonard Bernstein celebrated the fall of the Berlin Wall with a concert on Christmas Day in 1989.

Before the Konzerthaus, he passed the Schiller Memorial, a tribute to one of Germany's greatest poets. He realized he did not have much time. The president's opening address at the congress was about to start soon. Baker hurried through the heavy revolving doors of the Regent Hotel. As he entered the lobby, he noticed two gentlemen approaching him briskly. Both were young, mid twenties or early thirties, he estimated. Both were just over six feet tall and muscular. Both wore dark gray suits and grim faces.

"Dr. Baker," one man said. "Dr. Baker," he repeated. "Please follow me."

Baker stopped.

"Who are you? How do you know who I am?"

"Dr. Baker, this is a matter of national security," the man said, parting his coat just enough to reveal the Secret Service identification card on his belt.

"Follow me."

No "please" this time. The men took hold of Baker's elbows, turned him around, and led him onto the sidewalk in front of the hotel. A Mercedes was waiting, motor running, rear doors open, driver at the wheel. In front of the car were two Berlin motorcycle police officers dressed in green and brown summer uniforms, astride their green and white BMWs, blue lights flashing bleakly in the midday sun. The two Secret Service men guided Baker into the car and sat one on each side of him in the rear seat. The driver accelerated away onto Charlottenstrasse.

"Dr. Baker," said the officer seated to Baker's left. I am sorry, sir. But we had no time to explain. We're dealing with a national emergency. We're going to the intensive care unit at Charité Hospital. There, you will be met by the cardiovascular team of Dr. Jorg Schmidt, chief of surgery at Humboldt University."

Baker's surprise had changed to anger, almost fear.

"What the hell is going on here? Are you kidnapping me?"

"No, sir," the agent countered. "As I said, this is a national security matter. Approximately two hours ago, Air Force One landed at Tegel Airport. Something happened to the president while the plane was taxiing to its hangar. I don't know what. All I know is an ambulance was called. The president of Germany, the chancellor, and the mayor of Berlin were there to greet President Levenson. It never happened. When the plane stopped, the ambulance took him to the Charité Hospital."

"Very well, so we're going to the hospital," Baker said. "What do you want me to do? I have a lecture to give at the health congress in just a few hours. I'm addressing the European Congress of Vascular Surgery on aortic dissections. What are you going to do with me once we get to Charitee? And how did you find me, anyway?"

Baker waited. Curiosity and pride washed back anger and fear. The president was in danger, and they had come to him, Charles. Baker, M.D., famous cardiovascular surgeon, author of innumerable textbooks and scientific papers, chairman of surgery at one of the most prestigious medical institutions in the United States. He waited. "Dr. Baker, I want to apologize," the man said, though his tone did not sound apologetic. Let me introduce myself, please. My name is Harrington. The officer next to you is Farmer. The driver is Jordan. It's just that this is an unusual situation, we were all caught off guard and are a little on edge right now."

"Apologies accepted," Baker said with a smile.

Now he was in charge. They needed him, and being needed was his way of life. He was the doctor, they were the patients.

"You said you were caught off guard, what does that mean? Can you explain?"

"Yes, sir," the government man replied. He had begun to like this elderly physician.

"Doctor, our job is to protect the president of the United States. We plan Every step he takes meticulously for months before he takes it. Every minute, every second, every move he makes, we know. When it happens as planned, we know nothing should go wrong and are in our comfort zone. Our worst enemy is the unexpected. Naturally, we try to plan for all contingencies. But the unexpected happens. And it's happened now."

"You make it sound like someone's trying to kill the president," Baker said.

"We assume that someone always wants to kill the president. That's our job, hope for the best but expect the worst."

Baker sat for a moment and watched the motorcycle escort clear traffic ahead of them. They were efficient, but their task was not difficult. Germans respected authority perhaps more than any other people. In the past, it had cost them dearly. "Tell me why you came to me," Baker said.

"When the president got hurt or ill on the plane, his physician made a diagnosis," the Secret Service man said. "He said the president might need surgery on his chest. One of the president's staff had read in the newspaper that you'd be here in Berlin, giving a lecture. They decided that since you were available, and since you're the best, you should do the operation. Like I said, contingencies."

"One contingency you haven't thought of," Baker said. "There is a matter of, I guess you could call it etiquette, that needs to be addressed. I can't just walk into Charitee Hospital and take over. I have no privileges there, no right to practice medicine."

"Don't worry about any of that," Harrington answered. "We took care of it. The president's chief of staff spoke to the head honcho there, a Dr. Schmidt, I think."

"Yes, Jorg Schmidt," Baker said. "Excellent man, good surgeon. Jorg and I know each other from way back. He came to the U.S. to study with me and to learn some new techniques, my techniques."

"Yeah, that's right," Harrington continued. "When he heard it was you the president wanted, your German doctor had no problem. He even offered to be your first assistant, if you decide the boss needs surgery. I guess everyone knows you're the man."

Of course, they know, Baker thought. That's my job, that is what doctors do. Let everyone know you're the best. Not just the patients, them too, of course, they're important, but your peers, as well. Let them know all the time, never let up. You're better, you're always right, you don't make mistakes, and you're always one step ahead. And do it any way you can. Write books, scientific papers, lecture all over the world, talk to your peers, talk down to them, subtly of course, but let them know you're better. That's when you get the satisfaction of success, the satisfaction you've worked so hard for.

You look in the mirror and you know. Baker watched the motorcycle escort, the pomp and menace. He rather liked that, pomp and menace.

CHAPTER XII

Tel Aviv – Paris, September

MAZA SHAREF ALWAYS TOOK THE DIRECT route. He did not travel the way his agents did. Though he was the head of the Mossad, he had kept his existence a secret. He did not exist. The Israelis denied his existence. The prime minister of Israel did not control him. So he traveled directly. He took an Air France flight from Tel Aviv to Paris. The next day, he would fly from Paris to Berlin, arriving at nine a.m.

As soon as he had left the White House, he had made the only decision he could. He would not consult the prime minister; only he could make this decision. He was responsible for the security of Israel. It was clear. It was obvious. The president of the United States was now holding a gun to the head of his nation. As soon as Maza had stepped into the limousine, which took him from the White House to the airport, he opened his laptop and entered President Levenson into the Mossad computer files as a *"paka,"* a hostile. Before he'd boarded the plane back to Israel, he had telephoned the Institute to say that this would be an *"ain efts,"* or no-miss operation. The president had to be taken out. This was an operational emergency.

Sharef had put his team together. He knew they were the best. He knew they could do the job. This time, the stakes were the highest; this time, it meant the survival of his country and his people. Sharef had planned the mission thoroughly, efficiently, and, most importantly, deceptively. No one would ever know the Mossad was involved.

Sharef flew first class as a rule, but on this trip, he did not. The less attention he got, the better. This would be the most critical mission the State of Israel had ever engaged in. The nation was plotting against its greatest ally, preparing to wound its brother. If the prime minister knew, he would never approve. The prime minister would discuss it with the others and argue, and no decision would be reached. This had to be a Mossad mission. And he had to lead. After all, what do the politicians know?

Sharef left his aisle seat in the coach cabin and walked to the airplane's rear. He wanted to stretch his legs, and he needed a distraction. His mind had been preoccupied with all the recent events. He wanted a moment's rest to clear his thoughts. He stepped into the small galley in the rear of the plane to make idle conversation with one of the airline attendants. The attractive blonde attendant chatted briefly with him. Then she told him it was time to return to his seat. Drinks were about to be served.

Sharef returned to his seat and his thoughts. He had taken personal charge of this mission. This was unusual. Routinely, Israel's European agency, the *Yarid,* or "country fair," handled security measures there. However, this was far too sensitive. In addition, it was personal. Sharef had met Levenson in his office, on his turf, and he had been insulted, his people had been insulted, and Israel had been insulted. Levenson was just another politician. He had missed the point. He did not realize the danger. Sharef had tried to explain. He had given the president every opportunity to make the right choice.

It always comes down to this, he mused, as the plane reached its cruising altitude. Israel was on its own again. The U.S. had never fully understood Israel's struggle with the Palestinians, and now it refuses to recognize this new threat. Even the events of 9-11 seemed already forgotten. The Americans once again are too comfortable, too secure. They have not suffered often enough like the Israelis have, and until they do, they will not understand.

Sharef knew his mission. The *Yarid* had been put on highest alert. They had assembled the teams Sharef had asked for. One would be stationed at the Reichstag, Germany's parliament building, the other at Schloss Bellevue, the residence of the president of Germany, Allan Levenson's host. They were ready. Then suddenly it all had changed. Sharef had not been surprised. The Mossad always plans for the unexpected. With the president hospitalized at Charité, his roving team would take over. They would ensure that the unexpected worked in Mossad's favor and that Levenson would not reveal what Sharef had told him in the Oval Office. Had he broken his word? How had he put it? "You have the word of the president of the United States, and I guess I don't have to tell you what that means." Yes, Mr. President, you do have to tell me what that means.

The pretty blonde flight attendant smiled and asked Sharef what he wished to drink. He ordered a beer, a bottle of Heineken. Sharef knew that for this mission, he would not stay at a hotel, but at one of the Mossad's operational apartments. He did not want to be seen; he was not supposed to be here. The Israeli prime minister would never know that he or the Mossad was involved in the assassination of the U.S. president.

Sharef would directly blame the PLO. The PLO would assassinate the president. Americans would learn that they were again vulnerable. Once more, they would get a taste of the suffering that Israel had known for so long. And when they finally understood, they would be more firmly than ever in Israel's camp.

Sharef knew Dr. Baker, the famous American thoracic surgeon, was going to Charité Hospital to examine the president. The driver of the Mercedes taking him there was a Mossad agent. Several years ago, the Mossad had been successful in recruiting him. He had reported every move the local Secret Service officers made. At the hospital, the Institute also had its sayanim. Sharef would be well informed.

He knew he had two contingencies. One, Dr. Baker would operate on the president. In that case, the Mossad would have people in the operating room. Undoubtedly, Dr. Manfred Riff, head of anesthesiology, would administer the anesthesia. He was not only the top anesthesiologist in Berlin; he was the best friend of Dr. Jorg Schmidt, Charité's head of thoracic surgery. And he was a *sayan*.

In Sharef's second contingency, the president would not need an operation, or he would be transferred for surgery elsewhere. Sharef thought this to be the more likely event. The Americans would transfer Levenson to one of their own facilities, perhaps to one of their military bases, or they might even fly him back to the U.S. Of course, this depended on Baker's evaluation. The Americans would undoubtedly do if the president could be stabilized enough to allow a transfer. They would want him in an American hospital with American doctors. Sharef smiled. Yes, that's the American way, that's how it would happen.

Therefore, he had another plan. Undoubtedly, the Secret Service would not use an ambulance to return the president to the airport; they would want to get him there quickly. They would fly him from the Charité Hospital to Air Force One in a helicopter. Sharef had been in the business too long not to be able to predict the moves of his enemies. Anyway, before long, he would know for sure. He would know about surveillance at the airport, scheduling, and unusual security activity. One of Sharef's assassination teams had brought three Russian-made Strella missiles to Berlin. These had come not from Israel but from Bosnia, where the PLO stored them at one of their training camps. In one of their many arms deals, the Mossad had acquired a number of Strellas in the past. Sharef had known that one day they would come in handy. The weapon was one of the PLO's favorites.

Now they would link the PLO to the assassination. The Strella is not a particularly sophisticated weapon, but it is deadly, effective on slow-moving targets such as commercial airliners and helicopters.

The missile uses the U.S. "red-eye" system, and is propelled from a twenty-five-pound launcher that can be hung over a shoulder. Once fired, it finds its target by honing in on the hot exhaust of the engines of the aircraft. The weapon has a maximum range of just over two miles. It was perfect, Sharef thought, just what the doctor ordered.

Langley, Virginia, September

"Nicole, sorry. I hope I didn't screw things up with Bergman. But there was no other way. I had to do it. Our timetable has changed. I know the contact report you sent read routine, it's now gone to critical."

"Critical," Nicole replied in disbelief. "What happened?"

"It happened very quickly," he said. "The president is ill, very ill, and he's in a foreign country, a friendly, I assure you, but I still don't like it. We just got information from our Berlin station that your recruit Adam Bergman could be right in the middle of it all. That is why we called you. That's why you're here."

Nicole and her boss, the head of the CIA, the Director of Central Intelligence or DCI, were in an office on the seventh floor of CIA headquarters in Langley, Virginia. She knew "critical" meant top priority. What had changed in just a few days? Not long ago, she had been at the "Prime Fish" restaurant in South Beach, Miami, Florida, with Adam, a "developmental," as the CIA called them, someone they wanted to recruit. During their luncheon, her telephone had rung. Her instructions had been direct. Get to Langley, to CIA headquarters, immediately. Drop everything and get there.

So she did. She took a cab to Miami Airport, a flight to Washington, and another to Langley. As she rode up Dolley Madison Boulevard and into the two-hundred-and-fifty-eight-acre Langley compound, she knew she'd soon be in the middle of a mission. She could taste the adrenaline.

Nicole Amy Jefferson grew up in Cleveland, Ohio. Her father was an attorney, managing partner of one of the city's larger law firms. She had three older brothers; she was the only girl, and, not surprisingly, Nicole had grown up a tomboy. She didn't play with the other girls; she played with her brothers. She always thought they'd all been born just a year apart, and she could hang with them. She played basketball with them, she biked, she ran, she hunted, just like the boys. She was just as good and often better. On their annual ski trips to Colorado, she'd been the first to ski in the trees, and she was the one who first suggested helicopter skiing. There was no challenge she wouldn't meet.

Like her brothers, Nicole had gone to private school and excelled. She graduated first in her high school class at the Hawken School in the Cleveland suburb of Gates Mills and went straight to Princeton.

In her junior year, she studied abroad at Oxford, and that's when she decided she wanted to work overseas, she relished the adventure, the challenges. All her brothers had decided to follow their father into law. He had encouraged them to do so. He firmly believed that lawyers ran the country. Besides, he always said, law school teaches you to look at both sides of the coin, and that's important in life, no matter what you do. Nicole had thought about it. But she really didn't like the idea of being a lawyer. She knew her father's work, because often he brought it home with him. That wasn't what she wanted to do. However, she did it anyway and enrolled at Yale Law School. Her father was pleased. He thought he'd won her over.

Law school proved less than a challenge for Nicole. She graduated in the top ten percent of her class, and every reputable law firm on the East Coast was after her. Instead, she decided to join the CIA. She was not recruited; she was a walk-in. She had studied the organization closely. She knew of the many bungled operations, the Bay of Pigs, the assassination attempts on foreign heads of state. She knew that the "company," as it was called in the old days, was not well respected; indeed, many Americans resented the organization, and with good reason. After all, the early directors of the CIA, men like William J. Donovan, John A. Malone, Allen W. Dulles, Richard Helms, saw no conflict in running an intelligence organization within a free society. They also saw no reason to let the public in on what they were doing. However, those were the early days, Nicole assured herself. Things had changed in 1975 and 1976, when the Church Committee was assigned to look into the activities of the CIA. Senator Church, an Idaho Democrat, headed it. Then there was Gerald Ford's Commission, chaired by then-Vice President Rockefeller. Those committees had dug up a lot of dirt on how the agency had illegally intercepted and opened mail, kept dossiers on innocent Americans, infiltrated "dissident" groups in the U.S., and used LSD on unsuspecting citizens, and tried to kill foreign leaders. Worse, Nicole realized, all of it had been approved or initiated by American presidents.

After the Church hearings, Congress took a much stronger oversight role, and the CIA's operations changed drastically. Permanent committees were appointed to oversee the activities of the CIA and other intelligence agencies. The new CIA was as clean as any intelligence agency could be.

She'd decided to join. The adventure and the excitement were her true motivations, but she was also a patriot and loved her country. Having done her homework, Nicole knew that there five components to the CIA: four directorates and the Office of the Director of Central Intelligence. Of the four directorates, only one really interested her, the Directorate of Operations. This division does the human spying. It handles all covert operations. It employs approximately 5,000 people, and it's the most secretive division in the agency. The DDO heads it, the deputy director of operations, who reports to the gentleman Nicole was sitting opposite now, the head of the CIA.

The Directorate of Operations' mission is to break foreign countries' laws. The DO's agents perform espionage, which is illegal in most nations. The Directorate of Operations undertakes covert operations such as the overthrow or influence of foreign governments, political leaders, or political parties. This is done via secret funding, training, paramilitary operations, or, more often, recruiting. The DO recruits the agents of foreign countries who it thinks can pass along important information.

Nicole was sent to Camp Peary, Williamsburg, Virginia, when she joined the CIA. This was where she learned to be a spy. Over the year-long training period, there were courses in the detection of explosives, surveillance and counter-surveillance, how to write reports, how to shoot various weapons, and how to run paramilitary, counter-terrorism, and counter-narcotics operations. Most importantly, she learned how to recruit and run foreign double agents. After Camp Peary, she was sent to Harvey Point, North Carolina, for paramilitary training, then to Arizona for training in the desert, then to Panama for six weeks in the jungle.

Each assignment presents two options for the CIA case officers. One is to work undercover as a State Department employee or for the military. This is the safe way, with the protection of diplomatic immunity. If caught spying in a foreign country, officers are declared *persona non grata* and expelled. The second option is unofficial cover. This status confers no diplomatic immunity. If caught in a foreign country, a CIA officer can expect to be tried as a spy and be sent to prison, perhaps to the executioner. Several hundred CIA operations officers work under unofficial cover. Most pose as entrepreneurs or employees of American companies.

When Nicole received her assignment to recruit Adam Bergman, she was given unofficial cover. This would give her more freedom, more latitude. To preserve the illusion, CIA officers who work under official cover must perform some of the normal State Department or military duties, limiting their time for the CIA work. Nicole and the CIA had decided that recruiting Adam should be a full-time job. She would need all the flexibility she could get. She'd been told that the recruitment of Adam was a personal priority of the DCI, the Director of Central Intelligence. Adam Bergman was a suspected Mossad agent. Nicole was told to turn him, to make him a double agent. She knew this could be difficult. To turn a religious and nationalistic person was not easy. She needed to use all her skills, maybe more. And a man like this? He could kill her.

Generally, intelligence gathering inside the United States falls under the auspices of the FBI. But Executive Order 12333, signed by President Ronald Reagan on December 4, 1981, allows the CIA to gather intelligence in the U.S. so long as the target is foreign. Although Adam Bergman was an American citizen, because the CIA suspected him of working for Mossad, the agency decided to classify him as a foreigner. Though the CIA and the FBI are fiercely competitive, cooperation between the two organizations is not unheard of. After the reign of J. Edgar Hoover, they formed a joint operation, codename Courtship, which consisted of five FBI agents and four CIA officers.

To facilitate Nicole's recruitment of Adam Bergman, she was assigned to the CIA's Foreign Resource Branch, or FR. This division operates under commercial cover, and its primary function is to recruit foreigners visiting the United States. The FR is a closely guarded secret operating out of several American cities. Nicole was assigned to the Miami station. Once there, she was given another identity: a businesswoman working for the CIA under commercial cover in Miami. Her other identity was her true one: a CIA case officer.

The office of the man in charge of the CIA was not only spacious. It was luxuriously decorated. Tastefully, Nicole thought. Heavy wooden antique furniture and Persian rugs gave the office an ambience of peacefulness. Not what Nicole had expected.

"Nicole," the DCI said, "we have nonspecific information that something big is coming down in Berlin. Is it a coincidence that the president is in Berlin? I don't believe in coincidences. Now he's sick. I want him out of there as soon as possible."

"Yes, sir," she replied nervously. Yet she could feel the adrenaline rush, the excitement. This was the moment she had waited for, the moment she had trained so hard for.

"But if I may, sir, Germany is a friendly. And I'm sure their medical care is—"

"Look," the DCI interrupted. "I didn't bring you halfway across the country to hear your view on German medicine. I don't have time to explain. The CIA doesn't trust German doctors and the CIA doesn't trust Germany. They are not, repeat, not our friends. Europe is not our friend."

"What do you mean, Europe?" she asked in astonishment. "The European Union is now a CIA priority."

"Sir, I don't understand. Can you elaborate?"

"No, Bill can do that. He'll brief you downstairs. Then I want you on the next plane to Berlin. You'll report to our station there. Okay, go. We may not have much time. I just have this hunch. Don't ask me why, maybe it's all the years in this damned business. It's all going to come down Berlin. It often has, more often than any of us would like to remember."

CHAPTER XIII

Langley, Virginia, September

NICOLE WAS UPSET. AS SOON AS she left the DCI's office, she headed straight for the ladies' room. She needed to calm down, to regain her composure. Nicole decided that she did not like the man, her boss. He had treated her like a two-year-old; he had been abrupt and abrasive. He had not extended her professional courtesy; she felt she was due. She looked in the mirror, scrutinizing the beauty that usually got her deferential treatment. Not this time. She knew that she should not be so sensitive and not let it get to her. Thank God the next appointment would be a pleasant one. She knew it would be because the Deputy Director of Operations, or DDO, was a long-time friend of the Jefferson family. He and Nicole's father had met at the University of Michigan during their undergraduate studies. Nicole had approached the DDO when she decided to join the CIA, and ever since, he had taken an interest in her progress.

Nicole entered the DDO's office suite and introduced herself to the sixtyish, gray-haired woman sitting behind the desk in the sparsely furnished anteroom. The woman was typing on her computer and barely looked up to acknowledge Nicole.

"Oh yes," she said. "Go right in, he's expecting you. "And," she added, "he's been waiting."

Nicole walked into the DDO's office.

William P. Davis was sitting behind his large mahogany desk. His spacious, well-decorated office overlooked the grounds at Langley. He was a large man, six-foot-three and almost 240 pounds. Years ago, when he was the backup quarterback at the University of Michigan, much of his bulk had been muscle. Over the years, a lot of it had transformed to fat, or "adipose tissue," a much kinder term,

Davis had always thought. He was not fat; he'd just lost the definition and tone that regular exercise maintains. In his position as DDO, he had no time for that. He was in his early fifties, and his full head of brown hair was going gray at the sideburns. He didn't mind, he'd always thought the gray a mark of distinction and a hint of authority. In keeping with this image, he wore his customary pinstripe suit, dark gray today, with a light-blue shirt and solid dark blue tie. As usual, as the day had worn on, he'd shed the jacket and loosened the tie.

Davis was in charge of thousands of CIA case officers in the field. He thought of them as the nation's front line against foreign threats. He was convinced that the collection of HUMINT, in the CIA's dizzying array of acronyms, was the cornerstone of intelligence gathering. It wasn't spy satellites and computer profiling that got the job done; it was the CIA stations in 130 countries worldwide. The case officers and agents collected the raw data. Moreover, since September 11, 2001, they'd finally returned to their rightful place at the forefront of American intelligence.

The CIA had come a long way from its start in 1947. It has been the role of the CIA to acquire and then interpret information that indicates threats to the U.S. Based on the information received, it the

CIA then has a duty to protect the nation from harm. The information can also be used to further U.S. interests by manipulating foreign countries or their leaders. Davis thought the CIA had done both, sometimes well, sometimes poorly.

This time, there was no room for mistakes. That had become obvious the previous day when Davis's boss, the Director of Central Intelligence, showed him a copy of the President's Brief. This document, issued daily to the president by the Director of Central Intelligence, contained the most sensitive secrets in Washington.

Each day, it is the first order of business for the DCI. It is produced in the print shop at CIA headquarters at Langley, where the agency prints its forged documents, birth certificates, passports, driving licenses, and its propaganda books and leaflets.

Two copies of the President's Brief are taken from the print shop by six a.m. each morning. One copy is read by the DCI on his way from his home in Bethesda, Maryland, to the White House. The second copy is handed to the president during his morning briefing, usually around eight a.m. The brief is generally eight or nine pages long.

The President's Brief that the DCI had shown to Davis was not the most current; it was the same one the DCI had delivered to Levenson the day before he departed for Germany. Davis had not seen the entire brief; the pages he'd read concerned only a report from the CIA's Berlin station. The Berlin report was designated "critical," the CIA's highest level of urgency, but the DCI had at first hesitated over including it in the President's Brief. The report had warranted initially a grade of only five on the CIA scale; a twenty is the best grade, and a ten is very good. The Berlin report was not graded higher because the information it contained was based on just one source; it had not been verified by a second. In addition, his case officer did not consider the one source exceptionally reliable.

The DCI was convinced to include the report in the President's Brief because it suggested a direct threat. The DCI had even urged the president to cancel his trip. However, President Levenson would not hear of it. He had made a commitment, and he was going to keep it. "And to make sure I do, is your job," the president had told the DCI.

Now it was Davis's job.

When Nicole entered his office, William P. Davis stood up to greet her. She looked beautiful as always, he thought as he walked towards her and leaned slightly forward to kiss her on the cheek.

Though Davis was tall, Nicole was close to six feet in her heels. "Nice to see you again, Bill," she said with a smile.

He motioned to the leather couch in an alcove in his large office. He took a seat opposite, in a deep, cushioned chair. Between them on an antique coffee table was a book titled *Papers on the European Union,* compiled by the University of California.

Nicole noticed the book.

"I guess this is the topic of the day."

"First, tell me about your family, Mom and Dad, okay?"

"Oh, they're fine," she said. "You know how they are. Dad is busy, and Mom runs the house. Not much has changed. But I understand from Mom that you visited them not long ago."

"Yes. I was in Cleveland to speak at the Union Club and decided to make a long weekend of it. I stayed with your family and played some golf with your father. He's still the same hacker he always was. I don't understand why he enjoys the game. I guess he likes walking in the woods."

Their quiet laughter filled the sunlit room.

"I don't know what the boss told you," Davis said, turning to business, "but I assume he left it up to me to fill you in as usual. Europe is on the front burner—not the Russians, Western Europe, or the European Union. We've been watching developments there, and not all of them are positive.

Let's go back. After World War II, Germany recovered faster and more fully than anyone anticipated with the United States pouring in money to strengthen the defense against the Communist bloc. Even in 1950 some European countries were worrying again. France took the initiative. Jean Moneaut, a prominent French statesman, and Robert Schuman, then the French foreign minister, developed something called the Schuman Plan. The idea was to control the German economy and to encourage more harmony in Europe."

"Why would Germany go along with that?" Nicole asked. "Good question. The answer may be surfacing soon. But at the time the Germans let everyone know they'd play along, they were determined to calm the fears of future German militancy. So in 1951 the French and Germans integrated their coal and steel industries, which then to a large degree controlled economies. The French motive was as much economic as it was political. My guess is the Germans had the same motive. However, that early union was the seed. In 1957 they formed the European Economic Community, then the European Community in 1967, then the European Union in 1993."

Davis got out of his chair. "I am sorry, Nicole. I always get carried away. I neglected to ask you if you wanted a refreshment. Diet Coke, right?"

"Yes, thank you. That would be great."

He picked up the phone and briefly spoke to his secretary. Then he continued.

"The idea was to form an economic and political confederation of European nations. The most ardent supporters want it to be a United States of Europe. Moreover, my guess is that's where it's headed.

They've had their problems, some of the EU departments have been very successful, others haven't, but overall they've made remarkable progress for countries that have been bitter enemies for centuries. There are still a lot of hurdles. The most difficult probably is the whole concept itself. It requires member states to surrender at least some of their control of internal policy to comply with EU mandates. Some of the member countries have a problem with that, especially Britain, you know, 'This sceptered isle' and all that crap. For the EU to work that has to go away. The national identity has to be the European Union."

Davis paused and waited for Nicole to speak. She didn't. She had almost limitless patience. That was one of the things that made her a good case officer.

"You know," he went on, "the EU's problems are a lot like the problems our forefathers faced when the American colonies declared independence. We had essentially thirteen different nations. None of the colonies wanted to give up their sovereign status. As a matter a fact, they proclaimed that the united colonies are and ought to be free and independent states. Each state had the power to make war and peace, to raise an army or navy, levy taxes, enter into treaties, just like the members of the EU."

The knock at his office door interrupted him. "Please come in," he said.

His secretary entered, placed two diet Cokes on his large desk, and left without saying a word. He continued.

"But eventually the colonies all realized that they couldn't live without a strong central government. They created a national government to make laws, control commerce, levy taxes and exercise power over all the states. Each state had to give up some of its power. That's exactly what the EU members are struggling with now."

"So why doesn't the EU just build a government modeled after ours?" Nicole said, lifting her glass of Coke. "If it worked for us, why won't it work for them?"

"That's my point. I think they will. The question is whether the people will control it. What's troubling right now is that all the important positions are not elected; the EU ministers are appointed. Only their parliament is elected by the citizens, and it has very little power, mostly to veto, not initiate legislation. Undoubtedly, the EU will survive; it's only a question of what form it will take. No matter what, it will be a world power. Economically, it already is. It's one of the three major players in the world economy, accounting for seventy percent of world trade and forty percent of the world's GDP. The EU's GDP is larger than the U.S.'s and twice as big as Japan's. And we all know economic strength is the basis of political and military power."

Davis stood up and walked behind his chair. He put his hands on the back of the chair and looked at Nicole.

"Okay. End of political science lesson. Let's go to why you're here. Naturally, I can't tell you everything, but generally speaking, one of the agency's roles as far as the EU is concerned is to ensure they end up with the kind of government and leader in our country's best interest. We have reason to believe that the man you are working on to develop to be an agent, your developmental, and I guess he still is a developmental, that he may be critical in our operation to ensure that the right man ends up running the show at the EU. Let me put it this way: Adam Bergman appears to have the right connections. By the way, has he fallen in love with you yet?"

"Not yet," Nicole replied. "But he's on the way."

In the language of intelligence, to fall in love with an agent means to develop a relationship based on trust. It's the sort of relationship every case officer wants with a recruited spy. Nicole was no exception.

CHAPTER XIV

Berlin, September

DR. BAKER WALKED TO THE CORONARY CARE UNIT OF THE CHARITÉE Hospital, accompanied by the two Secret Service officers who had brought him there. The president's area of the CCU had been cordoned off. There were too many people here, Baker noticed at once. The doctors and nurses needed room to operate.

Baker approached the president. The president's personal physician, Nathan Cole, was at the bedside, along with many others. Baker immediately asked everyone but the physicians and nurses to leave the unit. He looked at the president and noticed he was resting comfortably in his hospital bed. The back of the bed had been elevated, allowing the commander-in-chief to sit up and breathe more easily.

"Is it an MI?" Baker asked

"No way, Charlie," Cole replied. "I haven't seen the results of the CT or the chest X-ray, but I have no doubt he had a type III aortic dissection. No doubt at all."

"Let's go to radiology and take a look," Baker said. "I hope you're wrong."

Together, they walked towards the elevator to take them from the seventh-floor CCU to radiology on the second floor. With them went a handful of Secret Service men. When they entered the viewing room of the imaging department, Dr. Jorg Schmidt, head of Charité's surgery department, met them.

"Jorg, how the hell are you?" Baker said, extending his hand. "Haven't seen you since you were in Houston."

"Yes," Schmidt answered. "Yes, you are quite right. It has been some years. I enjoyed every day of it. You are a wonderful teacher."

Baker smiled. He loved getting compliments from his peers; all doctors do.

"Well, I guess we have a situation here that might be right up my alley," Baker said.

"I think we do, Charles," Schmidt said. "Nathan and I have both heard the history and examined the president. Both of us came to the same conclusion. He has a dissection of the aorta, your type III."

"Type III is traumatic, just distal to the left subclavian artery," Baker said. "Let's see the X-rays, then I want to see the president. As you know, there are two or three ways to go. Operate at once, stabilize and operate later, or don't operate at all. Others have made a good case for never operating. I'm a surgeon. I like to operate. We also ought to get the opinion of an American cardiologist."

He said this in a way that only Americans can. He meant no insult to anyone. He assumed, as all American physicians do, that they were the best. Only they knew the state of the art.

By now, Schmidt's colleague and best friend, Dr. Manfred Riff, chief of anesthesiology, had joined them.

"No doubt about it," Baker said, as he examined the images of the CT that had been done on the president. "We have an aorta dissection here. Let's go see him, let's see if I have to get in there and fix it."

The physicians followed Baker out of the room. He had left no one in doubt that he was in charge. He radiated confidence. Nevertheless, he understood that President Levenson was in serious trouble. His chances of survival were not good. Baker knew, or thought he knew, that only he could save the president's life.

The doctors returned to the CCU, still pursued by their entourage. Baker had no idea who they all were, but he actually enjoyed it. He had always sought out the spotlight, and he had been there many times before, but never like this, never preparing to save the life of the president of the United States.

This was his moment, and he welcomed it. As he entered the area cordoned off for the president, he asked the group not to follow him. He wanted only Cole, Schmidt, and Riff to be there during the examination.

Baker first took note of the fact that the president was at ease. He seemed comfortable, in no acute distress. Baker knew the severe pain the president had experienced earlier had subsided. No doubt because Cole had been successful in lowering Levenson's blood pressure and had administered a narcotic analgesic. Nevertheless, Baker also suspected there had been a reentry of the dissection, where the blood once more had gained entry back into its proper channel.

The physical exam did not take long; surgeons' exams never do. The internists ask all the questions and do all the examinations. Baker took just two minutes with the president to confirm his diagnosis. The X-ray images told the story.

Baker left the president's bedside without speaking to him. He had asked the president not to talk while he examined him. When he had finished his examination, he walked away, the way he always did, the president would be no exception. As soon as he left the CCU,

Baker was surrounded by government people, Secret Service agents, the president's press secretary, and his chief of staff.

"Dr. Baker, tell me how the boss is doing," the chief of staff asked frantically. "I need to know. I have to inform the VP."

"He's stable right now," Baker responded, fiddling with his stethoscope and nodding his head, a gesture he often used to emphasize his medical opinions. "But we need to monitor him very closely."

"Will you operate? When will you do it?" the chief of staff persisted.

"Let me explain what we're dealing with here," Baker said. Then he went on to explain in layman's terms that the president was suffering from an acute aortic dissection. He had torn the lining of his aorta, the main blood vessel of the human body. There are different types of dissections, most of which are due to deterioration of the arterial wall. The most common cause is high blood pressure. Some dissections are caused by heredity disorders, but in the president's case it was trauma that caused the tear. The aorta arises from the heart, heads first upward toward the top of the chest, then it turns downward into the lower chest, and then into the abdomen. The turn is called the aortic arch. Several important blood vessels arise from this arch, the last one being the left subclavian artery. At the point where the left subclavian artery starts from the aortic arch, the aorta is held by a ligament, it's not free to move back and forth. Baker believed that when the president's plane came to a sudden stop, his torso was thrown violently back and forth. Since the aorta is fixed at this point, it would not move freely, and that resulted in the tear.

The tear characteristically occurs just beyond the left subclavian artery's point of origin, and this is where the president's tear was located. The aorta's outer lining, however, was intact, so that the blood pumped from his heart was escaping through tear and making a new channel in the wall of the aorta, and rupture frequently occurs. This can be fatal, Baker explained.

He paused and looked around the room, waiting for his words to sink in. The chief of staff got right to the point.

"So, can you fix it?" he asked.

"Maybe," Baker said. "If untreated, seventy-five percent of the patients die within two weeks. Sixty percent of those we do treat, and who survive the first two weeks, are still alive five years later. However, surgery isn't without risk, either. There is an approximate death rate of fifteen percent if we operate on an emergency basis."

"So, what should we do?" Cook, the chief of staff, put in again.

"Let me finish painting the picture for you," Baker answered. "The president's physician took the most important measure right away, he lowered the president's blood pressure. That's one reason why he appears to be resting comfortably. In addition, we got lucky. I believe the tear in the aorta has reentered the main channel farther down and this reentry is relieving the pressure in the false channel. As far as treatment is concerned, surgery isn't the only option.

Some doctors advocate no surgery at all, and there is data to back them up. This is what I recommend now, watchful waiting. We need to keep the president's blood pressure under control and let his body do the healing. If we do surgery, it's always better to do it on an elective basis."

"So do nothing?" Cook said. "Isn't that dangerous?"

"Frankly, I'm impressed with how well the president is doing," Baker said. "He's pain-free, comfortable; his blood pressure is under control. I recommend that right now we have a cardiologist look at him."

Cook finally relented. "Okay, you're in charge, doctor. But let me ask you, if you have to operate, are you comfortable doing it here?"

"Yes, I am," Baker replied. "This is a reputable institution; they have a fine cardiovascular team. Dr. Schmidt has volunteered to assist me, and he's perfect. He did some of his training under me in Houston. I'm told Dr. Riff, the anesthesiologist, is also an excellent physician. He would be in charge of putting the president to sleep."

The men in the room looked at each other. No one could appreciate the possible implications of his words. No one, not even Baker: anyone except for one, Dr. Manfred Riff, the anesthesiologist, the *sayan*.

CHAPTER XV

Berlin, September

THE ALARM CLOCK NEXT TO THE bed rang only seconds before the telephone. Adam Bergman heard them, but for a moment, he focused his eyes, ignoring both. He had slept well in his roomy Presidential Suite bed. Finally, he rolled over and picked up the phone. It was a recorded message, his wakeup call. He put it back on the nightstand and rolled back into his bed. No night spent with my fiancee, he thought. We're all professionals, all Mossad. Dinner had been short and conversation brief. There wasn't much to say; he only needed an address and a time. He had been given the time, not the address. He was to be there this afternoon. Moreover, he was to be sure he was not followed. He would learn the address on the day of the meeting.

He stretched, remembering the scent of her perfume, the excitement of her touch, the beauty of her face, her body. Nice fiancee, he thought, couldn't have done better myself.

He threw off the covers, got out of bed, and went straight to the slicks. He ran his hand along the top of the bathroom door and pulled out the string and hook: empty. Then he tried the rod in the bedroom closet: again, no message, no tools. He did not shower. Instead he pulled on his running gear and left the suite. He would take his run and check for surveillance.

It was six-thirty a.m. as Adam left the almost empty lobby of the hotel and stepped out onto the Pariser Platz. He noticed three other runners stretching in the street, two men and a woman. He turned to his left and ran toward the Brandenburg Gate, following his route. It would take him through the Tiergarten, Berlin's large city park, then back into the Stadtmitte, where he would run along the busy streets. These were the fast areas, crowded streets where a tail would have to close the distance to avoid losing him. This is where he would know if he was clean or not.

Adam picked up the pace. He didn't look back; he didn't have to, only a few people could keep up with him. Once he left the Tiergarten and rounded the Siegessäule monument, he would know if anyone had followed him. Adam turned around the large traffic circle at the Siegessäule and checked the people in the street. Only workers were on the way to the office, going about their business. As he ran back the way he had come, he looked for other runners. He saw no one else jogging along the road. He ran toward the Brandenburg Gate, through it, straight down the middle of the thoroughfare, which long ago had been reserved for the royal family. He crossed the Pariser Platz again and went up Unter den Linden to the Friedrichstrasse. Here, he turned right and headed toward the Gendarmenmarkt. There, he noticed the other runner.

Adam had just left Unter den Linden and turned onto Friedrichstrasse. The other runner was on the opposite side of the street, apparently paying no attention. She was running fast, close to his pace, and still there as he headed toward the Gendarmenmarkt. He was near the end of his run. He had to turn right at the square to reach his hotel. She was still behind him, not more then, twenty yards, she was keeping pace, not losing ground. Adam had not gotten a good look at her, but he sensed her presence. He knew she was there. He thought about accelerating his pace and losing the woman. But that was not the Mossad way. He had to confirm her presence, make sure she was following him. He didn't want to; he didn't want to abandon the mission and go home. He couldn't. Anxiety turned to anger. Damn it, this woman could wreck it all.

He decided to add another loop, another mile or two, back along part of his original course. He remembered what the Mossad had taught him: never lose your tail. Confirm that you're being followed, put on your cap, make the telephone call, and go home. I can't go home, he thought. I need to stay; I need to know my mission.

He did not look back as he passed the entrance to the Regent Hotel on Charlottenstrasse. He no longer sensed her. She must have gone straight when he turned on Charlottenstrasse. He had to make sure. He decided to add more loops. Each time he reached the entrance of the Adlon, he would turn and go another way. As he completed each circuit, he saw no one following him. He was satisfied; no need to put on his hat. The doorman handed him a towel and a water bottle as he entered the hotel lobby.

"Nice run," he said.

"Thank you," Adam responded, taking the towel and opening the water.

He walked through the lobby, which was quite busy now. He made his way to the bank of elevators and pressed the up arrow. A few feet behind another runner also stood waiting for the elevator. Adam sensed the perspiration, the heavy breathing. For a moment, he felt again the jangle of nerves. Had he missed something? Had he been followed inside? He told himself no, impossible, I made sure, probably just another jogger, some other guest who likes to go for a morning run.

When he stepped into the elevator, no one else followed. Why hadn't the other runner gotten on with him? Was he being followed? He had no proof, and without proof, he could not tell the Mossad. Besides, he could not go home. He had another job to do.

Pushing open the door to the Presidential Suite, he reviewed again the instructions he had received the night before: take your morning run, make sure no one is following you, get back to the hotel, shower and dress, and then meet us at our safe house in the suburbs. Be sure you are not followed. He would learn the address tomorrow, the day of the meeting. At the meeting, he would be given the details of the plan. Sharef would be there. There could be no mistakes, no slipups.

Adam went to the bathroom door, found the string, and gave it a pull. He noticed with a prick of excitement that this time it was heavy. Tugging with both hands he retrieved the package at the end of the twine. It was a .22 caliber Beretta, the Mossad's handgun of choice. A small piece of yellow paper was attached to the barrel, held in place by a rubber band. The weapon was loaded. He removed the paper, wiped the gun clean with a bathroom towel, and placed it on the bathroom counter. He examined the small piece of paper. The typed message was an address for this afternoon's meeting. He flushed it down the toilet.

Adam turned the shower tap on very hot and slipped out of his shorts and shoes. He shampooed, lathered, and relaxed. The doubts of earlier that morning, his fear of being followed, began to recede. He would be part of the mission. He would make sure of it.

Stepping out of the shower, he realized he hadn't yet checked the other slick. He wrapped one of the large bath towels around his waist and water still dripping from his torso, walked to the large closet in the living room. He opened the door and took down the bronze rod. Both ends were sealed with caps, which were easily removable. He pulled off one cap and turned the rod on its end. Nothing fell out. He banged it on the wood floor. Still nothing, so he took out a flashlight to shine it into the rod. Then he saw it, a small object halfway down. He took one of the wire clothes hangers from his suitcase, straightened it, and twisted it at the end. He pushed it down into the rod and a piece of paper fell onto the floor. He unrolled the paper, read the message, and then placed it in the ashtray on the large cocktail table in the center of the room. He struck a match and watched the paper burn. The message had not come from across the Mediterranean, from the Mossad. This message had come from another place. It had traveled across the Atlantic. By way of deception thou shall do war, he thought, as flames engulfed the small piece of paper.

CHAPTER XVI

Berlin, September

I T HAD BEEN A LONG TRIP for Maza Sharef, an Air France flight from Tel Aviv to Paris, where he had spent the night, then a 7:20 a.m. flight from Paris to Berlin. After arriving at Tegel airport, he had taken a taxi, and then two more, each cab to a different location. No tails, he had to be sure. No one could know, he assured himself, and he followed procedure. The last taxi dropped him at the Berlin Zoo, and he grabbed his small case and walked through the Zoo, checking carefully for tails. When he was certain, he walked outside to the black Mercedes sedan and climbed in.

"No Hebrew," Sharef said to the car's three occupants at once. "We only speak English. We are here to attend the Congress on Education and Health. We are representatives of the Canadian government."

The driver nodded and asked for directions.

"Do a run or two," Sharef said. "Let's make sure."

The driver, a Mossad *katza,* knew what to do. After an hour, Sharef decided that they were secure and that they would proceed to the safe house. He gave the driver the address, a villa in Dahlem, Bruemmerstrasse 62. Sharef had chosen the location carefully. He wanted privacy, yet he needed access to public transportation. One never knew when one might have to leave in a hurry.

He had considered the town center, Stadtmitte, but decided against it. His strategic headquarters should be removed from the action; the Mossad was not even here.

Dahlem is a fashionable suburb of Berlin. It is close to Stadtmitte, only a twenty-minute drive away, and has excellent public transportation. The bus and the U-bahn, the subway, were only forty yards from the villa. No one in the quiet suburb would think they were Mossad. The Freie Universität, the Free University of Berlin, was nearby. The locals were accustomed to strangers of all nationalities coming and going.

Sharef settled back on the leather couch in the library and listened to a clock as it chimed on a shelf on the bookcase next to him. A Sayan owned the villa. The family had recently left for a sudden holiday in Majorca, Spain.

Before Sharef arrived, the Mossad had made a few preparations. Special communications links had been installed, the windows facing the street had been bulletproofed, and a sophisticated alarm system had been installed.

A long day, Sharef thought, but now the pieces are falling into place. Still, good thing I am here to command. It's not every week that you kill the president of the United States. That afternoon, his Kiev, or assassination team, would meet him at the villa to receive their final instructions.

Sharef had covered all the bases. He had designed a detailed plan, he had accommodated the unexpected, and the unexpected had happened. The president was in a hospital, and he was within the Mossad's grasp. There would be no slips, no blunders. He was acting on behalf of Israel, although he had no official authority to do so, still, he knew deep in his heart that he was saving his nation—Israel, his children, and his state.

"I am sorry to interrupt you, sir," one of the young Israelis who guarded the villa said, "but what do you want us to do with all the weapons?"

"Which weapons?" Sharef asked.

"The rockets. There are three of them. The ones from the PLO camp in Bosnia. Where should I put them?"

"Leave them in the garage for now," Sharef muttered. "My team will know what to do with them."

Sharef woke with a start. There had been no alarm. The dream had woken him, the dream he often had. Ever since the Yom Kippur War in October of 1973, when the Egyptian invasion had taken Israel by complete surprise, Sharef had had this dream. It was more of a nightmare. Sharef had been only nine days from his twenty-ninth birthday when the invasion began on October 6. Only a few months ago, he had left the army, where he had risen to the rank of colonel and joined the Mossad. When he received the war news, he asked to be reassigned to his former unit, which he had joined on the front lines. This is where he witnessed all the terrors of war. This is when he learned how vulnerable his country was, how easily the existence of his children, the children of Israel, could be threatened. Since then, Sharef had never felt at ease, comfortable, and secure. And the nightmare kept reminding him not to forget. Israel had been unprepared. Even the Mossad was taken by surprise. Never again! He rose from the couch. He intended to take only a short nap before his team arrived. Now he was soaked in perspiration and breathing rapidly. He felt uncomfortable; he felt unsure, he told himself again that this was a benefit of his dream; it reminded him to be ready, to plan, and to take all precautions.

Sharef felt the tingling in his extremities, the lightheadedness. An anxiety attack, the same type he had been experiencing often since the Yom Kippur War. He never sought help, for he could not let anyone know that the chief of the Mossad had any weakness. That would be the end for him. Now he had to gather himself before his team arrived. He checked his watch, forty-five minutes until their arrival. He decided to go upstairs to the main bedroom, shower, and change his clothes. Most importantly, he needed to regain his composure. No one could know of his dream, no one should ever know of his doubts.

The villa at Bruemmerstrasse 62 did not have a bell or a knock. Visitors pushed open the front door and walked in. If they had gotten that far, they were welcome, the two Mossad officers on the street ensured that. Adam had no difficulty gaining entrance. He had parked his black BMW several blocks from the villa and stopped to have a beer at one of the pubs his grandmother had recommended. He had parked his car in the lot of the Alter Krug, a restaurant for more than 100 years. Before leaving the center of town, he had taken his last run. Although he had been unable to confirm it, he knew he was being followed. Stopping at the old restaurant, several blocks from the villa, he would try again to pick out his tail. Casually, he approached the small, quaint bar and ordered the local beer, a Schultheisser. The bartender immediately recognized Adam was not a local, for he did not speak the Berlin dialect. "Wie gehts?" Adam said to the obese bartender.

"Gut. Danke."

The bartender drew the beer from the tap. It took some time, and when he had finally filled the glass, he presented it with a certain amount of pride. He knew how to pour his beer, he knew you had to stroke it, he knew each beer needed that attention.

"Zum Wohl," he said and turned to the bar's only other customer, a man who had just entered.

"Danke," Adam replied and took a large swallow of the beer. Well, Grandma was right, he thought, a great beer and a wonderful old tavern.

He lifted his beer and glanced at the man standing next to him. Not a regular, too young, too muscular to spend his time in taverns in the afternoon. Berlin dialect, probably some Berlin yuppie who had decided to have a quick beer here on his way into town. But he would not take a chance. Adam decided to leave his car in the parking lot and walk to the villa. He did not glance again at his neighbor at the bar. He paid and walked out into the street. There was a beautiful garden behind the restaurant and many tables were occupied by diners enjoying the lovely afternoon. He strolled through the garden, appreciating the moment of relaxation. Yes, he thought, this is what we need to do more of in the United States, relax, take time out in the middle of the day.

He left the garden and went back to the street. He crossed the subway bridge, turned right on the Bruemmerstrasse, and walked toward Thielallee. The street was quiet; large chestnut trees lined one side of the thoroughfare, partially hiding the subway line, which ran in a small, narrow, man- made ravine between Loehleinstrasse and Bruemerstrasse.

He was being followed. He did not know by whom. He had a gut feeling the person who'd followed him during his run was not working with the man he had just seen. So, two different agencies. CIA? FSB, Russia's KGB replacement, German intelligence? The Mossad? The more the merrier!

CHAPTER XVII

Berlin, September

NICOLE FOUND HIM AT THE HOTEL adlon. She had left her hotel, the Berlin Hilton, which was located only a few short blocks from the Adlon, intending just a routine run. It was only a jog, the same one she took every morning to keep in shape, to keep off that extra pound or two, and to clear her head, to keep it all in perspective.

As she left Unter den Linden and turned onto Friedrichstrasse, she could not believe her eyes. He was twenty yards ahead of her, and there was no mistaking who it was. She recognized the long, smooth stride, the lean, muscular body. She saw his face when he made the turn at the Gendarmenmarkt and turned slightly to look behind him. She knew it was a trap, though he had not seen her, he had sensed a tail and now he wanted her to follow him, to confirm he was being followed. When he turned she did not. She continued up Behrenstrasse past the French Dome. Then she stopped. She had to find out where he was going, where he was staying, without Adam knowing he was followed. If he did, then it was over. He would have to go home, she knew that was the Mossad rule. And if he went home, she too would be pulled from the operation.

Nicole would not let that happen. She had waited for this opportunity and would not blow it now. She let Adam go. He had sensed her; it was that quick look as he turned the corner. That's when she knew. But she also knew he would rerun his route.

She hailed a cab and told the driver she wanted to take some sights around Stadtmitte. As she expected, the driver drove around the plaza and stopped the taxi on Charlottenstrasse in front of the Konzerthalle. He turned to his passenger and began to explain the plaza's history. Nicole did not listen. She was watching the sidewalk, looking for him. He would take another loop or two to find out about his tail. He had to make sure. She saw him running on the other side of the street. As he passed the cab, Nicole pointed toward him.

"That's my boyfriend," she explained. "Please follow him. Keep your distance. I want to surprise him."

The Turkish cabby nodded while putting the manual gear shift. They followed him up the Unter den Linden toward the Brandenburg Gate. Nicole got anxious. The boulevard was vast, and he was jogging on the opposite side of the street, separated by the broad, tree-lined and grass-covered median strip. Fortunately, it was early and the street was not yet crowded. She could not lose him now. Then he slowed and finally broke into a stride as he walked up the stairs to the lobby of the Adlon Hotel.

"Gotcha."

Mark Weiss was no slouch. He stood five foot-ten and weighed 185 pounds, all muscle. He was thirty-five years of age. He was a Berliner. His parents were Israeli, born and raised in Russia, and in the mid-fifties they had escaped and gone to Israel. Two years after he was born, his family had moved from Israel to Berlin. He did not know why. His father never told him, Weiss never asked. It had been Weiss's choice to join the Mossad and become a *katza.* He was one of the best *katzas* Sharef had ever trained. He was in charge of the German station, the station now on "daylight," the Mossad's highest state of alert. Although he had grown up in Germany, he was a Jew and an Israeli at heart. At age twenty-five, he had moved to Israel to first join the army, then the Mossad.

Weiss took a sip of Schultheisser. He had recognized Adam at the bar when he walked into the Alter Krug. Weiss had studied the photos given him by Sharef. Now, standing next to him, Weiss paid him no attention, yet he noticed everything. This was his target, the one Sharef had told him to follow. But Weiss was not there to tail Adam. He already knew his destination, the villa. Weiss was there to protect him, to make sure he was clean, not being followed. Sharef had told him this man was right now the Mossad's most important asset and that he had to be kept safe at all costs. Guard him with your life, Sharef had said.

Weiss took another swallow from his glass and turned his awareness a notch. Not once did Adam acknowledge his presence. But he could tell that Adam had spotted him. It's a delicate dance, Weiss thought.

Adam left the Alter Krug, and Weiss stayed where he was. He had studied the neighborhood; he knew all the streets were long and straight. He knew Adam would walk right up Bruemmerstrasse toward the villa. Bruemmerstrasse was straight, lined by chestnut trees; there was no way Weiss could run direct surveillance without drawing attention. Loehleinstrasse parallels Bruemmerstrasse, and the Berlin subway separates the two streets. Weiss decided to track him from the other side of the subway line. He knew it would be difficult. He knew he would not always be able to see his subject and that anyone else following Adam would inevitably choose the same strategy.

Weiss stepped outside three minutes after Adam finished his beer and left the Alter Krug. He watched him go through the garden and up Bruemmerstrasse toward the Mossad safe house. No one could follow him now. The street was straight, no curves, and no intersections to hide in. There was only one way to tail a man here, from Loehleinstrasse.

If anyone was following, Weiss wanted that person in front of him. So he waited a few more minutes before he crossed to Loehleinstrasse and turned toward their destination, the villa near the Thielplatz subway station. Weiss turned up the street and started in that direction. Immediately he noticed someone. She was young, rather attractive. She was walking leisurely ahead of him. Maybe she lived here.

He passed her, noticing her shapely legs. He also noticed her black hair, pulled back in a ponytail. He glanced at her as he passed, but she did not acknowledge him. She was walking slowly, as any local resident would. Weiss shifted his focus away from the woman back to the man he had been sent to protect. Adam would be a short distance ahead, but now he was not visible.

When Weiss reached Thielplatz he had a clear view across the narrow ravine with the subway tracks, to Bruemmerstrasse. Adam had stopped, turned, and started back the way they had come, obviously searching for tails, Weiss surmised. Adam walked twenty yards, turned again, stooped to straighten the cuff in his pants, and quickly looked in all directions. Then he stood and continued up the street. Thirty yards along he turned to enter the villa.

Weiss watched it all. He was satisfied. He too looked around, more slowly. No tails. The safe house was still safe.

"Good afternoon," the young woman said, passing him at the Thielplatz. "Beautiful day."

"Yes, it is," he answered with a smile, again noticing her long legs. She wore a white sweater, short black skirt and black sandals. Probably a student at the University, no one to worry about, yet he decided to make sure. He stopped and watched as she walked to the end of the small plaza in front of the subway station. She never looked back. She walked down the stairs to the subway platform. A local. But he thought he would stay and watch the station for a little while. He had been trained by the best; the Mossad took no chances.

CHAPTER XVIII

Berlin, September

NICOLE DID NOT GO FAR. SHE took the train to the next stop, Oskar Helene-Heim. She knew the Mossad safe house was near the Thielplatz; she had followed Adam Bergman that far when she noticed her tail. She wanted more. She tried to find the Mossad's temporary headquarters.

She climbed the steps to the street and walked back to the Thielplatz. She knew the Mossad safe house would be near the subway station. She also knew that if Adam had gone there for a meeting, others would join him. She would wait for them, and they would lead her to the safe house.

As she neared the Thielplatz, she reprimanded herself for her earlier impatience. She had been too anxious and too confident. She had followed Adam to this hotel and then to the Alter Krug without his noticing her. But she should have waited another minute or two before she followed him from the restaurant. If she had waited, she would have noticed the other man leaving. At that point, she could have followed them both. She had made a mistake.

She sensed the other man had decided she was not part of the game. She had to be careful. She had been noticed. His first look had been one of suspicion, but then the look had changed to that of a man admiring a beautiful woman. She had seen it many times.

"Adam, good to see you," Sharef said as Bergman entered the wood-paneled library. "It's been a long time."

"Yeah," Adam said, flashing a smile. "I kind of missed you and your spy games."

Adam liked Sharef. He looked up to him. In addition, he knew that their relationship was more than just co-workers. Yet, they never talked about it. They didn't need to. It was almost like father and son. Ever since he'd been recruited, Sharef had looked out for him. Sharef always went the extra yard for Adam. There was trust and respect between them.

"Well," Sharef said with a grin of his own. "Now you are in the middle of the biggest game you will ever play."

He motioned Adam to sit on the large, worn leather couch.

"How about a drink?"

"Sounds great," Adam said. "A cup of coffee would be fine, please."

There was one other man in the room. Sharef did not introduce him.

"Haim, get Adam a cup of coffee and ask the others to come and join us."

Sharef turned back to Adam. "How was your trip? Any surprises?"

"None," Adam answered. "Everything went according to your plan."

"No trouble getting here from the hotel?" Sharef asked, eyeing Adam's expression for any hint that he'd been followed.

"Smooth sailing," Adam responded with a grin.

"Wonderful. And how is your hotel room?"

Sharef smiled paternally. He liked to please Adam, but he also had to. He could not afford to lose his most valuable agent—not now, when all the pieces were falling into place.

"You got me the best suite in the hotel," Adam said. "I could live there forever."

"Well, you're number one, you deserve it," Sharef said. "And we have an image to keep up, of course. You are the successful investment banker."

At that point, the door opened, and Adam's dinner companions from the previous evening entered the room. Lisa, his supposed fiancee, looked as stunning as before. She wore tight blue jeans and a black blouse, and her long blond hair fell loosely onto her shoulders. She walked over to him, bent down, wrapped her arms around his neck, and kissed him.

"I have missed you," she said, sitting beside him. "Let's have dinner tonight. At your hotel. The restaurant is wonderful there."

"That's a deal."

Lisa leaned against him. The third member of the team, introduced again only as Jacob, nodded at Adam and sat in one of the deep leather chairs facing the couch. Adam felt uncomfortable with the man. Jacob never looked him in the eye, behaving as if Adam was not even there. At first, during their dinner at Borchardt's, Adam had thought Jacob somewhat of an introvert. However, as the night went on, it became apparent that Jacob was jealous. Adam wondered if Sharef knew Jacob's state of mind and decided Sharef was mindful of everything.

"Well," Sharef began, "we are here for one purpose, and it is the most crucial assignment the Institute has ever handled. That is why were you chosen? In my judgement, you are the best. We can not fail. My future is on the line. More importantly, Israel's very existence rests in your hands. You must succeed. The mission must be carried out tomorrow, the next day at the latest. By tomorrow morning, you will all be in place. By tomorrow morning, you will be ready to pull the trigger. As I said, there can be no mistakes. This mission will determine the future of our country, the future of the children of Israel. I am responsible for protecting this future and intend to fulfill my obligation."

"We all know of your dedication," Lisa put in. "Tell us what we need to do."

Adam thought Sharef might snap at the woman; Sharef hated to be interrupted. He fixed her with a gaze and continued.

"Let me go back and explain why we are here. Two weeks ago, I was forced to place a very important person on our *pacca,* the list of our enemies in the Mossad computer. That was not all. I had to decide that this enemy had to be eliminated. As you know, we don't do this without meeting stringent criteria, but this man met our most important criterion: he is holding a gun on our people. I had no choice. My decision was clear: no one, and I mean no one, will hold a gun to my people, not even the president of the United States of America."

"Hold it right there," Jacob interrupted. "Are you telling us we must take out the U.S. president?"

"Yes, Jacob, that is what I am telling you," Sharef said slowly. "I know they have been our allies. They have helped us as no other country has ever done. Yet, times have changed. Israel now has an opportunity to be a major player in world politics. This can mean everything for us. If we succeed, the Arabs will no longer be a threat. Just imagine it, Israel, Israelis finally controlling our own destiny. It can be done. We are not far from it. And it is the only way our country can survive. We need to step beyond our local rivalry with the Arabs;

we need to step up and enter world politics. There is one person who stands in the way of Israel right now, and that is the president of the United States."

"So tell us, how do we do it?" Jacob asked. "How can we even get close to the president?"

"Don't worry," Sharef said patiently. "I have it all worked out. We have our people. Some of them are in the hospital where the president is now, close to him. If what I think will happen does happen, he will be a sitting duck by tomorrow or the next day."

"I don't know," Jacob said, leaning forward in his chair. "The U.S. president is one of the best-protected people in the world. We should hear your plan, we should discuss it."

"No, Jacob, not tonight. You will be told when you need to be told. It may be only hours or minutes before I want you to strike. That is my decision. I will not change it."

Sharef fully intended to tell his team the plan details tonight. The more time they had to prepare, the more likely their success would be. Sharef knew that. He had been in the game a long time, maybe too long. This operation would be the climax of his career. He would single-handedly see that the small State of Israel became a world power. Not a power in and of itself; he was not delusional. But Israel could exert influence; control the right people who made the decisions.

Only minutes before his team assembled in the library, Sharef decided not to reveal the details of his plan. He did not know why exactly, but when he awoke from his dream, he knew he would not let himself or Israel be surprised again.

CHAPTER XIX

Berlin, September

"ADAM, PLEASE STAY, I NEED TO talk to you," Sharef said. Then he turned to the others as they stood to leave.

They all looked at each other. Silence fell over the wood-paneled room. It was an earnest and gloomy quiet that set in moments before soldiers leave their trenches to attack, moments before paratroopers make their jump behind enemy lines. The kind of silence that was filled with tension, when everyone felt alone.

"From now on, we do not meet," he said. "We will only communicate via the slicks. Check them every hour. One more thing: Adam is your leader. You will follow his command. Good night. Thank you for being here and for your dedication to your country. Israel will never forget."

Sharef approached Lisa and Jacob and kissed each on both cheeks.

"Baruch hasem," he said. Blessed be God, "And make sure you both leave separately. Jacob, out the front door. Lisa, around the back and through the gardens. I have been informed that a visitor appears to be interested in our villa. Let's take no chances."

Before Lisa left, she turned to Adam and put her arms around him.

"Don't forget our date tonight," she said. "I'm looking forward to it." Then she kissed him for a long time.

When she let go, Adam was flushed. Again, he felt he had lost control. He remembered that another woman, just as beautiful as Lisa, had managed to rattle him not long ago. He once more told himself he must control these situations and always be in charge. But he was not. Lisa quietly left the room.

"Adam," Sharef said, concern creasing his forehead, "I wanted to talk to you without the others. You now know our mission is to assassinate the president of the United States. I, we, have no choice. He represents a threat to our nation. It must be done, and time is short. There is a window of opportunity, and we must seize it. If we operate as we should, no one will ever know we had anything to do with it. Fingers will point at the PLO. I have it all worked out. I have decided your team will pull the trigger. Tonight I was going to share my plan with you, Lisa, and Jacob. Then I felt uneasy. Please don't ask me why. I have known all of you for years. I know your backgrounds, and I knew your parents. I have trained you, and I trust you all. But suddenly I felt unsure. I can't explain it. I guess I have been at this job too long; I no longer trust myself. This mission is the most important of my life, not just in my life, but in the life of Israel. If we fail, Israel will fail. All we have accomplished and fought for will be in vain."

Sharef paced back and forth on the Persian rug, which covered the hardwood floor of the library. This was as emotional as Adam had ever seen his boss.

"The time has come for us to be our own nation. No longer should we be puppets ruled by Washington. Don't misunderstand I fully appreciate the help the United States has given us. Nevertheless, we are no longer children who receive our direction from someone else. We are a mature nation; we have grown up. We are entitled to determine our own destiny. Do you understand what I am saying?"

"Yes, I do," Adam said slowly. "But how does the killing of the United States president make us an adult, as you put it? But maybe it is not for me to ask this question, mine is not to reason why."

"No, Adam, you have every right to, and I wish I could share every detail with you, because I know you would understand. To get to the point, things are happening in Europe that will change the balance of power in the world. There will be a United States of Europe, but the United States of America does not want this to happen, for a united Europe will give the U. S. a run for its money. They will challenge the world dominance the United States now holds and wants to hold forever."

"The United States wants world dominance?" Adam asked. "I don't believe that. The United States wants to be assured of world peace and that everyone can live freely in a democratic society."

Sharef stopped pacing and looked at him.

"Adam, Adam, don't be so naive. The United States is no different than any world power. The Romans, Hitler, and Stalin all wanted to control it all. The U.S. is no different. It sees a powerful European Union as a threat. Moreover, I agree, the new EU will be a dominant player; it will challenge the U.S. We need this counterbalance. The U.S. is getting too dominant. It is the only superpower left."

Adam held up his hand. He had had enough of Sharef's paranoia for one afternoon.

"I see what you're saying, the EU will be a major player. Why should Israel care? You're not Europeans."

"You are right," Sharef said patiently. "We are not Europeans. Yet many of our people are, and we understand the European mentality; we know what makes them tick. How many of our people still feel displaced from their homeland and wish to go back? However, that's not important now. I have a different vision. Adam, I have not shared this with anyone, but I know I can trust you. I know you will die for Israel."

"I am a Jew," Adam answered slowly. "Yes, my grandparents suffered greatly. Yes, I want to help. But I do not seek revenge; all I seek is justice."

"And justice is what I seek!" Sharef said. "Justice for Israel. This window of opportunity is also a window for Israel. The EU will be a major power. No one can stop that, not even the United States. Therefore, Israel must be in a position of major influence with this new Europe, maybe even in a position of control. Today, we are all too preoccupied with fighting the Arabs. That's not Israel's destiny; Israel's destiny is to be in control. We are the chosen people. We are God's children. Have we all forgotten that?"

Sharef smiled. "Sorry, I got carried away. Now we all assume that the new EU will be a reality, a real political and economic force. Moreover, we all assume that since Israel is not a European nation, we cannot be part of it all. Yet we can! As I said, my plan calls for us, the Israelis, to control the new Europe."

"But you still haven't told me how!" Adam watched closely for Sharef's reactiom.

"I can't answer that now," Sharef said. "But trust me, if our mission is successful Israel will control the new EU, and at the same time we will continue to exert our influence in the U.S. We will be in the middle, controlling both sides."

"Okay, fine," Adam said, giving up for now his hope of learning the details of Sharef's grand plan. "Where do I go from here?"

"You and your team must eliminate the president of the United States. He has information which cannot be made public, which cannot be shared with anyone else. It would jeopardize everything. Therefore he must be eliminated."

"You've told me that already," Adam answered. "You haven't told me how."

Sharef sat down in the old and worn brown leather chair in the library of the safe house.

"I was going to tell your team tonight, as I said, but then I felt uneasy. I don't know why. It was just a feeling I get once in awhile. No, let me be honest. There was an atmosphere in the room when we met with Lisa and Jacob, an atmosphere I did not care for. I have felt it before."

"I don't understand. Is there someone you don't trust?" Adam asked nervously.

"Adam I am also a spy. I have been a spy all my life, and with time spies develop a sense that tells you when something is not right. Eight out of ten times that sense is wrong, yet you cannot afford to ignore it. So tonight I felt uneasy, I know it sounds ridiculous, the best agents the Mossad has ever produced, and I am suspicious. Yet, I can trust no one, not my wife, my children, no one. This is a mission unlike any other. On my shoulders rests the destiny of the State of Israel. Do you understand? Do you know what I am saying?"

"Yes," Adam replied. "You're a very lonely man, too lonely. That's why you need me."

"I do trust you. I think I trust the others as well. I will tell you my plan for the assassination of the president. You are the leader; your team will pull the trigger. You will make certain that Israel will survive."

"You have my word," Adam said. "I will do what is right."

And Sharef told him the president would most likely be moved by helicopter from the hospital to Air Force One at Tegel airport. Sharef told him how his agents and *sayanim* at the hospital and within the president's security detail would keep him informed and supply him with all the details. He instructed Adam that his team would use two Strella missiles to shoot down the chopper and kill the U.S. president. He told him where he wanted Adam and his team to hide on the hospital's grounds to launch the two missiles. He detailed his plan, telling him all about the two Strella missiles. But the head of the Mossad did not tell him about the third.

"By deception, though, shall do war."

CHAPTER XX

Berlin, September

"NOH, I'M CERTAIN. THERE MUST BE a mistake. We reserved a room overlooking the plaza. Here's my confirmation. Can you check again?"

The registration clerk at the Regent hotel in Berlin looked at the two travelers, then began tapping at his computer.

Peter Schneider turned to his wife and smiled wearily.

"I'm sure it's just a mistake, honey," Katie Schneider said. "They'll find it. This is Germany, they don't make mistakes."

"Dr. Schneider," the clerk said at last. "I am sorry. There has been a mistake. Indeed, you did reserve a room overlooking the square. It has been given to another guest. I am very sorry, sir. We can offer you instead a suite overlooking the beautiful Gendarmenmarkt. The suite is one of our best. I can take you there and show it to you. Naturally, there will be no additional charge."

"That sounds great," Schneider said. "Mistakes happen. Don't worry about it."

The clerk came around the desk and motioned to a porter to take care of the Schneiders' luggage. Then he set off briskly across the lobby toward the elevators.

Schneider took his wife's hand and squeezed it.

"Follow the leader," he said.

As they crossed the crowded but quaint lobby, they admired the marble-tiled floor, the crystal chandeliers, and the tasteful paintings. There were no mistakes in the decor, Schneider thought.

"Dr. Schneider, Dr. Schneider!" The call did not come from the clerk.

"Dr. Peter Schneider," the voice echoed. "There has been an emergency. Dr. Schneider, please identify yourself!"

Schneider sighed. He wanted to ignore the page. He was on vacation, for God's sake.

He stopped abruptly and raised his hand, raising his wife's hand with it.

"I'm Dr. Schneider," he said.

The manager of the Regent, a small, officious looking man, rushed toward him.

"Sir, please excuse me. I am sorry to inconvenience you, but I received very detailed instructions. Once you checked in, I was told to call a local number, the Secret Service. They said it was a matter of national security. They also said the minute you arrived, I was to call this number, and someone was to come and get you. I was to keep you at the front desk. They will be here at any moment."

"What?" Schneider said, trying to keep up with the little man's words. "What do you mean, the Secret Service?"

"They are the Secret Service," he repeated. "That is what they have told me. And two of our motorcycle policemen are with them." "Katie, honey, you go ahead," Schneider said. "I'll be right back. I'm sure there's some confusion here."

Schneider turned and followed the manager, who was already hustling back toward the registration desk. There, Schneider noticed there were two men waiting. They did not look like hotel guests. Both were tall and muscular, and they wore dark suits and darker glasses. They had short hair and crew cuts, and neither smiled. As Schneider approached them, he glanced toward the entrance. Two Berlin motorcycle policemen sat astride their BMWs. Behind them, he noticed a black Mercedes, its driver no different from the two men he now faced.

The older of the two men standing at the registration desk turned and took a few steps toward Schneider.

"Dr. Schneider, sir, my name is Harrington," he said, extending a hand. "I'm with the Secret Service," he added in a low voice and quickly flashed a badge on his belt, just to the left of the buckle.

"We've got an emergency, sir, a matter of national security," he said.

"The president is ill, here in Berlin, sir. He's hospitalized at the Charité Hospital. Fortunately, Dr. Charles Baker was in town when the president became incapacitated, and he is attending to him now. Dr. Baker knew you would be here today, doctor, and he has asked that you examine the president. He wants your input. It's my job, sir, to get you there without delay. Please come with us. Oh, by the way, this is my partner, Agent Farmer."

Schneider nodded. He seemed to have no choice. So he followed his escort out of the hotel and went to see the president of the United States.

Sharef was informed immediately. Minutes after Schneider had climbed into the back of the black Mercedes, one of the motorcycle escorts, a *sayan,* had radioed the Mossad. Schneider was now en route to meet the president. This is what Sharef had to prevent; this would spoil his plan for Israel. In the library in Dahlem, Sharef squeezed the arm of his brown leather chair. He must not overreact. This would not be the time for the president to talk to Schneider. He would be a physician, trying to save the president's life. They would not talk politics now.

Or would they? Could he take that chance? Could he gamble the future of his country on a hunch? He felt unsure, and he did not like the feeling. He was always in control; he always knew his decisions were correct. Perspiration formed on his forehead. He had to make the most difficult decision of his life. He had not planned for this contingency. He had not anticipated that Schneider might visit the president this soon as a physician. He swallowed his cognac and inhaled smoke from his Cuban cigar. No. Do not react too quickly. Be patient. He knew how doctors thought. Schneider would be concerned only with his patient's needs. They would discuss nothing more. He knew enough about doctors to know that there was nothing more sacred to them than to be in that moment when they were superior, when people needed to rely on them. Schneider would be no different. There would be no other discussions. Not now, he was sure of that. But being sure is not enough, not in this business. Here, one took no chances. Here, one planned for all possibilities, no matter how remote.

He picked up the telephone on the antique end table and dialed.

"Lovebirds," a female voice answered. "Can I help you?"

"Code IOU," Sharef said slowly. "I repeat, code IOU. Only if necessary. Please confirm."

"Understood," the woman said matter-of-factly. "IOU. But only if necessary."

Sharef put the phone in its cradle. He had not wanted to make the call, but it was a contingency he had to implement. Code IOU meant the immediate assassination of the president, an attempt that it would entail significant risk to the Mossad. It meant the president would be assassinated the Mossad way, in front of many people, and shot several times. There would be no deception and no escape. He knew the head nurse of the coronary care unit at Charité Hospital would cooperate. She was one of the best agents the Mossad had ever recruited.

CHAPTER XXI

Berlin, September

SHAREF TURNED TO ADAM, WHO HAD waited patiently while his boss completed his telephone calls.

"Things are happening more quickly than I anticipated," Sharef said. "The time has come to bring you up to speed."

"Sounds good to me," Adam replied. "I knew when you first contacted me, I wasn't going to Berlin just to run the marathon."

"Actually," Sharef continued, "the marathon is part of the picture. I arranged to get you here because we at the office received some important information. The information helped us identify the probable president of the European Union."

"How can that be?" Adam said quickly. "Isn't that an elected office?"

"No. The Europeans are drastically changing the entire union, intending to create a sort of United States of Europe. And the people will not elect their president. He will be appointed."

"I wonder why," Adam said. "The U.S. system seems to work."

"That may be your opinion," Sharef said archly. "But a lot of people feel that a national election is too expensive, too corrupt and eliminates the influence of the people best qualified to choose. Often the wrong person is elected. Sometimes it's not even the person the people have chosen."

"Point to you," Adam admitted.

"The Europeans feel that the office of president is too important to let the people make the decision. After all, most voters are marginally qualified at best. Part of the reason we brought you to Berlin is to help make sure the right man, the right man for Israel, is appointed EU president."

Adam stared.

"I know what you are thinking," Sharef said. "And you are right, it sounds absurd. Believe me, it can be done. In any event, we must try. Israel's future depends on it. We rely too much on the United States. Let's be honest, without their money, we would not exist. Nevertheless, we pay a big price in return. We pay with our independence. Washington is forever interfering, dictating our policies. They are virtually running our country because they think their almighty dollar can buy anything. I am not saying Israel should abandon the United States. Clearly we cannot and do not want to do that. But Europe will be powerful, as powerful as the United States, maybe more so. And for Israel to thrive, no, to survive, we will need the support of this new world power."

This was not the whole truth. Sharef could not tell Adam that the prime minister of Israel had no idea of Israel's new policy, because it was not Israel's policy, it was Sharef's policy.

"I don't have to tell you that the information I'm sharing with you now is classified," he added, "urgent, tiger black. The prime minister and only a handful of people are privy to it."

The lie fell softly into the room. Adam thought Sharef's reasoning seemed sound. At least he could not think of any arguments to contradict him. Moreover, he knew that it was not his place to disagree. He should be more interested to know his own role.

"Adam, I know that it's highly unusual, in fact, it's unprecedented, for anyone but a *katza* to recruit an outsider. However, circumstances now call for us to be flexible, and I have reasons to believe that you're uniquely qualified to reach this person. Please don't ask me why, because I cannot tell you. But trust me, you are the most qualified person on the planet to get the job done."

"So you asked me to come to Berlin to try to recruit the future president of the EU to our side. Am I correct?"

"Correct," Sharef said. "That is your primary mission."

"Okay. Tell me about him," Adam said. "What is his name? Is he French or German? He must be German. They have a stronger economy. They have the money. Am I right?"

"Yes and no," Sharef replied. "Actually, he is American."

"American?" Adam said incredulously. "Why would the Europeans want an American to run their union?"

"Let me finish. He is American, but he is also German. He was born in this city and grew up here until he was fifteen, when his family emigrated to the United States. Here is his folder," Sharef said, handing over a manila envelope.

"It contains all his information, everything you need to know. Study it. You must learn this man and understand what he thinks and why he thinks it. I know you can do this because you have another advantage, which unfortunately, I cannot tell you now."

"I respect that," Adam said. "I know the game. How will I make contact? Where will I go?"

"You do not have to go anywhere. He is right here, in Berlin. You will meet him at a party. The invitations are in the folder. Yes, invitations. There is one for your grandmother; I know she loves parties."

"Thank you, Maza, that was very thoughtful. You are right, Grandma loves to be with people, and Berlin is her hometown. She was born here, by the way."

"I know," Sharef said. I know too well, he thought.

Adam leaned over and took the thick envelopes. Then he got out of his chair and extended his hand.

"Adam, sit down, please," Sharef said. "You are not going anywhere right now. You have already forgotten that the Mossad wants you not only to recruit one president but to assassinate another."

They both began to laugh.

"Recruit one and kill another, Adam said. Now that is a handful."

"A week or two ago, I flew to Washington," Sharef continued.

"I met with the president of the United States. The Mossad had decided he needed to be included in this, to be part of it. Well, not completely, but we wanted him to feel that we were sharing, that this is a cooperative effort. This was a mistake. We misjudged the man. I thought that since he's a Jew, he would understand. He didn't. To make a long story short, I gave him information during our meeting that was top secret, and he threatened to use the information against us, against Israel. I don't think it was an empty threat. I don't think he has shared the information with anyone yet, but he will when it is to his advantage. We can take no chances. He could destroy our plan. That is why he must be eliminated. We discussed it earlier. It needs to be done, and I already have two teams in place. Then the unexpected happened: the president fell ill. Obviously, this changed everything. President Levenson is now in a hospital. I hear he may die anyway, without our help. However, we have to be sure. This has to be an *ain efes,* a no-miss operation. One possibility is that they will move him out of the hospital here. They may fly him to one of their European military bases or, more likely, fly him home. As I told I think they'll move him, but his American doctor, Charles Baker, will make the decision.

Baker has asked for another opinion from an American cardiologist who recently arrived in Berlin. And guess who that is? His name is Dr. Peter Schneider. He is the probable future president of the EU, the man you need to recruit."

"Is this a game?" Adam asked. "Did someone arrange it all? It's too big a coincidence."

"No. There is an international health conference in Berlin." Sharef continued, "The president was to speak there and many important people were invited, Baker and Schneider among them. Now, if they do not move the president, if they operate on him at Charitee

At the hospital, then everything will be taken care of. My hunch tells me they will want to get him out. You know, the Americans think only they can do it right. Therefore, if possible, if his medical condition allows it, they will move him. If they do, it will be tomorrow. Dr. Schneider is evaluating him now. Baker already thinks he can be moved. If Schneider concurs, they will move him tomorrow by helicopter."

"Well," Adam said, "I have a lot of work to do. I'd better get going. And don't worry, it will be done."

He got up and gathered another folder containing information on the missiles and their placements.

"You can leave by the front door," Sharef said. "Mark took care of everything."

"Who's Mark?" Adam asked.

"He is your guardian angel. I never let you go anywhere without one."

Sharef stood up, and both men embraced. As Adam left the safe house, Jacob entered the library.

"We are on our way, Jacob," Sharef said, "keep an eye on him, but always have Mark in front of you. Adam knows only about two of the missiles. You will take care of the third."

Jacob nodded and left the villa. Adam would never know. By way of deception, Sharef thought, thou shalt do war.

CHAPTER XXII

Berlin, September

NICOLE WANTED TO RETURN TO THE Thielplatz to continue her surveillance. She knew that Adam had entered one of the villas on Bruemmerstrasse near the Thielplatz subway station. Earlier, she had not seen which villa. She wanted to find out.

As she neared the small plaza in front of the subway station at Thielplatz, she saw the man. The same man who had passed her earlier. He was standing at the edge of the square of the subway station near the entrance to Schwarzer Grund, the park which abutted the station. He was enjoying an ice cream bar. Nicole was sure he was Mossad. He was running interference. Now she had to abort her surveillance. Now she would not find the Mossad safe house. Not today. She had been outwitted, and it infuriated her.

Adam left the villa and walked to the bus stop at Bruemmerstrasse. He caught the two-decker yellow Berlin bus just as it arrived. He took it to the Kudamm. Then he got off and hailed a taxi. He asked to go to the Brandenburg Gate. Here, he left the cab and strolled leisurely along Unter den Linden, and he thought as he went. There was much that needed to be done in the next twelve hours. He had to study the plan to deploy the missiles. He had to meet with Jacob and Lisa to coordinate the attack. He remembered Sharef's words: minimize risks. And he recalled he had a dinner date with his grandmother, who had arrived earlier in the day. What about his dinner with Lisa at his hotel? It would be no problem. He would ask Grandma to join him and Lisa. She would enjoy the company, Grandma loved people. Moreover, there was one more date he had to arrange, a date that would make all the difference.

"I think you are right, Charles," Schneider said to Baker as the two left the CCU of the Charitee Hospital. "Type III aortic dissection. He is stable now. You managed him well. If I didn't know better I'd say you are a cardiologist," he added with a smile. "If you want to move him back to the States, I see no problem, Schneider continued. "His BP is fine, I think he will do all right."

"Thanks Peter," Baker replied, "you know I like to operate, but I thought it would be wise to get someone else to evaluate the president. Then I heard you were in town and, well, it was no brainer. Lucky guy, our president. He gets hurt in a foreign country and guess what? Two of the best doctors at dealing with this kind of ailment are right here. I hope I will be that lucky. Anyhow, I will make all the arrangements to get him home," Baker added, "I'll need to talk to the president's people. The faster we get him home the better. We'll get a chopper to take him to Air Force One at Tegel. Do you want to go along?"

"No," Schneider said quickly, thinking of his wife back at the hotel. "You don't need me to be there."

"Okay, Peter," Baker said, shaking hands. "If anything changes at night, I know where to reach you. I'll talk to the Secret Service, tell them we're getting out of here tomorrow. And I'll meet with the head nurse of the CCU right away."

Adam completed his stroll without any surprises. He went to the Hotel Adlon, to the concierge's desk, and asked him to contact his grandmother and Lisa and let them know they were invited to dinner at eight.

He unlocked the door to his suite and immediately checked the slicks. Both were empty. He sat on the living room couch and laid both folders in front of him. Each was about an inch thick and had a white sticker attached. One read "Dr. Peter Schneider, M.D., President of the E.U.," the other read "PLO." The PLO folder contained the missile information. This was the more urgent of the two. His date with Dr. Schneider apparently would not be for several days. He would have plenty of time to study that folder. The other folder held information he needed to know now.

Sharef had been meticulous. He had determined where the missiles were to be sited. One was to be shoulder-launched by a team member, and Adam was to decide who. The other was to be launched remotely. They were to be fired five seconds apart.

He read the instructions. The missiles were to be in place only minutes before the president's helicopter lifted off from the Charity Hospital helipad. Adam would be told just minutes before lift-off where the missile locations would be. Sharef was taking no chances.

As he read the instructions through a second time, he stopped. Something was wrong. He wasn't sure what. It was just a feeling that all the pieces did not fit. What is it, he thought, why can't I put my finger on it?

The plan appeared to be perfect. Sharef had chosen the proper ammunition; the missiles were a favorite weapon of the PLO; this would look like a PLO hit. Adam went over it again. Two missiles, the primary remotely controlled, the backup shoulder-fired. Two missiles. No chances. That's how the Mossad worked. When it killed, it killed with determination. It made sure.

Two missiles. But Lisa had told him the Mossad had brought three Strella missiles to Berlin. Yes. She had said three missiles, not two.

So where was the third missile? Why hadn't Sharef told him about it? Then he knew.

"By way of deception thou shalt do war."

CHAPTER XXIII

Berlin, September

THE TELEPHONE RANG ONCE, TWICE, THREE times. Maximillian von Habsburg was patient. He knew it would be answered. They both had agreed on the day and time of the call. It was just a formality. He would phone to say that all was going according to plan. It was essential to let William believe he was running the show.

Finally, a voice on the other end said, "May I help you?" "Yes, please," Max said. May I speak to the prince?" "Who may I say is calling?"

"It is Prince Maximillian von Habsburg."

"Of course, your highness, he will be with you immediately. He has been waiting for your call. He's in the rose garden. Just a moment, please."

A minute later: "Max, Max, is that you?" "Yes, William. How are you?"

"I am well, thank you." The voice on the other end sounded a little winded. "Please forgive me. I waited for your call, but when it didn't come, I got upset. I thought something had gone wrong, so I went into my rose garden to relax."

"I'm sorry, William, but I'm only ten minutes late. Let me apologize. The traffic today in Innsbruck was much heavier than usual, and I left my cell phone at home. I'm sorry if I caused you any worry."

"Well, now that I hear your voice, I know all is okay," William said. But you are usually so punctual. We are getting so close. I still can't believe it. Max, tell me this will succeed."

"William, you have my word. Everything is going according to plan. Things could not be better. You should be pleased."

"Pleased? Max! I am in heaven. I am so excited! All has been arranged. The party after the marathon will be great. Everyone is coming, everyone who counts. The Germans, the French, of course, our man Schneider. It's all going the way we wanted. Schneider also accepted the brunch invitation on Sunday, when we will sit down and really discuss business."

"William, please remember, "Max said forcefully, then reminded himself to maintain a moderate tone, "you have agreed to let me run the show during the brunch. This is very important. Of course, you are always in charge. However, I will know more of the people attending who will make the decisions. Leading the way and showing them the right direction will be easier. You know what I mean."

"Of course, Max, that goes without saying. You are my right-hand man."

"Grandma, you look lovely. I'm so glad you're here," Adam said, approaching the table at the restaurant Lorenz Adlon on the first floor of the hotel. She was sitting next to the window overlooking the Brandenburg Gate.

"Any trouble with your flights? Is your room okay? Did your luggage get here?"

"Honey, calm down," she said. "Everything is wonderful."

He leaned over and kissed his grandmother.

"So great to see you. I worried about you. I never wanted you to travel alone, but I couldn't help it. I'm sorry."

"Stop it, Adam. I know how to take care of myself. Remember, I have taken care of you. You worry too much. Besides, you seem to forget this is my hometown."

"I know, Grandma, but still I worried."

"Do me a favor, darling," she said. "Sit down, have a drink, and relax. I think you're overworked. You seem to have too much on your mind."

"Yeah, I did have a tough day."

He sat next to his grandmother and looked around. The restaurant was a quadrant with a large white column in its center. A mural of the sky adorned the ceiling, and the walls were paneled with Canadian cherry wood. He had a grand view of the Brandenburg Gate.

The place was buzzing, and there was no empty table in sight. He called for the waiter, who was dressed in the traditional black tie, and ordered a glass of Pinot Grigio. His grandmother was already enjoying a Berliner *Weisse mit Schuss,* a beer with raspberry juice that she had not had for more than fifty years.

"Grandma," he said, "I hope you don't mind if someone else joins us tonight?"

"Well, if it's a girl, I welcome it. You know, Adam, it's time you thought about settling down. You're not getting any younger."

"Please, Grandma, please. We've talked about this before. I know you got married when you were very young. It was right for you. You met the perfect person. Grandpa was made for you. But you must give me time. I need to be sure. Tonight it's a woman and it's not business. I only met her a couple of days ago. She's beautiful, you'll like her."

"As long as the possibility exists and as long as she is Jewish," she said. "Don't worry, I won't embarrass you."

When she walked into the restaurant, heads turned. She did look beautiful. Her low-cut, tight-fitting gown accentuated the lines of her body, and her long blond hair caressed her shoulders. Confidently she walked toward the table.

"Hello," she said, addressing Martha Bergman. "I am Lisa, a friend of Adam's."

Adam rose quickly. "I'm sorry," he said. "I should have made the introductions. Lisa, you took me by surprise. You look stunning. You're absolutely beautiful tonight. Grandma, don't you agree?"

"Yes, she is," she replied. "But child, please sit down. It seems my grandson has forgotten all his manners. I think you have a spell over him."

Lisa smiled and gently rubbed Martha's shoulder as she took a seat. Adam noted she was not wearing her engagement ring.

"Your grandson is special, I think," she said and smiled at Adam. "Well, he certainly is to me," Martha Bergman replied. "But it seems that you have captured his imagination. He behaved like a schoolboy while we were waiting for you."

"Grandma, you know that's not true. I'm already in deep trouble here," he said.

"All right, darling, I will just be like a fly on the wall. I won't say anything." Then she did. "Lisa, you don't look Jewish, are you?"

"Yes I am, as a matter of fact I am Israeli. I work for the embassy here."

"Oh my goodness, are you the Israeli Ambassador?" Martha asked.

"No, no. I do work for him, though."

"Okay, Grandma, that's it," Adam said. "You promised. No more talk like that. Let's have a nice dinner, no more interrogation."

"Yes, of course. I'm only trying to get to know Lisa. She seems to be such a nice person. She is beautiful and intelligent. Moreover, she's Jewish. Really, Adam, what are you thinking? You two seem like two perfect lovebirds."

Lovebirds, little did Adam's grandmother know the meaning.

CHAPTER XXIV

Berlin. September

ADAM BERGMAN KNEW HE HAD TO be careful. He knew he would be in charge of two of the Strella missiles that were to kill the president of the United States. But he did not know where the third was. He was sure there was a third. He vividly recalled Lisa telling him that the Mossad had brought three Strella missiles to Berlin. He was sure they were meant to be aimed at the president. Even if he tried to find out the whereabouts of the third missile, how could he prevent the attack? Asking questions now, probing for information, was not a good idea. He had to find another way, a way to make sure Sharef never blamed him for the failure to assassinate the president. Sharef had to trust Adam as much as he trusted any person. Of course, Sharef never really trusted anyone. That's all right. As long as he didn't suspect Adam, he could find a way to abort the attack that would not link him to it. He had to give the appearance of following the Mossad's plan. Therefore, he decided to arm and carry the shoulder-held missile personally. Only then would Sharef fully trust him. Once the weapons were in place, there was only one way to derail the assassination: Sharef's target, the president, could not be on the helicopter.

These were Adam's thoughts as he dined with his grandmother and Lisa at the Lorenz Adlon restaurant. It was easy to think and plan, because Lisa and his grandmother were engrossed in conversation during the entire dinner. Occasionally, they would turn to him. He would smile and nod. That was enough.

Before the dinner, Adam had planned to meet with Lisa afterward to try to find out about the third missile. Now he knew this would be a mistake. Instead, he would take Lisa for a walk across the plaza and tell her where she was to meet him to fire the remotely launched Strella. And he would tell her that he would carry and fire the other. However, he had to make sure there would be no target. How? The Secret Service had to change its plan to evacuate the president. And when it did, no one could know about the change. Adam knew the Mossad had people very close to the president. That was how Sharef anticipated their every move. Yes, Adam had to be careful, very careful indeed.

Nicole was exhausted and disappointed. She was also angry with herself. She had failed. The Mossad had outwitted her. She was furious and frustrated.

Nicole left the Thielplatz and headed back towards Oskar-Helene-Heim on foot. She walked briskly. She wanted to run. She tried to get back to her hotel as soon as possible. After all, she had found the approximate location of the Mossad's safe house. Or was it? How could she be sure? Maybe Adam Bergman had just been visiting someone, a relative, perhaps, or a friend. No, she could not contact her station chief and tell him that she'd just located the Mossad safe house. First, she had to make sure. Not today, she had missed that opportunity.

She took the subway from Oskar-Helene-Heim to Stadtmitte, the station close to her hotel. As she entered the Hilton lobby, she had a frivolous thought. Why do Americans always stay at American hotels? That's the agency, she told herself, probably was getting a discount.

She entered her room and saw a dozen red roses in a vase beside her bed. She retrieved the card fastened to one of the flowers. It was a computer-generated note. It was brief. It read: "Tomorrow at precisely 8:30 a.m., be in the French Dome, in the restaurant on the ground floor." There was no name, no signature. She didn't care. She knew she would be there.

"Let's go over this once more, Dr. Baker," said the president's chief of staff. "You are telling us we should fly the boss back to the United States."

"That's precisely what I'm telling you," Baker responded. "All of us, most importantly Dr. Schneider and I, have decided the best course of action is to get him back home. He is stable enough to make the trip. Once he's back, we'll re-evaluate him. Maybe we'll do surgery, maybe not. But right now, we think this is the best action."

"I keep hearing you think," the chief of staff said. "That makes me uncomfortable. Are we risking the life of our president based on what you think?"

Baker decided he had heard enough. He was not used to having his medical opinion questioned, not even by the president's chief of staff. What the hell did he know about medicine?

"If you think differently, do it your way," he said. "But you assume the responsibility. By the way, I don't recall you telling me where you went to medical school."

Baker turned to leave.

"Please, doctor, please," the chief of staff said. "I did not mean it that way. You are the expert. We will listen to you. We will get him back to the United States. I've already discussed it with security. We'll put him on the chopper at ten a.m. tomorrow morning."

Baker was in no mood to discuss this further with this man. He was not used to someone doubting his decisions. This is my turf, he thought; here I'm the president.

Adam knocked on the door of Room 417 at the Adlon Hotel. It was almost midnight. He knocked again.

"Just a moment, please," he heard his grandmother say at last. "I'll be right there."

A moment later, his grandmother opened the door.

"Adam, darling, what's wrong? Come in. Are you in trouble?"

"Grandma, I am so sorry to disturb you so late."

"Don't be silly, I was just lying in bed reading. I'm not tired at all. Maybe it's because I'm so excited to be back in my hometown, breathing the *Berliner Luft,* the Berlin air. Please sit down, let's talk. That Lisa, you really should get serious with her. She is such a wonderful woman."

"Grandma," he interrupted. "I'm sorry to barge in on you like this, but I knew of no one else who could help me. I've got a dilemma."

"Then Grandma will fix it. No doubt, it has something to do with your love life. Am I right?"

He had not thought about it quite that way. Yes, that was the way to portray it. He hated to use his grandmother, but there was no other way. He was stuck.

"Yes, Grandma, there is another girl. She is also here in Berlin. They don't know about each other, I mean Lisa does not know about

Nicole. Nicole, that is the name of the other woman. I met her not long ago in Miami Beach. Now she's here in Berlin. I don't know why. I know she's a runner, so maybe she is going to run the Berlin Marathon."

He had known it was she. When he had gone for his run in Berlin, he had known someone was following him. He turned his head slightly and caught her in his peripheral vision. He had thought she would follow him further, but she had not. She had not made the turn onto Charlottenstrasse. Now he felt more confident that the hunch he had about her true identity was right. Today he would be counting on it.

"Well, anyway," he continued facing his grandma, "Nicole left a message at my hotel today. She wants to meet me at the French Dome tomorrow at eight-thirty a.m., and I can't be there. I promised Lisa we would spend the day together. We have plans to go to the Spreewald, I want her to see it. But you know it's a bit of a drive and we need to leave early."

He paused. "Really, Grandma, let's just forget about it. I don't want you involved with my problems."

"Nonsense, Adam. That's what grandmothers are for. Is Nicole Jewish too?"

"Yeah, I don't know. I never asked her."

"Well, never mind. You seem to like both of them equally. I want to meet her. Let's have dinner with her, okay? That's my price for doing whatever it is you want me to do tomorrow."

"Fair enough," he said. "All I want you to do is go to the French Dome. She'll be there at eight-thirty, in the restaurant. You'll recognize her at once. She's beautiful, black hair, usually tied in a ponytail. But don't talk to her. Just give her the envelope and walk away. The envelope will have my message, my apologies, and now I'll add the dinner invitation. Is it a deal?"

"Of course, no trouble at all. You know grandmas love to be matchmakers, and I'm no exception. I promise not to interrogate her. I can wait for that until we have dinner. Don't worry, Adam, I will do it."

He knew she would. He knew he could count on her. He also knew that she would speak with Nicole. She wouldn't be able to resist. But a few words were not too high a price to pay to secure the life of the president of the United States, he thought, as he handed the envelope to his grandmother.

CHAPTER XXV

Berlin, September

MARTHA BERGMAN LEFT HER HOTEL ON the Pariser Platz by seven-thirty a.m. She was an early riser. Already she had had her breakfast at the cafe of the hotel. For a long time, she had been looking forward to once again eating a proper German breakfast, the coffee, the fresh rolls and butter, all the cold cuts. That was how it used to be, how her late husband and she had enjoyed each morning. Strolling across the Pariser Platz, she headed directly toward her old home. It was the reason she had returned to Berlin, to see the house again. It was where she had experienced all her happiness and then all but sadness.

As she stood staring at the building, the memories came back. What a wonderful time. We had everything; everything, until the Nazis came and destroyed it all. She lost her husband, and she lost her son. She had no choice. God, please help me, she thought, help my son forgive me. She had been young then; there had been no one to help her. She hoped she had done the right thing. She knew she had. She knew because God had rewarded her with Adam, her grandson. How could she ever love anyone more? Tears ran down Martha Bergman's cheeks. She had done what no mother would ever do: give up her son. It had been the only way to save her child.

She turned away from the building and slowly continued up Unter den Linden to her destination at the Gendarmenmarkt. Here she would meet Nicole Jefferson and deliver her grandson's message. A message for lovers, she thought. How exciting, how long has it been since I thought about lovers?

She entered the beautiful French Dome and took a few minutes to walk around. Although she was early, she was anxious to meet her grandson's friend. She then went to the restaurant to wait.

Nicole was also early. She was the only one in the restaurant, and Martha recognized her immediately. She was beautiful, a natural beauty. Yes, my grandson has taste.

Nicole was dressed casually in jeans, running shoes, and a loose blouse. Her long black hair was tied back in a ponytail. She looked nervous, Martha thought. She had forgotten what love can do to you. Martha did not deliver Adam's note at once. She was five minutes early. And Martha wanted to use her grandmother's way this time.

"It's a beautiful morning," she said nonchalantly as she walked toward Nicole.

"Yes, yes it is," Nicole replied, noticing for the first time the older woman's tasteful clothing. "You have the look of a Berliner," she continued.

"Well, thank you," Martha said. "Yes, I was born, grew up, and spent my formative years in Berlin. This is where I started my family. But then I had to leave, and I have not been back for a long time, too long a time."

"That's sad," Nicole said. "We should always keep in touch with our roots. They're what make us who we are. I'm sorry if you have lost that."

"I returned to ensure my roots are still here and alive."

"I hope they are," Nicole said. "Without roots, who are we? How do we explain ourselves, I don't mean to others, but to ourselves. I think it would be very, very difficult."

Martha Bergman was starting to like this young woman.

"You don't realize how right you are," she said. "But I am sorry to natter on. You don't want to spend your morning listening to an older woman. At my age, we always talk about how it should have been. You should talk about how you want it to be at your age."

Nicole smiled. "It sounds as if you have been thinking a lot."

"Well," Martha replied, glad finally to have a chance to bring up Adam, "I have a grandson. I raised him. He is maybe three or four years older than you are. He and I are very close. He confides in me. He and I talk all the time. It keeps me young, makes me understand what's going on. Don't get me wrong, we don't always agree. In fact, we rarely do. The beauty of our relationship is that we always reach a compromise. I guess that's what love does. It helps us understand the other."

Martha looked at her watch. "I'm very sorry," she said abruptly. "I hope you will understand. I hope that we will meet again. Please forgive me."

Martha handed her a small envelope.

"He said you must read it immediately," Martha explained. "Later, he will call you. It was a pleasure meeting you, and I hope to see you again. I know I will. *Auf Wiedersehen.*"

She turned and walked quickly away, back into the plaza. Nicole did not move. Slowly, she opened the envelope. There was a computer-printed note. It was brief:

"The president must not be on the helicopter. You have ninety minutes to save his life. Be careful, they have people close to him."

A hoax? Nicole went to the nearest pay phone and called the CIA's Berlin station number.

Adam had to know. He waited until precisely nine a.m. to call his grandmother's room. He needed to get to the Charity Hospital grounds to fulfill his mission, but he did not want to leave until he knew his grandmother had delivered the message.

"Adam, darling," his grandmother responded after several rings. Her voice sounded winded. "I just walked in the door. Your friend Nicole is such a wonderful person. I love her. I see your dilemma. Please forgive me; I never knew you had such problems. You have two beautiful women in town and you are attracted to both. No wonder you are preoccupied."

"Grandma. Yes, you're right. Sorry, I have been preoccupied. Did you give her my message?"

"You know she is not just beautiful," his grandmother went on. "She has brains too. We talked for a while. I promised you would take her out to dinner. And she said that I could be there too," she fabricated.

"Of course, of course, Grandma, I'll do it." he replied impatiently.

"But did you give her the envelope?"

"She is one of the brightest people I have ever met. She is so sensitive, so caring. I agree. She is a true dear."

"Grandma, please," he said. "Did you give her the envelope?"

"The envelope, of course, honey. I gave it to her at eight-thirty a.m., just as you told me."

"Grandma," he said, "I can never do without you. Now I have one more job for you, you have to go with me to that party, the party after the Berlin Marathon. Remember, it's a grand party at one of the most famous Berlin homes. You said you knew them, you promised me you'd come along."

"I'll go on the condition that you bring Nicole as well." "Grandma, you have my word. I will."

As he said this, he again realized he had exposed himself. Now Nicole knew, and now he had another job. He had to take care of Nicole Jefferson.

CHAPTER XXVI

Berlin, September

THE BEIGE MERCEDES-BENZ BENZ TAXI LEFT the Charité Hospital at precisely ten a.m. There was no escort, no Berlin motorcycle policemen. The taxi pulled away from the area marked "Deliveries Only." It went slowly into the street. It was in no hurry. It appeared empty but for the driver. Just a taxi going for its morning fuel-up at one of the gasoline stations, maybe a doughnut and coffee for the driver. Yes, it happened all the time. No doubt, that's where the taxi was heading.

At ten a.m., the helicopter lifted off the helipad at the Charité Hospital. All night, it had been guarded. Early in the morning, a team of Secret Service agents prepared the chopper with all the necessary equipment the U.S. president needed to get to Air Force One. The head nurse of the coronary care unit coordinated the entire evacuation plan.

All he could do was smile. Yes, the *sayan* thought, the president was in that helicopter. The *sayan* was one of several Berlin policemen guarding the chopper. Of course, there are the Americans, too, he told himself. All those guys in the dark suits are Secret Service.

He shifted into the seat of his BMW motorcycle and looked up at the sky. In about thirty seconds, he knew the fireworks would begin.

At precisely thirty seconds past ten a.m., the explosion occurred. The helicopter had just left its pad and was barely above 300 feet when lit by a flame. For a moment, it whirled wildly in the air. Then it exploded and fell to the street in flames.

Adam dropped the missile and launcher. He had seen the fireball. Sweat was forming on his palms, and he wiped them again on his pants leg. Had she done it? He wondered. All he could do now was hope Nicole had had time to scrub the target. He left the missile and launcher on the roof of the medical school building, only five hundred yards from the hospital's helipad. The weapon was clean; his surgeon's gloves had made sure. Sharef had insisted that all the guns be left in place. Obviously, he knew what he was doing. He was leaving a trace, a trace leading back to the PLO.

Adam quickly left the grounds of Charity Hospital. He walked for a while, then he took the subway, then the bus. He was headed toward Wannsee, far away from the scene. He would have the entire day to himself. He had told his grandmother he was going to the Spreewald with Lisa, but Lisa was now returning to Israel. Her mission was over. How unfortunate, he thought, as he gazed out the window on the bus to the Wannsee, one of Berlin's most beautiful lakes. I really liked her, and I will never see her again.

Adam needed time to himself, so he got on a boat, had a beer and a Wiener, one of the Berlin hot dogs, and got mentally ready for the next mission, the mission for which he had been called to Berlin in the first place. His cell phone rang.

"Yes," he answered, "I am on a boat."

"I know," a woman said. "In another twenty minutes, the boat will make a stop. It will dock for half an hour. Get off and call back. You know the number."

"I will, but please, I am sorry, I do love you, I just needed some time."

"I understand. Just call."

They were good, Adam thought; yes, the Mossad was the best.

The taxi did not stop for gasoline, coffee, or a doughnut. The beige Mercedes taxi drove directly to Tegel airport. It did not pull up to the departure area, but it went to the north end of the airport. The fence was opened to allow the entry of the cab. It continued to the hangar where Air Force One was parked. As soon as the taxi stopped, there was chaos. People were everywhere; a gurney with a man was eased from the back seat and quickly transferred onto the plane. The president was put on board Air Force One, accompanied by his chief of staff and his personal physician.

In ten short minutes, the plane was airborne, headed for the United States.

CHAPTER XXVII

SHAREF RECEIVED THE TELEPHONE CALL AT two minutes past ten. He had been ready.

"It is done," said the man.

"Excellent," Sharef answered, then added, "I need to know which missile did the job."

"The second one, the one remotely controlled. But the other two were also in place. They were ready, as you planned it."

"Very good. Now I want all of you to leave. You know the exit plan. Everyone gets out immediately, everyone but Adam. He has another job to do. Is he clean?"

"No doubt about it. He had the second missile on his shoulder. He was ready to shoot. You can trust him."

"Okay, pull out, and let the PLO take the blame for killing the president. Don't wait; I want all of you out of here, Lisa and everyone else. Jacob, you stay, and Mark as well. Understood?"

"Yes," the man replied, "just as we planned. Most of us are already on our way. Don't worry."

"Fine," Sharef said. "Don't call me here again. I'm preparing the second step of our operation. Killing the president was an inconvenience. Now it's time to take care of a more critical task. Thank you all for a job well done."

Sharef got out of the leather chair and went to the door. His aides had already packed his bags—he no longer needed to be here. The rest of the operation could be handled long-distance. Now it's all politics, all diplomacy. Now all the pieces will fall into place.

The North African Desert, September

They were huddled in a tent in the North African desert, but only a few in the group were Arabs. Most were Europeans, men, and women—twelve in all. They listened closely to the radio transmission.

The helicopter carrying the president had been shot down. The president was dead. It was a Strella missile, one of their own. They looked at each other in disbelief. Then they smiled. Sure, it was the PLO. Let the world think we have such power, the power to kill anyone, even the president of the United States.

Berlin, September

"Nicole, you just saved the life of our president. If you feel like sharing, I'd be curious to know where you got your information. Or maybe you'd like to tell the president yourself. I'm sure you'll be meeting him. Congratulations."

Nicole Jefferson was listening on a secure line at the American embassy. It was her DDO.

"Thanks," she said. "Really, I only did what anyone else would have done."

"Give it a rest, Nicole," the DDO said with a smile in his voice. "One of your first assignments, and what do you do? You save the life of the president. I've been in this business for twenty years and I never even got to tie his shoelaces. You're an instant hero. We want you back here. We want to make sure the chief understands why he's still alive, because the CIA saved his ass."

"Hey, slow down," Nicole responded. "As I recall, I have another job to do, and I want to finish it. What about bringing Adam Bergman over to our side?"

"Forget it," the DDO answered, "we need you back here. We need credit where credit is due. The president needs to understand that without us he'd be coming home in a plastic bag. This is important to the agency. I guess the Secret Service did help. But without you our chief would be dead by now."

"Look," she said sharply, and even she was surprised at her tone. "You play politics, okay? I'm just a case officer and I have a job to finish. Tell the president that it was my pleasure to save his ass."

"Do you know what you're saying? You'll be invited to the White House, you'll meet the president, have dinner with him. You'll get a promotion, you can name your job. Get on the next plane; I'll arrange a military flight. The CIA needs you here."

"Remember our meeting in your office?" Nicole said. "You told me that the stakes here in Europe were very high. Forget about politics for once. I'm not a politician anyway. You don't need me to claim the credit for the agency. I want to stay here. I don't want to leave this case."

The DDO relented. "Okay, stay in Berlin. You're right, it is essential. I want to hang the PLO bastards who tried to kill the president."

William P. Davis, "Pistol" Davis, as everyone called him, put down his telephone receiver at his office in Langley, Virginia. He had to ensure the credit for saving the president went where it belonged, to the CIA. He had a plan. There had to be a hero, he thought, so why not me? After all, he ran Nicole; she was his responsibility. Who was to say he wasn't the one who showed her where to get the information that saved the president's life?

Yes, the DDO thought, that's how we'll play it. I'm the one who saved the commander-in-chief. I'll meet him at Andrews Air Force Base when he arrives. It was my operation. Without me, Nicole would have never been in Berlin. Without me, the president would be dead right now.

Berlin–Washington, September

Air Force One had reached its cruising altitude of 33,000 feet, and the pilots had leveled the plane. They thought it would be a smooth ride, or so the radar showed them. Now they could relax. They were about to leave German airspace and cross the English Channel.

"Mr. President," the chief of staff said softly as he approached President Levenson on his gurney. Are you okay? Is there anything I can get for you?"

He had been reluctant to approach his boss after take-off, for the commander-in-chief appeared to be sleeping. Finally, he had decided to check.

"Mr. President," he repeated.

No response.

"Mr. President," he now said, raising his voice. "Are you okay?"

Again, there was no answer.

"Dr. Cole," he said, "get over here immediately. I think we have a problem. I think the boss needs help."

But help was too late. The president was dead. His weakened aorta had ruptured. It had happened so quickly that he could not call for help. The president's physician knew it immediately. His first thought was that they had all been wrong. Baker, he, and Schneider all had thought the president had been stabilized. They had been bad. The aorta had ruptured, and the president had bled to death. In an instant.

Cole knew there was no chance to revive him. He asked for a blanket. It was printed with the flag of the USA. He placed the blanket over the dead body of his friend, the president of the United States. Tears ran down his cheeks.

"Yes, another cognac, please. I would appreciate it."

Sharef relaxed as he reclined in his first-class seat aboard the Air France flight back to Tel Aviv. Everything had worked in his favor. That's what happens when you plan, he thought, you anticipate all the possibilities. There was no one better than he.

Sharef raised himself slowly from his seat. He was tired. The first-class section was empty, so he strolled toward the back of the cabin. He sat down in an aisle seat and took a swallow of the cognac. He earned it, he thought. He took out the telephone from his armrest, swiped one of his credit cards, and called the safe number. It rang once.

"Lovebirds," he said. "I need an update."

"Yes," came the response, a high-pitched female voice. You will be pleased. While the mission did not go entirely according to plan, the result has been the same. Can you provide details now?"

"No, no, not now. Brief me when I am back home. Not now."

"Yes, sir, but I repeat: We won."

Sharef hung up the phone. He looked around. No one had noticed him changing seats and making the call.

He stood up and went back to his seat. He sat down and smiled. Yes, he thought, we had won. From now on, Israel would be in control.

Berlin, Wannsee, September

The Wannsee sightseeing boat made its first stop, and Adam Bergman was the first one off. He went straight to the restaurant, just fifty yards from the dock, and walked to the men's room. When he exited, he appeared relaxed, entirely at ease, and he strolled to the bar and ordered a beer. Most of the ship's passengers had arrived at the restaurant by now. Adam picked up his beer from the bar, took a drink, and left. He carried his beer onto the patio. It was a beautiful day. He passed the public telephones, then shook his head as if he had just remembered something.

"The office," he mumbled.

He turned, drank another beer, and walked to the bank of telephones. He picked up the receiver and dialed the number.

"Darling," a woman answered, "I have waited to hear from you. Why did you not call? Grandfather died; he is dead. He did not die in the helicopter, he was not on it. He died on the plane on his way back home."

"I'm so sorry," Adam said. "I'll get back right away. What a tragedy."

He had succeeded, at least temporarily. The president had not died in the helicopter; he had been killed on Air Force One, on his way home. Nicole had been successful, and now Nicole knew too much. His plate was not getting any emptier.

The sightseeing boat left the dock without Adam. He had decided to get back to work. He knew all too well that he still had a job to accomplish—several jobs—and he needed to do them all.

CHAPTER XXVIII

Berlin, September

PETER SCHNEIDER STEPPED OUT OF THE shower in his suite at the Regent Hotel.

"Honey, come and look at this," his wife called from the living room. "Hurry!"

"What is it?" he asked, drying himself with one of the hotel's oversized towels.

"Look," she pointed at the television. "The president is dead."

"What?" he said, letting the towel drop. "You're kidding. What happened?"

"They said he was in the care of Dr. Baker. They said Baker made a mistake. They are saying it's Baker's fault."

The TV screen showed the anchorwoman giving the details again: the president of the United States had been on his way back to Washington on Air Force One when he had died of a ruptured aorta. The camera cut to the president's chief of staff, standing at the dais in a hastily called press conference:

"The president needed surgery, and the decision was made to transport him back to the United States. The decision was made with advice from the best doctors in the world. It's a tragic day, and

I ask that all of you go about your business and remember that our government is strong. Although we are saddened by this tragedy, we have work to do, and we will continue it."

A reporter shouted a question: "Are you telling us that moving the president was a bad idea, that that's the reason he died?"

"We're not prepared to say at this time," the chief of staff said. "Obviously, there will be a full medical investigation and the details will be made available as we get them."

Schneider stood in disbelief. He had heard enough bureaucrats in his career to recognize the implication now, blame would be shifted to the doctors. The politicians were doing the first thing politicians always do in time of crisis, cover their ass.

Schneider also knew he was at least partly to blame. He, Baker, the best doctors at Charitee Hospital, the president's own physician, all had concurred. It was safe to move him. Get the president back to the United States. They had all felt confident with the decision. They had all been wrong, some of the best minds in medicine. He reminded himself why he wanted to change his career, why he had to leave medicine. He had been in this position too often. Too often he'd dealt with patients who were ill beyond help and who still expected the impossible, a miracle. Then when it didn't happen there was nothing but blame, blame for the medical profession, blame for the doctor.

Schneider didn't want to be a part of it any longer. I should have gone into law, he told himself, not for the first time. Who runs Washington, the Senate, and Congress? Lawyers. Their interests will always be protected. They make the decisions, not doctors.

Now Schneider knew he had to do something else. He had to do something different, to accomplish his goal, a goal he had set for himself many years ago. A goal that said I want to do all I can to help, to help my fellow citizens, to help human beings, to help humanity.

Nicole walked into her room at the Berlin Hilton and collapsed. My God, she thought, what is happening to me? Finally, I'm in the middle of the game and don't know how to play. No one tells me anything. I need help, she thought. I need to talk to someone. She heaved a sigh, opened her eyes, and saw another bouquet, twelve red roses next to her bed. There was a card too.

She jumped up and stared at the flowers. Then she allowed herself to open the card. She read it twice, then a third time. She could not believe it. She had done it. She was invited to the most crucial party in Berlin, the post-marathon celebration at Prince William von Hohenzollern's palace. I need a new dress, she thought at once.

They worked in the same office, for the same boss, on the same assignment. Both had the same goal. But they disagreed on one point: one thought the man he was to follow was a friend, the other thought he was an enemy.

At first, Sharef had intended to have Jacob watch Adam Bergman's back. That was the natural choice, because Jacob was part of Adam's team. But Sharef realized there was poor chemistry between the two men. The reason was apparent: Jacob was in love with Lisa, truly in love with her. Lisa ignored him. And when Lisa met Adam, she was infatuated with him, no question about it. Even Jacob, especially Jacob, could see it, and immediately disliked Adam and did not trust him. So Sharef changed his strategy. He assigned Weiss to protect Adam and kept Jacob to watch him. He knew Jacob would do his job passionately; he wanted to find fault with Adam. And when you control a person's emotions, Sharef knew, you control the person.

Sharef was certain Jacob would be the ideal bloodhound. Of course, Sharef had told Jacob that he trusted Adam implicitly. Adam was one of his best men. But it was Mossad policy to trust no one.

Jacob had welcomed his assignment. He wanted Adam to make a mistake; he desperately wanted him to fail, and he wanted to be there when it happened. Jacob dreamed Adam was, in fact, a foreign spy, a double agent, and he would expose him. At first, Lisa would scorn him, he knew. She would tell him he was jealous. But when she realized Jacob was right, she would adore him. It would drive them close. Now Jacob was hoping his dream would come true.

This day, however, he was having serious doubts. He had just watched Adam himself shoulder a Strella missile and display every intention of firing it; he had watched him order Lisa to press the button and shoot the remotely controlled missile that downed the helicopter. Yes, it was unfortunate that the president had not been on board, but as much as he wished it, Jacob could not blame Adam. No question about it, Adam was faithful to the Mossad.

On the other hand, Weiss had developed a real affection for Adam. He was his guardian angel, and he took the assignment seriously. He followed Adam everywhere, but he did not know about Jacob. That was the Mossad way.

Weiss had followed Adam on the boat ride. He had caught a taxi and followed the bus Adam took. Adam knew about Weiss. Sharef had told him. The Mossad took no chances. They were the best in this business. They would protect Adam. They would make sure no harm would come to him. It was a comforting thought. Adam felt secure. He knew he was well guarded.

Adam had returned to his hotel, changed his clothing, and gone for his daily run. He knew Weiss was behind him. He could almost hear his breathing. He smiled.

Abruptly, his senses switched to full alert. Turning a corner, he noticed a man running thirty paces behind his guardian angel, Weiss. What surprised Adam was that he knew the man. It was Jacob, the third member of his team. Adam was perplexed. What was Jacob doing here? Was he also assigned to protect him? Sharef had not mentioned him. Maybe he had forgotten. No, Sharef does not forget. As he ran, he decided there must be another reason why Jacob was following him. He made up his mind to find out. He had a hunch. Sharef had not told him everything. And Adam gambled. He would risk his mission; he had to know what Sharef was up to.

When Adam got to the Adlon Hotel, he immediately went to one of the public telephones and called the secure number in Tel Aviv.

"Yes," a woman answered in a business-like manner.

"This is Adam Bergman. I'm being followed."

"Just a moment, please."

It took another ten seconds.

"You know that Weiss is with you."

"It's not Weiss," Adam said.

"Just a moment."

This time, the response took longer. Adam now knew why.

"It's okay; the boss says not to worry. Continue with your assignment."

Now Adam was sure. He was not told to go home or to a movie. He would not have to put on his cap; he did not have to abandon his mission. Sharef had ordered him followed by someone else, and this was no guardian angel. Adam had caught Sharef at his own game. Sharef did not trust him. Of course, he reminded himself, Sharef trusted no one.

CHAPTER XXIX

Berlin, September

NICOLE WAS STILL READING HER INVITATION to the post-marathon party at Prince William von Hohenzollern's palace on Friday evening, when the phone rang. It was the United States Ambassador to Germany. He was brief and to the point. She was expected at the embassy in thirty minutes.

Nicole called the concierge and asked for a taxi, although she could easily walk to the embassy. She did not want to waste any time. She went to the bathroom to freshen up, then she left her room. She took her invitation to the party along.

She got into the taxi, asked for the U. S. Embassy, and settled back in the rear seat to read the invitation more carefully. It was printed in a formal, ornate typeface, and a handwritten note was on the back. It said: "Pick you up at seven-thirty at your hotel. Tired already? Adam."

She smiled. He had remembered the line she'd used when she picked him up on their run in Miami Beach.

"Nicole! You there? Can you hear me?"

"Yes," Nicole responded, "I hear you quite well as a matter of fact." She was sitting in the ambassador's office at the Berlin U.S. embassy. She was alone. Langley had insisted on it. The ambassador disliked leaving the room, but he had no choice. He knew where he stood in the pecking order.

"I have terrible news," said Pistol Davis, DDO of the CIA, and Nicole's immediate supervisor.

"The president is dead. They say the doctors screwed up. We did our job. Now it's time to move on and focus on the primary assignment. You have to get to our man, to Bergman. Time is running out. We know the Royals are planning to move soon. They have a timetable, and somehow this guy Adam Bergman is involved. We don't know how. That's your job to find out."

"Apparently, the president knew how Bergman was tied in but never told anyone. It's up to you now. And there's something else. We have information that indicates there's a link to Bergman's grandmother. Her name is Martha, Martha Bergman. The ambassador will give you a folder with all our information about the Bergmans. We are counting on you. I think something big is about to happen. Can you get to Bergman? Oh, and one other thing, there's a party sponsored by the Royals. We think the party is part of their plan, there you may be able to find out more of what's going on. Try to get invited."

"Sure," Nicole replied, savoring the rare chance to tell the DDO something he didn't already know. "But there's something I want from you. If I can get into that party, and if I can arrange for Adam to be my date, will you pay for a new dress?"

"A dress?" the DDO said. "What are you talking about?"

"Well, naturally I need a new dress to go to the party. Or did you not think about that?"

"No, no, I didn't," Pistol Davis said. "You buy any dress you want. The agency will pay for it. Just be there, and be there with Bergman."

"Alright," she said. It will be difficult, but I'll work on it."

She smiled as she placed the receiver back on the telephone on the mahogany table in the large office of the U.S. ambassador to Germany.

Boys will be boys, she thought, and boys are one thing I know how to handle.

Peter Schneider was exhausted. He was also elated. He had done it. He had finished the Berlin Marathon and, better than that, he had run a personal record. His goal had been three hours and thirty minutes, but he had done much better, he had run the marathon in three hours, fourteen minutes and thirty three seconds. His best ever. What a race! The course had been perfect, the weather ideal, slightly cool. Not a cloud in the sky. He took a deep breath. He felt a true sense of accomplishment. He knew he had accomplished many things in the past, accomplished goals that to many people would look much more illustrious than a marathon time. Not to Schneider. A 3:14:33 at his age was one of his greatest victories. All he wanted to do was to find his wife and share the moment. Yes, he thought. If you put your mind to it and prepare for it, you can do it. You can do anything. I'm ready; I'm ready for the next challenge. He wondered what it would be.

Adam Bergman had also finished the Berlin Marathon, forty minutes and twenty-three seconds before Schneider crossed the line. But Adam was not satisfied. He had not met his goal. He had run a 2:34:10. Not bad, he thought. But he had wanted to get under 2:30, and he knew why he hadn't. His training had been erratic, his tapering uneven. His work had interfered. One day, he would run under 2:30.

William was not disappointed. William had trained hard. William had done everything according to the book. William had no job to distract him. William finished the race in 3:27:58. When he finished, he felt great. He was not breathing hard. His muscles had not cramped. He could have run for another few miles, he thought. When he reached the twenty-mile mark, the marathon's traditional "wall," he was not ready to quit. Twenty miles is the point at which most runners have used their bodies' store of carbohydrates, their primary energy source. Then the body has to switch to a different fuel: fat. William knew that burning fat is more difficult if you are not trained for it. Nevertheless, it is a more efficient fuel. There are more calories in fat than in carbohydrates. William did not hit the wall. He had trained for it. He had been ready. I did it, and I did it faster than I thought I could. I feel great. I feel no pain; all I feel is a sense of accomplishment. A perfect day, he thought, and tonight I will have an ideal party.

Nicole ran through the finish line. She finished the marathon, and she was happy with that. She had set no goal for herself, no time to beat. She just wanted to finish, and she was elated when she did. She looked at the clock mounted at the finish line. It read 3:24:48. She could not believe it. She obviously had finished the marathon in less than three hours and thirty minutes. She felt good; now she knew she could do it all. That's what a marathon does to you, she thought. It makes you realize that you can reach any goal you set for yourself. It was near noon in Berlin, and Nicole knew she had an important date that night. She also knew she needed a dress, so she had to go shopping. There was not much time to waste.

He spent more time in the shower, much more than he usually did. His body needed the relaxation. It's strange, he thought. I still feel as if I could go running right now. I don't feel tired at all.

Finally, after fifteen minutes or so, he stepped out of the shower onto the bathmat marked with the emblem of the Hotel.

"Katie," he called out, "what should I wear to the party?"

"Honey, it's casual. Just wear slacks and a nice dress shirt. I laid it out on your bed. Hurry up. We don't want to keep the Prince waiting," she said with a snicker, for she knew no one would notice them.

The taxi left the Adlon Hotel, traveled only a few short blocks, and pulled up to the Hilton Hotel in Berlin's Mitte district.

"I'll be just a minute, Grandma."

"Okay, but hurry, darling. We don't want to be late and miss anything."

Adam made his way into the lobby and saw his date immediately. She was more beautiful than he remembered. No, he thought to himself, not attractive, more than that, stunning, striking, physically arresting. Her dress clung to her. Nicole saw him then and flashed a bright smile. Her hair hung loose and flowed over her shoulders, caressing her skin.

He was speechless again, and he cursed himself for this weakness. He must change. Tell her anything, he thought, don't stand here like a schoolboy.

"Nicole. You look beautiful tonight. The last time I saw you, we jogged on the beach in Miami, remember?"

"Yes, I do," she replied. "You certainly know how to follow a woman."

"Well…" Now he was embarrassed again; he could feel his lips growing stiff, his brain fumbling.

"Well, I saw you were here, in Berlin," he said after a moment. "So, yes, naturally, I thought we should get together. You'll enjoy the party tonight. The prince is supposed to throw some of the best parties in Berlin."

"That's what I've heard," she said. "By the way, how did you know I was here, in Berlin?"

"Oh, I saw you in front of your hotel the other day," he lied. "You were getting into a taxi. I called your name, but I guess you didn't hear me. Let's get going," he smiled. "I've a taxi outside, with my other date."

"Well, that's no surprise," she said good-naturedly. "I always figured that one woman would not be enough for you."

"It's my grandmother. I hope you don't mind. She will only stay a bit and then take a taxi back to her hotel. She loves parties. She loves this city. She was born here, you know."

"No, I didn't." Nicole lied, for she had studied the CIA folder on the Bergmans. She knew everything about them, everything the CIA knew.

They arrived at the curb, and Adam took a quick step and opened the taxi door.

"Grandma, meet Nicole," he said. "Nicole, this is my grandmother. Well, her name is Martha, but she actually prefers Grandma."

"Hello," Nicole said, not missing a beat. "Pleased to see you again."

"Yes," Martha Bergman replied. "I'm glad you kids worked it out. My goodness, you look beautiful tonight. Adam, how do you do it? All these beautiful women."

Adam squirmed a little.

"Grandma, please," he said, sliding into the front seat next to the driver.

"We're going to the Grunewald," he told the driver. "Let me find the address. It's at Prince William–"

"Oh," the driver interrupted. "You are going to the party at the prince's house. Don't worry, I know how to get there. There probably is no taxi driver in Berlin who does not know his address. You will have fun tonight. His parties are Berlin's best. Not that I have been there, you understand. I have only heard about them. In the past, the prince has invited some drivers; that's how he is. He loves people, and particularly his Berliners. Do you need a ride back, later tonight?"

"Yes, we do," Adam said. "I mean, my grandmother does. She's going to leave early. At some point, we'll leave, too, unless the prince asks us to move in."

The taxi driver laughed. "You never know," the driver said. He reached for the dashboard.

"Here is my card. Have someone call me and I'll be there to pick you up."

Adam put the card in his breast pocket.

They rode in silence for a time. Then Martha Bergman said, "Nicole, can I ask you one question?"

"Sure," she said. "Ask as many as you like." "Nicole, are you --"

"Stop it, Grandma," Adam said, turning quickly in his seat. Then, checking himself, he softly added, "Please, Grandma, no more questions."

Martha Bergman smiled at her grandson and looked out the window at the tree-lined street. There would be another time, later in the night, and then she would ask her question again.

CHAPTER XXX

Berlin, Grunewald, September

THE TAXI CRUNCHED TO A STOP in the gravel drive before the magnificent, brightly lit palace. Two attendants in black tuxedos and bow ties jumped to open the rear doors of the car.

"Welcome to the home of Prince William von Hohenzollern," the older of the two men said. "May I please see your invitation?"

"Certainly," Peter Schneider responded.

"Honey." He turned to his wife, patting his pockets. "Did I give it to you?"

"No, you picked it up off the nightstand when we left the hotel."

"Oh yes," Schneider said at last, reaching into the back pocket of his slacks.

"Here it is."

The attendant glanced at the card, then looked again.

"Oh, Dr. Schneider," he said. "Just a moment, sir. Please wait here. It will not be but a minute or two."

"Is something wrong?" Peter asked.

"No sir, not at all. The prince asked to be informed personally the moment you arrived. He wants to greet you right away. Just a moment, please," he said, then turned and hurried up the stairs.

So much for not noticing if we arrived late, Katie Schneider thought. Then she felt her husband's hand take hers. They stood together and looked for the first time at their surroundings. The palace was built of stone and marble with a beautifully weathered slate roof. Schneider counted nine chimneys. He estimated the house must be at least 35,000 square feet. It was immense, yet not out of proportion considering the grounds on which it stood. They had driven in through a large ornate iron gate, past a guardhouse located just off a quiet street in the beautiful Grunewald, Berlin's large forest. The driveway was at least 500 yards long, lined by chestnut trees and a split rail fence. They glimpsed a pasture through the trees and several horses bending to graze. Nearer the palace, the driveway looped into a circle, and in the center of the circle stood a large fountain decorated with many lion heads; around the fountain was a lush rose garden, all of its flowers in full bloom. The weather was perfect, a beautiful September evening, a slight breeze, not a cloud in the darkening sky.

"Dr. Schneider," a man said, interrupting his reverie. "I am so pleased to meet you and your lovely wife."

Schneider turned to face the prince and was surprised. He had expected a much older man, perhaps heavy set, indeed more regal. But the man who took his hand had a youthful look. He looked much younger than a man close to sixty. He was deeply tanned, well built, with an effervescent smile and excellent English. Schneider liked him immediately. Then the prince took Katie Schneider's hand and kissed the back of it. She smiled and blushed.

"I cannot tell you how thrilled I am to meet you both finally. You know your husband is a very distant relative of mine, Mrs. Schneider. I pointed it out in the invitation I sent you. I wanted to be sure you accepted. Well, let us get all the formalities over with. After all, we are family. So may I suggest that you call me William, and I call you Katie and Peter?"

"Of course," Katie replied, "I guess, since we're family."

"Well, let's drink to that!" The prince turned toward the older attendant.

"By the way, may I introduce Heinrich, my butler? He is the best. If there is anything you need, anything at all, Heinrich will take care of it."

"Would you like the champagne now, Prince?" Heinrich spoke a more heavily accented English.

"Yes, please, Heinrich, a toast with my cousins from America."

Heinrich handed each a champagne glass and poured from a bottle of Cristal.

"Thank you, Heinrich," the prince said, then raised a glass. "Here is to us. To Katie, Peter, and me. Let us look forward to a long relationship. Here is to family."

Nicole had spent many hours formulating a strategy for this night. She would go to the party with Adam and have fun, but at the same time, she would do her job. In fact, the two went together. She thought the more I enjoy myself, the more convincing I'll seem to him. After all, I need to earn my dress.

She had read the agency's file on the Bergman family. She knew all about Joshua, Martha, and Adam. She had also studied the history of the European Union and the CIA folder on Dr. Peter Schneider. Her boss, the DDO, had told her that Adam was important and that he was a link to exposing the secret that the president had taken to his death. However, the real link, the DDO had added, was his grandmother, Martha. No one at the CIA knew exactly how or why, they had heard only rumors, faint signals from the field, obscured by static. Then confirmation came that the agency was onto something of great importance: the president had known the truth. Someone had told him. The information was so important that someone had tried to assassinate the president. They had failed. Now the president was dead anyhow. Nicole needed to find out what the president knew. And so she had developed her plan: Adam and Martha Bergman must meet with Peter Schneider at the party, and she, Nicole, had to be there.

"Max, Max, come over here," William shouted as he led Katie and Peter into the elegant, circular foyer of the palace. Twelve Ionic, sixty-foot marble columns lined the circular candle-lit room. The floor was Italian marble and covered by large, red Persian carpets. Many crests of the former Hohenzollern Empire lined the walls. The crest of Mark Brandenburg had been hand-painted on the high ceiling.

The room was crowded. People were standing shoulder to shoulder, most holding champagne glasses. Mozart's music, played by a cellist, a violinist, and a pianist, was barely audible over the crowd's chatter. The guests' dress was as varied as their ages and nationalities. Some wore black ties, and others were dressed in very casual attire. There was much excitement in the crowd, and the mood was festive.

Then William saw him. Max was standing in a circle of a dozen guests. He was the center of the discussion, holding everyone's attention. He obviously was wheeling and dealing, William thought. He was a Habsburg.

"Max," William called. "Max, please, come over here. There is someone I want you to meet."

Max excused himself from his attentive audience.

"Katie, Peter, this is my best friend, Max," William said, beaming. "We have known each other ever since childhood. We are like brothers, Max and I, we are like family. So he is part of us all, part of our family."

Maximillian von Habsburg, direct descendant of the last Habsburg emperor, smiled as he greeted Katie and Peter Schneider. Again, Peter was surprised. Once more, he had expected an older person who was also more aloof and distant. But this man was no older than he was. Moreover, this man exuberated warmth and friendliness. He did not put on the air of a prince. His dress was casual: tan slacks, a black shirt, and a black V-neck sweater. He had the jovial face and the slight potbelly of someone who knew how to enjoy life.

"What a pleasure," he said, "I can't tell you how much William has anticipated your visit. William loves family, you know. He could not wait to meet you when he found out you were related. And neither could I."

Then he kissed the back of Katie's outstretched right hand, as William had done. He looked Peter right in the eye, put his arms around him, and hugged him.

"Thank you," Schneider replied. He immediately liked this man. Although it felt strange, he felt like he was reuniting with old friends and family he had not seen for a while.

"We, too, Katie and I, have looked forward to this moment. When we first got the invitation, we thought it was a hoax, a mistake. My parents never told me, but they probably didn't even know. I'm glad William did his homework. By the way, William, how did you figure out who I am?"

"That's a long story," William answered. "As Max said, one of my hobbies is my family. I have studied my ancestry closely. It is something of a concern to people of our background, as you might imagine. Max, for instance, knows every Habsburg in the world, no matter how far removed from the family tree."

"I understand." Schneider felt a bit of a peasant among men talking about two of the oldest royal families in Europe. "I'm pleased myself to find out about the family I still have here in Germany, in Berlin, where I was born."

"Well, now you are one of us," William said warmly, as if sensing Schneider's nervousness. "And we won't let you get away. There is an old saying: 'Once a Berliner, always a Berliner.'"

"Let's drink to that," Max said as Heinrich poured more champagne.

"And I understand that you ran the marathon," Max added. "You are an avid runner, I hear, just like William. Must be the Hohenzollern genes," he smiled. "We Habsburgs would rather eat and drink. We are not so driven as you are."

"Maybe I have some of the Habsburg genes as well," Peter replied. "Eating and drinking are the other two things I enjoy. Could I be part Hohenzollern and part Habsburg?"

They all laughed. Yes, Max thought, he is our man. He has it all, charisma, good looks, intelligence. He will make a fine leader. No, he corrected himself; he will be a fine man for me to lead.

By now, Schneider was completely at ease. He was enjoying himself. So was Katie. Everyone seemed to be paying attention to them. They were the center of the party. Katie could tell her husband had immediately taken to both the princes. He seemed to innately relate to them.

"Katie, Peter," William said, motioning to the crowded room. "I want you to meet some of our guests, some of my friends. I hope' you do not mind. Max, come along, please. You already know them all. But Peter, you must meet our chancellor, our president, the premier of France, all the important people who run the EU. I think I saw Boris Becker earlier and Kirill Petrenko, the new conductor of our orchestra. Do you mind?"

"Mind? Not at all," Katie Schneider said immediately, thinking of Boris Becker. "This is wonderful."

"And the Kaiser, William," Max interjected. "They must meet the Kaiser."

The Schneiders raised their eyebrows in surprise. Max and William exchanged a glance and smiled.

"Of course they will meet the Kaiser," William said. "Kaiser Franz Beckenbauer, Germany's greatest ever soccer player."

Nicole knew she would find him. She had studied the photographs, she knew his face. It was only a matter of time. However, the party was thronged with guests. There were more than 500 people. Slowly she moved through the crowd, searching. Adam followed her, his grandmother just keeping pace behind. Martha Bergman stopped to chat at every opportunity, obviously enjoying herself.

As Nicole paused again to wait for Martha to catch up, she realized that this woman obviously liked parties even more than her grandson thought she did. She was someone used to meeting people, someone who loved the excitement, loved being with people. She had had a lot of practice, years ago.

"Nicole, darling, this is such a wonderful party," Martha Bergman said, as she made her way through the crowd. "Don't you just love being here?"

"I do," Nicole said with a patient smile. "I'm so glad you and Adam asked me to come along."

"Well, between you and me, remember, I never said this, but between you and me, Adam thinks you are special."

"He does?" Nicole said, trying for Martha's sake to look embarrassed. "How do you know? Are you sure?"

"Child, I know because I am a grandmother. You don't get this old unless you know things like this."

A group moved past to get a drink, and Nicole saw him. He was not more than twenty feet away. People shaking his hand, clapping him on his shoulder, and engaging him in conversation surrounded him. There he was, looking just as he did in all the photographs she had studied. She took a breath and moved off toward Peter Schneider.

Making quick excuses to the guests she had shooed past, she was soon standing directly in front of Schneider, surrounded by at least ten people.

"Dr. Schneider, how nice to see you," Nicole said broadly. "I can't believe it, running into you like this, here in Berlin. You must have run the marathon. Oh, I'm sorry. Perhaps you don't remember me. I was a nurse in the CCU, remember?"

He did not remember. Then, he reminded himself, physicians rarely remembered their nurses, the people who were always there but never got the credit they deserved.

"Yes, of course," Schneider smiled, "I remember. How nice to see you. What are you doing in Berlin?"

"I ran the marathon. I'm sure you remember. We used to talk about it when you made your rounds. I guess you never thought I'd do it, did you?" she said as perkily as she could. "Well, here I am. I did it."

"That's wonderful," he said, sensing others were listening to this rather inane conversation. "I do remember. I'm glad you made it." Schneider was getting embarrassed.

"Dr. Schneider," she went on, "the only reason I did the marathon was because of you. You inspired me. I still remember you making your rounds in the CCU in the morning in your Nikes. That's when you told me you planned your life around running. And I told myself, well, if a doctor can do it, I can do it."

"Yes," Peter said, "I do remember." He was still drawing a blank. "Oh, by the way, Dr. Schneider," she said now, turning, "I would like you to meet my date, Adam Bergman, and his grandmother, Martha."

Martha Bergman was standing right next to her, determined not to miss a moment of the party. But her grandson was not there. He was a few feet away, chatting with another guest.

"Adam, Adam darling, come over here," Nicole called to him. "I want you to meet Dr. Schneider. I used to work with him."

Adam heard her and stopped in the middle of his sentence. He quickly excused himself and walked over.

"Dr. Schneider, a pleasure to meet you," he said. "Nicole has told me so much about you. And please let me introduce my grandmother, Martha."

Schneider took Adam's hand, then bent to kiss Martha lightly on the cheek.

"A pleasure," he said. "Please meet my wife, Katie."

They all took a moment to shake hands and exchange the obligatory kisses.

"Katie dear," Martha Bergman said, "how do you know Nicole? Is she family?"

"No," Katie responded. "I think she worked with Peter. I hear she's a nurse."

"How wonderful," Martha said. "I love medical people. They are so dedicated to helping others."

"Yes," Katie Schneider said. "That's what my husband used to think."

"Used to think?" Martha asked. "What happened? Why does he not think that way anymore?"

Katie Schneider decided she liked this older woman. She wanted her directness. She was someone she could relate to and talk to.

She turned and noticed her husband and Nicole's date were already engrossed in conversation. It was probably medicine or politics, she thought. In any event, she decided she would rather speak with the older woman.

"It's a long story," she said. "Are you sure you want to hear it?"

"When you are my age," Martha Bergman said, "you love long stories."

Nicole stood between conversations, wondering which she should join. She decided quickly.

She would join the women. That is where you learned the most.

CHAPTER XXXI

Berlin, Grunewald, September

T HE PARTY EXCITEMENT HAD REACHED ITS peak. Several dignitaries had arrived, including the president of France and the chancellor of Germany. William and Max were busy introducing Peter Schneider to all the proper people. The people they needed to make sure their plan would succeed.

Nicole had been told this party was important; it was part of the plan of the Ring. Surely, reason would dictate that she should stay close to her date, to Adam, who appeared to be part of it all. But Pistol Pete, the DDO, her boss, had told her the real key lay with Martha, Adam's grandmother. And Nicole's instinct told her to stay with the women. Somehow, she knew, this is where she would find the key, the answer the CIA sought.

"Do you mind if we sit for a moment?" Martha Bergman said, putting a stray lock of hair back in place. "I get tired these days. I can't walk and stand as much as I used to."

"No, please, not at all," Katie Schneider said, gesturing to a doorway across the ballroom she had spotted earlier. "Let's sit down. It looks as if there's a library over there. We can sit and talk. Nicole, will you join us?"

"Yes, if you don't mind," Nicole answered. "I don't want to listen to a conversation about politics or golf. Let's sit down and chat."

"Thank you, dear, you are so thoughtful. How lucky your men are to have such wonderful ladies. I had the most wonderful man. It was long ago. But I will never forget him."

The three women found their way into the palace library. It was the room where Max and William enjoyed their Padrón cigars after dinner at the Schildkroete Restaurant. Again, a fire was blazing in the large floor-to-ceiling fireplace. The room was empty, and they sat down in the deep brown leather armchairs placed around an antique card table. Music filtered from one of the bands playing at the party. It was classical, soothing, and it lent itself to conversation. "So why are you here tonight?" Katie Schneider said to Martha Bergman when she was settled.

"Do you really want to know?" Martha answered. "I am an old woman and so it will be a long story."

"Please, tell," Nicole encouraged her, giving her a daughterly pat on the hand. "Tell her this is your hometown, where you were born, where you grew up."

"I guess Adam told you all about me." Nicole was caught off guard. She had made a mistake. Adam had not told her, the CIA folder had. "Yes, yes he did," she answered quickly. "He loves you very much."

"Yes, I'm curious," Katie put in. "Please tell me."

"Well, I was born here," Martha began. "And here I married the most wonderful man. He was an artist, a poet. Every day with him was like a poem. I could not have asked for more. We had everything, a villa in town, a villa at the Wannsee, parties every night. My husband was the center of universe. Everyone loved him, everyone adored him. Then the war came and destroyed it all. My dream was over. And when I was heavy with child, our firstborn, my husband killed himself."

"What happened?" Katie said. "Why did he do it?"

"Well, Katie, we are Jewish. When the Nazis came, they tried to kill us all, but not our family, not Josh and me. He was too famous, too important. But finally he broke, he could not stand it, he wanted to be with his people."

"How sad." Katie looked at her. "You must have suffered terribly."

"But that's all in the past now," Martha answered. "Now I am happy. I have my grandson. That's all that counts. He is why I am living; he is my will to continue."

Nicole reminded herself she had a job to do, but still she felt for the old woman. How much she must have suffered, and how much she must have forgiven. A remarkable woman.

"But what happened to your baby?" Katie asked, not willing to let the story end.

"Oh, my baby, he, he was born prematurely, only a few days after my husband killed himself."

"And where is he now?" Katie urged on.

"Well, after he was born, right after, I took my baby and we fled Germany. We went to the United States. There I raised him, he got married and had a son, my grandson, Adam, and then he and his wife died in an accident when Adam was fifteen. I have raised Adam ever since. He really is my son, my love, my heart and soul."

Tears had formed in Katie's eyes.

"Grandma, you have suffered so much. Does it not hurt to come back here now, to the place where all the hurt began?" Nicole asked.

"No," Martha said immediately. "I love being back here. This is where I was born, my roots are here, and I feel I belong here. Do you understand?"

"I don't," Katie replied. "But my husband would. Peter was born here, too."

"Really?" Martha said. "Peter was born in Berlin. You know, I could tell. I knew he was a Berliner. I sensed it. There was a certain familiarity, a commonality; I sensed that your husband and I had something in common. You know there are not many left, us true Berliners. I guess it's just an old woman's intuition."

"Yes, he was born here near the end of the war. His family did not emigrate to the United States until he was fourteen or fifteen. So he spent many of his formative years here. Moreover, he's proud of it. He still calls himself a Berliner."

"Well, that's what Berlin does to a person. No other city does it. It captures you. You can never let go. I feel the same way, Berlin will always be my home."

"Your true home?" Nicole asked. "You've spent most of your life in the U.S."

"As I said, my roots are here. You can't change that. I was born a Berliner and I will die as one."

"It's funny," Katie continued. "We have so much in common. Your son, Adam's father, was born here near the war's end. So was Peter, my husband. Peter is a doctor. And I think he still brags about the fact that Berlin's, no Germany's, best doctor delivered him, Dr. Sauerbruch, was his name."

"Dr. Sauerbruch," Martha Bergman asked, surprise in her eyes. "Are you sure he was the doctor who delivered your husband?" "Yes, I'm sure," Katie said. "I think he was famous, at least that's what Peter always tells me. He's proud of the fact that he delivered him. I guess it's a doctor thing."

Suddenly, Martha was uneasy. Nicole noted the change in her demeanor. The older woman was breathing heavily. She no longer smiled. But clearly, she wanted the answer to one more question. Or did she? Nicole could see something she wanted to know but could not ask. Perspiration appeared on Martha Bergman's upper lip. When she spoke, it was almost a whisper.

"Tell me, Katie," she said so faintly that the other two women could hardly hear her. "Where was he born, and what is his birthday?"

"Peter was born at the Charité," Katie said, "on October 15, 1944." Now she knew. Finally, the older woman knew.

Nicole did not know. She sensed it. She could feel the answer was there in front of her. Right in this very room, in the library of William von Hohenzollern, the direct descendant of the Hohenzollern Empire.

Martha Bergman did not look well. She was slumped in her chair, breathing hard, and tears ran down her cheeks.

"Nicole," she said in a voice barely audible. "Nicole, I need to go home. I need to go back to the hotel. Could you arrange it, please?"

"Of course, Grandma. Are you ill? Should we call a doctor?"

"No, no please," Martha said quickly, "I am fine. Don't call Peter. Please don't. Let's not bother him. It's just that I had a long day. I need my rest. Just get me a taxi, please!"

"No," Nicole said firmly. "I'll call Adam, and he will decide. You definitely don't look well."

"Child, I am fine," Martha said, just as firmly. "Now I must insist. You and Adam stay here and enjoy the evening. Katie too. I cannot tell you how much I have enjoyed your company. You are such wonderful people."

"But I would feel so much better if you would let my husband check you out," Katie said, "just to ensure you're okay. Please, it will only take a minute."

"It's not necessary," Martha said. "I don't want any fuss. I'm sorry if I upset you all. I'm fine. It's been a long day."

Nicole knew better from her training: Never take anything at face value. The conversation had upset Martha Bergman. The discussion of Peter Schneider, his place and date of birth, had triggered it all. Now, she also knew where she had to go. She was close to the answer, close to the information that the president of the United States had had no opportunity to share.

Weiss and Jacob were bored. They hated surveillance. They knew nothing would happen for hours, probably not all night. They had followed Adam to the Grunewald palace and were now positioned in the woods near the front gate. There was no reason to go further, no reason to take the risk. If Adam were to leave, he would leave by the front gate, and they would see him.

But Weiss felt uneasy. He knew someone else was out here with him, in the woods of the Grunewald. He made a decision. He knew he had time; Adam would be at the party for a few hours, and at the party, he was safe. Weiss decided to take out the other pursuer. Silently, he doubled back through the woods to the estate entrance. He was careful, making his way in a long arc. It took him almost an hour. He did not know exactly where the other man was; he had not seen him. But he knew he was near the gates of the estate. That's where a professional would be.

Weiss carried a Beretta, like all Mossad *katzas*. He had to get close. He knew he had to be facing this man. It would not be easy, but he would do it. His mission was to protect Bergman. And someone else was out there, in the woods of the Grunewald, who had a different mission. Weiss would stop him.

Adam Bergman liked the doctor at once, and the feeling was mutual. Schneider felt this young man, whose date was the beautiful nurse he could not remember, was special. During their first conversation, they both found they had much in common. Both were runners, both had just completed the marathon; Adam's grandmother was a Berliner, as was Schneider. They had much to discuss, so they hardly noticed their women had left to speak alone.

"Please, Peter," Max von Habsburg interrupted the two men's conversation. "Please introduce William and me to your young friend."

"I'm sorry," Schneider said. "This is Adam Bergman. Adam, this is Prince Maximillian von Habsburg and our host, Prince William von Hohenzollern."

"I'm Pleased to meet you," Adam said, flashing a smile he hoped would convey the innocence of a wide-eyed tourist. I'm grateful you invited me. It's a wonderful party."

Max and William took turns shaking his hand.

"Are you a friend of Dr. Schneider?" one of the princes asked.

"No. No, I am not. I am a banker. I work for Ross Bank."

"Of course," William said. "You are their representative. I apologize that Morris could not make it, but I'm glad we have someone from your esteemed institution."

He turned to Max. "Max, these people do some of my investing. They are a small Wall Street bank but do an excellent job."

"I would love to sit down with you sometime," Max told Adam. "I'd be interested in learning more about your bank and the services you provide."

"Great," Adam replied. "I'm not going back to the States till the middle of next week. So maybe we can meet on Monday or Tuesday. I mean, if that's convenient for you."

"Let's make it Tuesday," Max said. "I would prefer the morning, but let me call you at your hotel next week, and we can set up a time and place. Where are you staying?"

"At the Adlon."

"Oh, a great hotel. I think it is Berlin's best."

"Adam, Adam," came a voice, carrying a note of urgency that made all three men turn. "Adam, can I speak with you briefly, please?"

It was Nicole.

"Of course. Gentlemen, please excuse me."

Adam turned and followed the Nicole into the library. "It's your grandmother."

"What happened? Is she okay?"

"I think so," Nicole said. "But she wants to go back to the hotel. She says she's tired. Katie suggested her husband look at her, but your grandmother refuses. She wants me to call her a taxi to take her back. I insisted you speak with her first. It's strange, the three of us were just talking and suddenly your grandmother got very upset. She just wanted to leave."

"What were you talking about that upset her so much?"

"That's just it. It was just girl talk. Nothing specific, nothing I can put my finger on."

The lie slipped into the festive air.

CHAPTER XXXII

Berlin, September

EISS WAS WITHIN TWENTY-FIVE YARDS BEFORE he saw him, crouched in the bushes just inside the gate of the estate. He was camouflaged in a dark green shirt and dark brown pants. He had positioned himself close to the driveway.

Weiss reached into his pocket and slid out his Beretta, then the silencer. Slowly he threaded it onto the barrel. It would get difficult. He had to get very close. Then he got the break he needed. Cars were coming down the long driveway, leaving the palace, and his target was focused on the departing automobiles. The sound of their engines covered Weiss as he made his move, walking in a low crouch to within ten yards of the figure kneeling before him.

He took aim at the back of the man's brown haired head and squeezed the trigger. The man's head jerked, the man pitched forward. He stood over the body and squeezed the trigger four more times. Then he turned the man over and could not believe what he saw. My God, he thought, what have I done? Why did no one tell me? "Maza, Maza," he mumbled, "you should have told me. Maza, what is happening, what is your game?"

Weiss sat in a crouch. He smelled the sour cordite and the coppery scent of blood and thought for a long while. What does this mean? There was a lake not far away. This was the logical choice. He dragged the body to the lake and tied a large rock around the dead man's waist. Then he pushed the body into the water.

It was almost one in the morning when the taxi left Prince William von Hohenzollern's palace.

"I have a wonderful idea," Adam told Nicole in the Mercedes cab next to him. She was resting her head on his shoulder.

"Well, let's hear it," she said. "I love wonderful ideas."

"Let's have the cab drop us at the Pariser Platz at the Brandenburg Gate. Then we can walk along Unter den Linden, go to the Gendarmenmarkt, and then to your hotel. It's such a beautiful evening, and a little walk would do us both good."

"Okay, let's inhale some of this special air, this *Berliner Luft*. I love to walk at night."

The taxi dropped them at the curbside of the Hotel Adlon. Adam paid the driver and wished him good night as he took Nicole's hand. Then they set out leisurely along the wide boulevard, lined with lime trees. It was indeed a beautiful night. Many couples were enjoying a walk.

"Nicole, tell me," Adam said after a time. "Why are you in Berlin? Did you follow me from Miami to be my date tonight?" "Of course. Don't beautiful women follow you around the world all the time?"

"Seriously. I want to know."

"Okay. I am a spy. I work for the CIA. You're my target."

"Are you going to kill me?" he asked with a smile.

"No," she answered. "I'm supposed to fall in love with you. Those are my orders." They both laughed.

"Please, Nicole. Tell me the truth."

"Sorry," she said. "I just love to tease you. It's so easy. No, I came here to run the marathon. I've always wanted to visit Berlin, and the marathon was a great excuse."

"Will you be going back soon?"

"Not right away. I've got a little work to do next week. I'll be back in Miami by next weekend for sure. What about you?"

"I'm heading back in the middle of next week. What kind of work do you do? I know you're not a nurse."

"You're right. I just said that so we could meet Dr. Schneider and the others," she added quickly.

"Why did you want to meet Dr. Schneider so much? How did you know about him?"

Nicole had made a mistake.

"Well," she said, thinking quickly, "he was standing there speaking with the prince, and I wanted to meet Prince William and Prince Maximillian. I've heard so much about them. Pretending to know Schneider, let me cut in and meet everyone."

"But how did you recognize Schneider? How did you even know his name?"

"Oh, that," she said. "On my flight from Washington to Berlin, I was sitting next to this American doctor going to Berlin to attend the Health Congress. He talked for hours about it. He had a program he showed me. That's where I saw Schneider's picture and his name. He was listed as a speaker."

Nicole suspected Adam knew who she worked for. After all, he had asked his grandmother to deliver the note to her. Nicole decided to play along. She saw him nod, but she did not see the faint smile that played across his lips. Adam smiled because he was sure. After all, he had relied on it. That's how he had saved the president of the United States. But he would wait for the call, for confirmation.

"Well, we're here," Nicole said, interrupting his thoughts. "My hotel. Thanks for a lovely evening. I enjoyed myself very much."

"Will I see you again before you return to the States?"

"I'd like to, but I have some work to do," she said. "Call me later this afternoon. I'll know better then."

She put her arms around his neck and kissed him. Adam felt the warmth of her body. He felt her thighs pressing against his. Then, suddenly, she let go, turned, and walked quickly into the lobby of the Berlin Hilton. She did not look back; she was already thinking about what to do next. She knew where she had to go and which records she had to examine. She hoped they were still there, not lost or destroyed at the war's end or in the chaos that followed. Then she realized that tomorrow, or today, since it was past one a.m., was Saturday. The record room would not be open on the weekend, nor at the Charity Hospital.

CHAPTER XXXIII

Berlin, September

THE LIBRARY AT THE PALACE OF Prince William von Hohenzollern was filled with cigar smoke. Three men sat, sipping cognac and smoking the two princes' favorite cigars. William had bought the anniversary edition of the Padrón cigar to surprise his friend Maximillian. Smoking Padrons together always seemed to strengthen their friendship. Now they had a new friend, another man to bond with. It was one-thirty a.m., and the guests had gone. As usual, the party had been a great success. Now, Max and William could relax. They settled back in the deep, comfortable leather chairs and enjoyed their cigars. So did Schneider. He felt among friends. He knew it had happened quickly, but it happened quickly because of the chemistry. They had much in common; they thought alike. They did not speak; they relaxed, smoked cigars, and drank cognacs. This is what friends can do.

Katie Schneider was enjoying the company of Maximillian's wife, Claudia. Claudia was a handsome woman, ten years younger than her husband. She had short brown hair and dark brown eyes.

Claudia was talkative, inquisitive, and did not mind sharing her opinions. Katie liked her openness, her directness. They were sitting on the porch overlooking the magnificent estate and sipping glasses of wine. They, too, were relaxing; they, too, had bonded. After all, this was family, and now that all the others were gone, they could relax, secure in the knowledge they were among their own.

William drew on his cigar. Slowly, he released the smoke. Then he broke the silence in the library.

"Peter, Max," he said, "this is one of the best moments of my life. Really, I have a new friend and so do you, Max. However, he is not just a friend; he is family. As I sit here, I ask Where have you been? It's as if you are my brother, someone I have sought for so long. It's strange. It's the nature of family. Somehow, we know we belong together. Wouldn't you agree, Peter?"

"William, I must be honest. As I told you earlier, when I first received your invitation, I thought it was a mistake. Once I got to Berlin, I felt a little different, not much, but I felt more comfortable. After all, I was born here; I grew up here. Then, when I got to your home and met you, William, that's when I knew. I knew this was my home too. I can't tell you why exactly. However, the moment you and I met, there was something special. I guess that's family. Yes, I do agree."

"Absolutely," William replied. "Heinrich did not have to point you out to me. I would have known. Yes, I knew we were related on a very distant basis. I looked into it. A long time ago, one of my great uncles married someone in your family. It was long ago, but you know genes. Here we are, I feel like you are like my brother, a brother I never had." "Let us hold it right there," Max interrupted. "This is too much Hohenzollern talk, too much Prussian. Are you sure he's not really related to my family, the Habsburgs?"

"Max, you are right," William said. "I am sorry. After all, this is the twenty-first century. No longer are we fighting each other. I did I don't want to imply that Peter and I were different from you. We are all Germanic. We all have the same roots."

Schneider could not believe the evening. It all had happened so fast. He had met many influential people. But Max and William controlled it all. They had decided who he was to meet and for how long. He did not understand why. He was surprised that anyone had paid attention to him and Katie. He seemed to be the focus of the party. William and Max had made sure of it. Then, when William introduced him as family, it made sense. They all knew his distant cousin, Prince William. Why shouldn't they know him? He was family.

"Peter," William said, "tonight you are staying at my home. Heinrich has already prepared your room. No sense going back into town. It's too late. In fact, I would like you to stay here as long as you are in Berlin. My home is your home. Please, I insist. Heinrich will cancel your arrangement at the Regent. Stay with me. If you need to go into town, one of my drivers will always be available. Besides, I really want to show you Berlin, and the surrounding area, the Mark Brandenburg."

"Yes. Who better to show you than someone who has owned it all for over five hundred years?" Max put in.

Schneider did not know how to respond.

"Peter, tomorrow we will go for a run. I will run with you through the beautiful Grunewald. There is nothing like it, I assure you."

The North African Desert, September

They were huddled in their tents in the North African desert. They had just received new information: their missiles, the Strella missiles, had failed. Yes, a helicopter had been downed, but the president had not been on it. This changed the mood in the tent. Most of the members of the splinter group of Al-Qaeda were already drunk. So were the mercenaries. They had begun to party earlier when the news broke. A Strella missile had killed the president of the United States of America. One of theirs. Quickly, their leader had taken the credit. They were angry now that they had learned the President had not been in the helicopter. This was an embarrassment, an insult to them. No doubt, the leader thought, the Israelis were behind this. He left the tent to look at the stars in the clear night sky. He needed to clear his thoughts. He needed to leave the tent where the mercenaries were drinking, gambling, and fighting with each other. His orders were to stay in the desert, train the mercenaries, and prepare them for the acts Allah demanded. And he knew the day would come when his people would conquer, when all the infidels would die.

No longer did he notice the stench of unwashed human bodies, the smell of marijuana, the language of tongues loosed by alcohol, the frustrations, the loneliness. Too long had he lived in the tents, too long had he lived with the mercenaries. They did not understand his cause; they did not believe in Allah.

The Israelis had arranged events to make them look like bumbling fools. Now the Arabs needed revenge, to show the world they were a force to reckon with. They had done it before. They must do it again. They needed a new target, the Arab leader thought. Once more, he looked at the sky. Then he knew. They would kill the European Union's president-to-be, Dr. Peter Schneider. This way, they would get even.

He smiled. Yes, they knew about Peter Schneider, too. The Mossad might think they are the best, but Al-Qaeda had its way. The man had called from Basel when the Strella missile sale went down. And

Jacob called often. But their most important asset was in the midst of all the action and decisions.

As he returned to the tent in the North African desert, he looked up into the endless star-strewn sky. *"Ala bub, Allah,"* he said. Whatever will be, we will leave it to Allah. Of course, he would not. A plan was already forming.

Tel Aviv, Israel, September

News travels fast, even from the tents in the North African desert.

"We can't let this happen," Maza Sharef said into the telephone at Mossad headquarters in the Hader Dafna Building in Tel Aviv. "Call the Berlin station and our European headquarters in Brussels. Put the best team together. I want him protected. And remember, no one can know, especially not Schneider. If a mosquito comes close, I want it swatted. Am I clear? Protect him like our prime minister. No, protect him better. I'm counting on you. The fate of Israel rests on your actions."

Sharef put down the telephone. Those damned Strella missiles. Maybe he'd made a mistake. Perhaps he should have done things differently. He had thought they were home free. But they never were. That was the destiny of his people. Sharef surveyed his plain desk. They will try it, he thought.

Al-Qaeda will mount an operation to kill Schneider. How would they do it? They would not pull the trigger; they will use someone else. Sharef came up with three possibilities, three terrorist groups to choose from. First, it would be a European group, Action Directe of France, the Italian Red Brigade, or Germany's Red Army Faction, or RAF. Which would it be? At first, he thought it surely would be the obvious: the RAF. After all, Schneider was in Germany now, and Sharef knew the terrorist group wanted to strike quickly.

That was too obvious. No, Sharef thought, the terrorists are devious, and therefore they will pick the French. In addition, they will pick the French for another reason as well, if French terrorists kill the EU president, it will undermine the close relationship the German and French heads of state now enjoy. That too appeared too obvious. No, he thought, they would pick none of these. They would use the unexpected; they would use the PKK. After all, the PKK, or Kurdistan Workers' Party, had a strong foothold in Germany. This country has more than 500,000 immigrants of Kurdish origin. It is estimated that the PKK has a force of 10,000 in Germany and an additional 40,000 supporters. The RAF helps to train them in the guerrilla camps. Moreover, lately, the EU has become a target for this Turkish-based terrorist group. Yes, it will be the PKK, Sharef was almost inevitable. No matter how soon, he would know for sure. His people would find out. The Mossad would be ready.

CHAPTER XXXIV

Berlin, Grunewald. September

THE SUNDAY BRUNCH AT PRINCE WILLIAM von Hohenzollern's palace took place in the rose garden. Heinrich and his staff had prepared tables there. It was a beautiful setting on a beautiful September day in the Grunewald in Berlin. William had insisted, and Max had agreed, that they should meet in the garden. It obviously was an idyllic place for a brunch, but that was not their primary reason. They were concerned about security. They had heard of no imminent threat, but you cannot be too careful, they had agreed. Before Schneider had moved into the palace early on Saturday, William and Max had the house swept for bugs and added three additional security guards. Now six armed men protected the estate.

To be certain, William had instructed Heinrich to set up the brunch in the rose garden, and he had done so only an hour before the first guest was to arrive. He mused that the only bugs we would have now would be the Japanese beetles that love my roses, particularly the yellow ones.

It was a brunch for the princes. Only they had been invited, only they would vote. Max had been careful in selecting the Royals. The fewer the better, he had always thought. It would be much easier to control a handful. But Max could not leave out any family that was influential. He had been careful when forming the Ring over a year ago. First, he decided to include only those royal houses that had influence in France and Germany, which would control the EU. Ultimately, he knew, it would be the Germans, but, again, no sense taking chances. No reason to ruffle feathers, not now.

One royal house he did not mind snubbing was the English. Max did not want the British Royals involved. He did not trust them. Moreover, they were not real Europeans anyway. They were not Continentals. And they had much too close an allegiance to the United States. Max knew very well that the British used the Americans; no love lost there. But that's the nature of the Brits. You can't trust them. So he excluded them. Yes, they were family; the Brits might reasonably have been included. Every family has its black sheep; the British Royals were Europe's—no British Royals in the Ring.

All the others were at the brunch: the Bourbons, the Habsburg-Lorrains, the Hohenzollerns, and the Saxons. Each house had sent the head of the family. They all were of similar ages, except the prince of the house of the Lorraines. He was only thirty-two years old, but Max did not mind. He was an impressionable person, and he and Max had a long-standing relationship. Max had known him since birth; he was family; they all were. They shared the same genes.

The atmosphere was formal. Most princes wore blazers with the crest of their respective royal houses. Heinrich had meticulously prepared the table in the garden. There were no place cards. Heinrich had used silverware and plates engraved with the banner of each of the princes' former empire. The seating was determined by protocol. The most powerful royal would sit at the head of the table.

Yet it was also a gathering of relatives, of uncles and cousins, no matter how distant, who all still knew they were family. Max had made sure they all understood the common cause, their reason for being there. Once more, their families, our family, as Max liked to say, would rule Europe. Today, they would meet Schneider, and they would vote. Max had no doubt Schneider was their man, and he was equally confident that Schneider would accept.

He was right on both counts. All the princes were impressed with Schneider. They liked his looks, demeanor, intellect, and charisma. They also wanted his background. Born in Germany, a blueblood like the rest, yet raised in the United States, the heart and soul of democracy. Yes, they agreed quickly, he was the perfect choice. Once Max had met Schneider and spent the evening with him at William's party, he knew that selling him to the Ring would be easy. Schneider would sell himself. Max knew all the other princes; how they thought, and what they wanted.

The one unknown was Schneider. Max had worried about him at first. Would he take the position? Would he understand? How should we present it to him? Max knew he would have to do the selling, and it would not be easy. All day Saturday, he had planned and rehearsed. After brunch, the princes would all meet in the library of William's palace, without Schneider, and there they would vote.

They did, and the vote was unanimous. Each shook Peter's hand, hugged him, and invited him to their estates. Each of them really liked this man. Now, Max's work began. It was up to him to ensure that Schneider accepted the position. It was up to him to see that the princes would control Europe again, this time for good.

"Peter, what do you think?" William began. "Did you like those fellows? I am sorry they asked so many questions, but they really wanted to get to know you."

William, Max, and Peter were seated on the veranda overlooking the four-acre spring-fed pond, which was adorned with blooming water lilies. A trout occasionally surfaced to disturb the still surface of the lake.

"Oh, I didn't mind at all," Schneider said. "They were all very nice. You're right, they did ask many questions. I guess they really wanted to get to know me. Is that what you do? Is that what royal families always do when they meet an unknown relative?"

Max smiled. Schneider had been surprised and a little uneasy during the brunch. Now the time for questions was over. Now it was time to lay all the cards on the table. He sensed it was what Schneider wanted. He could see it in the man's eyes, that faint gleam that comes to any man who catches the scent of power. Besides, he is a doctor. They want the facts, the data. That is how they make their decisions. "Peter," Max began, "I would like you to listen to me, and please listen carefully. Everything we have told you is true. You are related to William, although it is a very distant relation. Both William and I think the world of you. Truly, we believe we've made a friend for life in just a day or two. That is why I feel compelled to be honest. So does William. Let me go back. When you first received the invitation to attend William's party, you thought it was a hoax or a mistake, remember?"

"That is what I thought."

"Well," Max continued, "it was neither. It was part of a well-designed, carefully prepared plan, a plan that will change the balance of power in the world. Wait," he held up a hand. I know this may sound melodramatic, but hear me out, and then you can be the judge and tell me if you agree. Have you heard of the European Union?"

"Yes, of course," Schneider said. "Politics is sort of a hobby of mine."

"Well, I will not examine all the history and the details. However, if you want more information, please stop me and ask. I will answer all your questions to the best of my ability. The EU is changing. It is reorganizing itself. It has been realized that its current structure is inadequate. In the future, the EU will be more like the United States of America; it will be the United States of Europe. In addition, with all that, the EU's presidency must change. The new EU president will have unprecedented powers, much like the U.S. president's, because the EU will be a world power and rival the United States. Understand me, we do not want to challenge the United States, but we all should agree that a balance of power is good for everyone. After all, your U.S. constitution, calls for a balance of power even within your own government. The Europeans and the world now feel that the United States is too dominant. I believe that this is true. We need to establish a balance. We need checks and balances. You have it in your constitution; we need it in world politics. The EU will provide this. There is no doubt."

"Well," Schneider said. "I agree, that is what democracy is all about. But you're thinking not about democracy in one country only, but democracy worldwide."

"Exactly, Peter. You understand," Max replied. "I knew you would. We need to establish a worldwide democracy. We need a balance, a balance of power."

"Max. You should be a politician. You should run for office, the office of President of the World. I would vote for you."

I am running for that office, Max thought. However, I will not be elected. I will achieve this position the Habsburg way.

"Peter, the EU will be a world power, and our government will be very much like yours, with one major exception, the office of the EU. The President will be a powerful one, maybe even more powerful than the office of the United States president. But our president will not be elected; he will be appointed."

"Appointed? How? Why?" Schneider asked.

"Well, look at your elections," Max went on. "The costs, the competition, all of the name-calling, the bad politics, and finally the man who wins loses. No, we Europeans think that this decision is too important to leave to the voters. After all, let us face it that most people do not know or care what it is all about. Should they have a say? Many of them do not even pay taxes."

Schneider laughed.

"Peter," Max began again. "In one year, the new president of the EU will be appointed. The people you have met at the party and, most importantly, the men you have met today, will decide on the new president. They will say who will lead Europe with this new and unprecedented power. Peter, I have talked with all of them, and we have decided. We want you to be president of the European Union."

A trout plopped across the pond surface, a silver flash, then it was gone.

"Max, I'm sorry. What did you say?"

"I was asked to find the most qualified person for the office. I selected you. Before you say anything, think about it; you have all it takes. You are our man, and now, today, everyone has agreed. The rest will be a formality. Of course, we must go to all the heads of state and the EU people, but as I said, this is only a formality. You will be appointed."

"When, when would this happen?" Schneider asked, looking first at Max and then at William.

"Peter, you will be the United States of Europe president approximately twelve months from today," William said.

William had been silent. Max had wanted to run the show, and William had let him. William knew the Habsburgs; he knew they thought they could outwit anyone and were the consummate politicians.

Then Peter surprised them all. His answer was expected. They all knew he was a man of reason, a man who would see the whole picture, a man who would understand. But he surprised them with the quickness of his decision, with his direct approach.

"Very well," he said. "I'll do it. I'm your man. But I want to talk to Katie about it. And I want to be the first to do so."

Peter knew he had surprised everyone. He had thought about world politics many times in the past. Often, he had lengthy discussions with colleagues at Harvard, not physicians, but scholars of history and political science. Yes, Schneider was an American, and he loved his country. He believed in the principles that made America great. He was also concerned. He feared that America had become too strong, too dominant. He thought no nation should be dominant. History has taught that when a single nation exercises too much power, it invariably leads to disaster. The founding forefathers had foreseen this. But in those days, they looked only within the U.S. government and put in place assurances that one branch of government would not dominate the others. They never anticipated their country would become a world power and dominate world politics. Schneider was convinced that they would have created international checks and balances if they had. He believed in liberty, in justice for all, not just for Americans. He also believed in checks and balances. That is why he supported a strong European Union, a force to counterbalance the U.S. The E.U. would ensure there was not only the American way.

Max smiled, stood up from his chair, and approached Peter. Peter stood up also, and the two men embraced. Then Max kissed Peter on both cheeks.

"Peter," he said, "I knew. I always knew. You are our man." Schneider patted Max on the shoulder.

"Don't worry," he said. "I will take care. I will take care of it all."

Max knew he would. Physicians had large egos, they were ambitious, they were intelligent, they always wanted to control, and yet they wanted to help; they were suckers for a cause. Doctors, he thought, are just like the Royals.

"Max," William said, "let's celebrate. What a day! Heinrich," he called. "Please bring us another bottle of champagne."

"Yes," Max said, "let us have a toast to the new president of the United States of Europe. But give me a moment; I must make a short telephone call. Excuse me."

Max walked off the veranda and crossed the large ballroom to the library. He picked up the telephone and punched in a number.

"It is done," he said. "I want you here now. At once. I want him protected. No one, no one is to get close to him. I want the best, and I want them put in place now. Do not waste one minute. Do you understand?"

"I do," a man responded in a military tone. "No one will get close to him. There will not even be a mosquito that can bite him now."

The man put down the receiver of his telephone. He smiled. He was not a mosquito. He was the owner of a private protection agency. And he was a sayen.

CHAPTER XXXV

The North African Desert, September

"ALLAH BUB ALLAH," HE SAID AGAIN softly as he sat in his tent in the North African desert. But this time Allah will need help, he thought. Moreover, I will need help, as well. From the Red Army Faction? They seem to be the perfect choice; they are German and will be ready to strike at once. But no, the Israelis will anticipate this choice. Besides, he thought, I need to make a significant statement. I need to let the world know that we have power. So then the French. Yes, the terrorist group Action Directe. They will pull the trigger. It will be easy. No, not the French. They would not be ready to strike quickly enough and have been too inactive. He needed someone who had a strong presence in Berlin and could strike at once. And he needed someone who also despised the European Union. The PKK. Yes, the PKK will fulfill my mission. No one knows this Peter Schneider, the supposed future president of the EU. He will be an easy target. However, we must strike quickly, while he is still unprotected.

Little did he know, as he sat in his tent, that he was already too late. Not by much, but still too late.

Berlin, September

Overnight, Peter Schneider became the best-guarded man in the world, although he did not know it. He did not realize that Maza Sharef and the Mossad had dedicated all of their European resources to protecting him, and the Ring had done the same. No one would be able to get close to him.

William had convinced Schneider and his wife to stay at his palace. He had several reasons for wanting the future president there. He wanted to be close to Schneider, to get to know him well, to gain Schneider's confidence and friendship, and to make him feel part of the family. Most of all, he needed to protect Schneider, and he knew that this could be best accomplished if Schneider stayed with him.

Katie had been the first to agree. She loved the surroundings and the luxury, and she knew she would be the only woman in the palace. Schneider did not object. He liked William and his company. Naturally, he loved all the comforts of the palace. However, he had another reason: he needed time to understand what he had gotten himself into.

The ambulance left the Hotel Adlon and sped towards the Charité Hospital. The older woman was resting on the stretcher in the back. The siren blared and lights flashed, but it was a quiet Sunday afternoon in Berlin; traffic was light. The paramedics had made the correct diagnosis after arriving on the scene. The older woman had suffered a myocardial infarction, a heart attack. They had started an intravenous line and administered morphine. A cardiology team the two paramedics decided that she would meet them at the emergency room. She would be in good hands, and she would pull through.

The concierge at the Hotel Adlon had immediately called Adam Bergman's room to let him know his grandmother had taken ill and was being taken to the Charité. But there was no answer. So the concierge quickly went to Adam's suite and used his key to open it. The suite was empty. He returned to the lobby and approached the doorman of the hotel to inquire whether he had seen Mr. Bergman leave. The doorman had. Adam had left the hotel approximately forty minutes earlier, dressed in jogging attire. No doubt, he would be back soon, the concierge thought. And no sooner had he returned to his desk he saw Adam walk into the lobby.

"Mr. Bergman," he called out. "Please, I need to talk to you for a moment.

"What is it?"

"Well, it is your grandmother. She is ill. No reason to be alarmed. We called an ambulance and she is on her way to the Charitee. She may be there already."

"Took ill?" Adam said sharply. "What happened? Is she okay?"

"Yes sir. The paramedics think she had a mild heart attack. They took care of her right away. She will be fine."

"A heart attack. My God! Please call me a taxi.

"Yes, sir."

Adam walked to one of the public telephones in the hotel lobby. He dialed the number that rang the telephone at William von Hohenzollern's estate. He knew Schneider was staying there. Heinrich, the butler, answered the telephone. Adam asked to speak with Dr. Schneider.

"Of course," Schneider responded after Adam had explained his grandmother had taken ill. "I'll meet you in the coronary care unit. I can be there in twenty minutes."

Tel Aviv, September

Sharef was reminded almost at once that his network was the best. He knew immediately that Martha Bergman was at Charitee Hospital and that she had had a heart attack. He was also informed that Adam Bergman was on his way to the hospital and that Peter Schneider had been asked to go and examine the old woman. He knew all of this because Heinrich, William's butler, had made contact. Heinrich was a *sayan*.

Now Sharef worried. If the old woman got very sick, perhaps near death, she might reveal all to Schneider and her grandson. That is not what Sharef wanted. He wanted to set the stage, and he wanted to do all the explaining. He had to do it. He could not take chances. Sharef decided he must go back to Berlin. He needed to be there, to be in control. Unlike his archenemies in the North African desert, he feared he would be too late.

Berlin, September

Schneider hurried to the front door of the palace of William von Hohenzollern. A large Mercedes was waiting for him to take him to the Charity Hospital. As the limousine left the driveway and pulled onto Koenigsallee, a helicopter hovered above, and two cars followed. "Do you have him in sight?" one of the drivers of the two cars cars shouted into his two-way radio.

"Roger, I've got him. Stay back. Don't follow too closely," the pilot of the chopper answered. Schneider did not notice. He did not see how well he was being protected.

It was the end. Martha Bergman knew it. She felt comfortable after the paramedics had given her the drugs. As a matter of fact, she felt pretty well, almost silly to be going to the hospital. But as soon as she arrived, she felt more pain, much more pain. Her breathing grew labored. It would be over more quickly. She struggled; she wanted to stay alive, she wanted to see her grandson before she died. But then she was told that Peter Schneider was on his way to examine her, and now she felt a new pain, emotional pain. She had lived with it for so long, had hidden it from everyone, had ignored it, and had pulled the blinds and the shutters. She had done exactly what her husband, Joshua, had done: trying not to see or face it. Tears ran down her wrinkled cheeks. The pain in her chest she could cope with, but the emotional pain was far worse. She did not want to die this way; she wanted to die in peace. So she made a decision, she would struggle to survive, she knew how to do it, until Peter and Adam were at her bedside. Then she would tell the truth.

"Do not worry," the man said in a heavily accented voice. "We can take care of it. Yes, I know he is on his way to the hospital. Be assured he will not put his foot into the front entrance. My best people are there. He will be dead before he gets there. You have my word on it."

"Don't fuck it up," the Arab said. "I'm counting on you."

"It will be done."

He was wrong. It would not be done. Instead, the Mossad would do what the Mossad wanted done. The three-member PKK assassination team had no chance. The Mossad knew their plan already; they knew every detail. The Mossad also slept in a tent in the North African desert.

The terrorists would be stationed near the emergency ward entrance. Yes, they would be heavily armed. But their plan was crude, so crude that the Mossad thought it might be a decoy. It was not. It was all the Kurdish terrorists could muster. Fanatics made poor professionals. The three Kurds died quickly, minutes before Schneider arrived at the hospital. Each was shot in the head, four more bullets from close range. They were shot in public. In front of the emergency ward entrance, in front of several people. The assassins left the bodies where they fell. Almost leisurely, the two gunmen entered the car that waited for them.

CHAPTER XXXVI

Berlin, September

"NICOLE," THE MAN SAID OVER THE phone, "I want you on the next plane to Washington."

"Come home?" she said. "You're kidding. What happened to my mission? What about my target, Bergman?"

"It's over, Nicole," said Pistol Pete, her DDO. "Sorry. You did a great job, but you are no longer needed there."

"What are you talking about? I just made contact. He's starting to like me, trust me. Give me a few more days, and I'll have him. Isn't that what you wanted?"

"It was. But the situation has changed. We have new information that makes your job unnecessary. Sorry. You're off the case, starting now. Do you understand?"

"No, sir, I don't understand. However, I will follow orders. I will be back as soon as possible. I'll catch the next flight."

"Fine. Come to Langley. I want to explain things to you. You'll understand."

Nicole hung up the phone. She was angry. All they would ever let her see was a piece of the picture; she would never be entitled to see it all. She exited her chair in her room at the Hilton and started throwing clothes into her suitcase. She would follow orders. But she would do something first.

Adam Bergman was in his suite at the Adlon. He had just called Schneider and they had agreed to meet at the hospital. First, he had to change out of his sweaty running gear. He took a quick shower and dressed in casual clothes. The telephone rang and he jumped.

"Adam, everything is going according to plan. You have done a wonderful job, as usual, I might add. Your country is proud of you. I know your grandmother is ill. I hope she'll get better soon. These are trying times. However, don't forget your primary objective. If we're going to control Schneider, you need to win his confidence. I don't need to remind you. You're our best man. By the way, you're right, she is CIA. They have just called her off the case. She's coming back to D.C. on the next plane. I guess the two of you will have to fall in love some other time."

Adam's boss at the National Security Agency had not even waited for a reply.

CIA, Adam had been right. Then the phone rang again. "Yes," he answered impatiently.

"It's me. It's Nicole."

"Nicole, can I call you back later? My grandmother's sick. I'm on my way to the hospital now."

"Is she all right?"

"I don't know. The concierge said she looked okay when the ambulance picked her up."

"Then I'll be quick, Adam. I have to return to the States immediately, and just wanted to say goodbye. However, there's something else I need to tell you. I didn't tell you the truth last night about your grandmother. It wasn't just girl talk when she got upset. We were talking about her husband and her baby, your dad. She told us your father was born prematurely at Charité Hospital and that she took him with her when she fled to the United States."

"Hold it," Adam said." Is this one more CIA game? My dad wasn't born in Berlin. He was born in the U.S., after Grandma went there."

"No, Adam, listen. I'm being honest with you, that's not what your grandmother told Katie and me last night. Moreover, when she really got upset was when she found out Schneider was born at Charitee. She was stunned when Katie told her that Dr. Sauerbruch, I think that was his name, performed the delivery. Then she asked in a whisper, as if she didn't want to know, she asked the date of Schneider's birth. When Katie told her, your grandmother immediately wanted to leave the party." Nicole's voice faltered. "I don't know why, but I thought you should know."

"It's strange," Adam said, not able to conceal his interest. "Grandma always told me dad was born in the United States. I wonder why. Well, thanks for telling me this. I'll ask her about it when she gets better."

"Please, don't let anyone know I told you. It's important. No one can know."

"You have my word."

"Adam, when you get back to the States, please call me."

"You have my word on that too."

The shower and the phone calls had delayed Adam. He and Schneider arrived at the hospital at the same time. They ran into each other just outside of the coronary care unit, the CCU. They shook hands. They embraced. Solemnly they entered the CCU.

Schneider stopped quickly to pick up Martha Bergman's chart at the nurse's station, in the center of the unit. He studied it while Adam waited. The old woman had suffered a myocardial infarction, and it had extended since she had entered the hospital. The damage was severe, and she was now in heart failure. The cardiology team at the hospital had recommended immediate surgery, an angiogram; maybe balloon angioplasty or open- heart surgery to revascularize. Martha Bergman had refused. She wanted no such help. She had told them all she was born here and she wanted to die here.

Tears were evident as Schneider and her grandson approached. She appeared comfortable, not gasping for air. Yet she was crying. She took their hands and squeezed them.

She spoke so softly that the two men could not hear. Adam leaned over until they were cheek to cheek.

"You are my grandson, Adam. You always will be. I love you. You were my life. But I am ready to join your grandfather. This is my wish. This is not goodbye. It is *Auf Wiedersehen*. I know we will all meet again, your grandfather, your mother and father, and I. So please do not cry, do not despair. This is my wish. I want to die here, here in the city where my husband took his life. Please give me a kiss and then leave me alone with my doctor."

"Grandma, please," he said. "I want to stay with you."

"No, Adam," she said. "Please, leave me now. I love you." Reluctantly he obeyed.

"Take care of her. I'll wait outside," he told Peter as he left the CCU.

"Peter," Martha whispered. "Please listen to me."

Schneider leaned close and put his ear close to Martha Bergman's mouth.

"Please, Peter, hold my hand. You are my son," she whispered. "God, please forgive me. I had to do it. I had no choice. I wanted you to live. Please understand. You were born here, at the end of the war. I did what I had to do. I know God understands. I switched babies to give you life, to give my baby life. Peter, you are my true son, the son of Martha and Joshua Bergman. Adam is my grandson. I beg you, don't ever tell him different." Her voice was almost inaudible.

"God, please forgive me," she said once more.

Schneider had seen people die before, but today, it was different. Never before had he seen someone die so gracefully, eagerly, happily, and at peace.

Schneider was always in control. He took pride in it. That, he thought, was one of his attributes. Now, as the woman was dying, he lost control. He leaned over her and cried. And he did not cry softly. He sobbed. He vented. He let go of all control. Too much had happened to him in the past few days. The woman dying in the bed in front of him was his mother, and no sooner had he found her than she was gone. Now he had his own secret to keep from her grandson, Adam. Schneider wiped his eyes and face. He needed time to sort it all out.

As he left the CCU, Adam was waiting for him. They looked each other in the eye, and Adam knew his grandmother was gone. And Schneider knew he would never tell. He would never disappoint Adam and say Martha Bergman was not his grandmother. "Adam," Schneider said, "I want you to understand I will always be there for you."

CHAPTER XXXVII

Berlin, September

SCHNEIDER WAS SITTING WITH HIS WIFE on the veranda at William's palace. They talked about Martha Bergman's death and waited for Adam to join them for lunch. They had invited him because they knew this was a time when sharing was important. Their host, William, had left with Max to go to Brussels to keep paving the way. Peter was to join them there the day after tomorrow.

Heinrich interrupted to let him know he was wanted on the phone. He took the call in the library. It was tapped and it was taped. The Mossad was listening. The security around Schneider was airtight, but the phone call got through because it was Maza Sharef. "Dr. Schneider," he said. "You don't know me, but I must share some essential information. Obviously, we all have the same friends; otherwise, I cannot talk with you now. I suggest a private meeting. The information I have is personal. May I suggest the meeting place? How about Jagdschloss Grunewald at ten a.m. tomorrow? We can walk through the forest from there, just you and me. There is only one hitch: You cannot tell the princes about this. It must be you and me alone."

"Just a moment," Schneider said. "Who are you? I need to know."

"Let me just say this. You are Martha Bergman's son. Or you think you are."

Schneider was stunned. How did the man know? "I agree, let's meet," Schneider said.

"I want no one there, do you understand? He and I will be there only once I meet him at the Jagdschloss. It will take thirty minutes, then he will be back at the *Jagdschloss,* and you will resume your protection. He must be protected like no other person. Do you understand?"

Sharef hung up the phone with a bang. He had been too late. The older woman had died. He did not know her last words, but he could guess. He had lost control.

"Peter," Adam Bergman said in the palace library. Peter, Katie, and Adam had finished their lunch. Adam had asked to speak to Peter in private.

"I know I shouldn't do this, but it's right. And I will overwhelm you with information. But I can no longer hold back. I have to tell you all." He shifted in his seat and crossed his long legs.

"Yes, I'm the grandson of Martha Bergman," Adam said. "Yes, I came here to run the Berlin Marathon. However, I have to tell you more because I trust you. I can't deceive you. I came to Berlin on assignment. I work for the Ross Bank, but that's not why I'm here."

"Why did you come?" Schneider asked, "I came here to recruit you."

"Recruit me? What do you mean?" Schneider said.

"Well, it's very complex," Adam began. "Everyone, the Americans, the Europeans, the Israelis, they all think you have a chance to be the next president of the EU. So naturally, they all want a piece of you; they all want to control you. I'm ashamed to be a part of it. I work for the U.S. Government, the NSA, the National Security Agency. The Israelis think I work for them, the Mossad. I'm a double agent. Somehow, they all think you and I have something in common, but I don't know what. I think it was my grandmother, but I don't know."

"Slow down, Adam," Schneider replied. "It had nothing to do with your grandmother. I talked to her before she died. She loved you, but don't let anyone use that against you. Do you understand?"

"Yeah, I do. But something's wrong. The other night at the prince's party Grandma got very upset when she learned you were born in Berlin and delivered by Dr. Sauerbruch. In addition, when she learned your date of birth, she got agitated. It's all very strange. She also told your wife and Nicole that my father was born here in Berlin. However, that's not true. She's told me the story since I was a child, she escaped Germany when she was pregnant and then a midwife delivered my father in Manhattan shortly after she arrived."

"Who told you all this, Adam? I guess I already know. It's obvious."

"Yes, I guess it is. I'm sorry, I promised her not to let anyone know."

"Don't worry about it. As far as your grandmother is concerned, you have to remember she was getting old, probably losing part of her memory. That's not unusual for people her age. I'm certain whatever she told you is the truth. She loved you very much. You were like a son to her. Don't forget that. And, Nicole, okay, I am sorry, I hardly know her, but if she told you your grandmother got upset when she learned about my place and date of birth, then Nicole misread your grandmother. Clearly, something else was bothering her. My professional opinion is that she probably had a mild heart attack then. It only makes sense in view of what happened to her the next day."

"You're probably right. That's the more rational explanation. Sometimes women rely too much on their intuition."

"I know you took a real risk, you probably jeopardized your career to tell me who you really are. No one will ever know, Adam. You have my word."

"Thanks. It's funny, I always knew I could trust you. You were like family the minute we met. That's why I wanted you to know. I want no one to take advantage of you."

"Adam, I think I'm getting a hold of it all. I think I know what's happening."

Mark Weiss, Mossad *katza,* Adam Bergman's guardian angel, knew about the meeting at the *Jagdschloss.* He had access to all the telephone calls that came into Prince William's estate. Mark knew he would have to do it again. He would have to leave Adam unguarded. It would not be long, he knew, just half an hour, the same half hour that Sharef would be alone with Schneider in the Grunewald. Because that is when Sharef would be unprotected, and that is when Weiss intended to find out what game Sharef was playing.

It was a misty Monday morning in September. The forest, the Grunewald, looked almost eerie. A light mist covered the trees, and the visibility was poor. Nevertheless, Sharef saw him at once, standing in the cobblestone courtyard of the 450-year-old *Jagdschloss.* He was Schneider was dressed in running attire: a Nike sweatshirt, sweatpants, and running shoes. Although it was cool, Schneider was perspiring. He had left the palace early and taken his daily jog to clear his mind and be ready for the mysterious rendezvous. He knew the man he was about to meet was important. He knew, or rather he sensed, that after this meeting, he would be able to put together the pieces of this puzzle. After today, he would understand what was happening.

"Dr. Schneider," Sharef said softly as he approached. "Dr. Schneider, I am Maza. May I call you Peter?"

"Of course," Schneider replied. It is a pleasure to meet you. Your telephone call surprised me. But I knew I needed to see you."

"That was very perceptive of you. Let us get away from the Schloss. Let us walk down to the lake. There is not much time, so if you forgive me, I will be direct. I am the head of the Mossad, the Israeli intelligence agency. I know that takes you by surprise, but it should not. Everyone knows, or thinks they know, that you will be the future president of the United States of Europe. Naturally, they all want to influence you. I know all the players. We are only one of them. It is my job to make sure you understand our interests. I wanted to meet with you before Martha Bergman died. I wanted to be the one to tell you who you really are. However, I was too late. She died before I could get to Berlin."

"How did you know Martha?" Schneider asked.

"Well, you know, we Jews, we stick together. Josh and Martha Bergman, we were always close to them. And now we are close to their grandson, Adam."

"Okay," Peter responded slowly.

"I am guessing that the old woman told you the truth, did she?"

"Yes, she did. She told me I was her son. She had switched babies at the Charité to save her newborn. She was in a panic. She was desperate. When we met at the prince's party, she found out I was born in Berlin, at the Charité, and delivered by Dr. Sauerbruch on October 15, 1944. She knew then I was her son. She put me in the crib when she took the other child."

They were now near the lake, and the sun was slowly burning off the mist. It would be another beautiful day.

"So, Dr. Schneider, you are the son of Martha and Joshua Bergman. You are a Jew. You realize that?"

"Yes," Schneider said.

"And how do you think the Ring, the Royals, the princes of Europe, will respond when they find out?"

"I don't know," Schneider replied. "I really have not thought about it."

"Well, doctor, do you think the European aristocracy will allow a Jew to run their empire?"

"Where are we going with this? You told me time was of the essence. Get to the point."

"Peter, you are destined to be the most powerful person in the world. Most of the leading countries know it, and they want to control you. They want to claim you and convince you that you belong to them. I am an Israeli. I, too, wanted to have influence over you. I was convinced that this was the only way Israel could survive. Therefore, I wanted to contact you to tell you that you are really a Jew. I made every effort to get back to Berlin to meet with you before Martha Bergman died. I wanted to be the first one to tell you who you were. I was certain that if I did, I could convince you to be with us, to be a Jew, to help Israel survive."

"What happened? It sounds like you changed your mind."

"No, I didn't. I still love Israel. But on my way to Berlin, something happened that caused me to change my plan."

"What?" Schneider asked.

"I received some information that made me question everything. At first, this information stunned me. Then, the more I assimilated it, the more it became clear that I needed to share it with you. No one else but me knows what I am about to tell you."

Sharef had thought long and hard about this. Not long ago, he remembered sharing very important information with another important and powerful person, the president of the United States. And that had been a mistake. But today, Sharef knew he had made the right decision. The man he was walking with was not like the president of the United States. This man is honest, Sharef thought. He is fair. He will do the right thing.

"All your life you thought you were an American," Sharef said. "Then the other day, you were told you are a Prussian. Yesterday, you became a Jew. I guess you really do not know who you are, or where you came from, to be more accurate."

"That's true. Right now I'm pretty confused."

"Well, Peter, I am no different."

"No different? What do you mean?"

"I, too, do not know where I came from. Let me explain. Your mother, Martha Bergman, told you the truth. She did switch babies at Charitee's obstetrical ward on October 15, 1944. However, what Martha did not tell you, what she did not know, is that four boys were born that day at the hospital, and all of them lay in their cribs there. When Martha switched babies, the lights were out, and it was night. She could not have read the names on the cribs. Remember, she was in a hurry and a panic."

"What are you getting at? I don't understand?"

"Peter, I know you have experienced much turmoil in the past few days. I am sorry. I really do not want to make things worse. What I'm saying, though, that Martha did not know whose baby she took and into what crib she put her baby."

"Okay, okay," Schneider said. "Let's go back, Maza. Do you know the identity of all four male babies born on October 15, 1944, at Charitee Hospital?"

"I do know. That is the information I received while I was going to Berlin. That is why I changed my plan."

"Will you tell me?"

"Yes, I believe you should know. I will tell no one but you. And I will let you decide what to do with that information."

"You have my word I won't use the information to harm anyone."

"I know that, Peter. That is why I am telling you. The last names of the four male babies born at the Charité Hospital on October 15, 1944, were Rubin, Bergman, Schneider, and von Hohenzollern."

"Repeat those names."

"Rubin, Bergman, Schneider und von Hohenzollern." Schneider leaned against the nearest tree. They had reached the shore of Lake Grunewald. The mist was slowly disappearing, and the sun was showing its face.

"Rubin, Bergman, Schneider und von Hohenzollern.

"Maza," he said, "you obviously know what this means. Explain it."

"I will," Sharef said, "but only if you are sure you want me to. Remember, there will be only two people in the entire world who will know this. You and I."

"Explain it. I think I know part of it, but explain it."

"I think you have met them all, or almost all. One of the babies born then is no longer alive, Adam's father, Daniel Bergman. On the other hand, maybe that is not who he really was. We may never know. You have met the other two. You know William von Hohenzollern, the direct descendant of the Hohenzollern empire. Although again, I am not sure that's who he really is. Then there is one name left, Rubin. That was my name. After WWII, my family emigrated to Israel and changed their name to Sharef. Of course, I knew you and I had the same birth date. But I did not think I was born in Berlin's Charité Hospital. That is the information I received from a close friend on my way to Berlin. I had asked him to research the medical records at the Charité. I needed to know all about you."

Both men kept walking along the shore of the calm lake.

"It was not easy to locate the records," Sharef continued. "Usually, they are purged after several years. Because of the turmoil following the war, this was never done. My friend was able to locate the files."

Schneider had sat on the grass at the shore of Lake Grunewald. His mind was working feverishly.

"Why did you not know your place of birth?" Peter wanted to know.

"My parents had always told me I was born in Solothurn, a small town in Switzerland."

"Why?" Peter asked.

"When I received the medical records from the Charité, I called my father to verify my place of birth. Finally, he told me the truth. His best friend, a friend from early childhood, had become one of the highest officials in the Nazi party. That is why my family was allowed to stay in Germany. When my father decided to emigrate to Israel a few years after the war, he was afraid that his friendship with the Nazi might prevent the move. So he made up the story about Solothurn. I do have family there. My aunt, my father's sister, still lives there."

"Maza, let me make sure I understand."

"Go ahead."

"Four babies, four boys, were born at Charitee Hospital on October 15, 1944," Schneider said. "Rubin, Bergman, von Hohenzollern und Schneider."

"Yes."

"Your name is or was Rubin, mine is Schneider, Adam's name is Bergman, and William, Prince William, is William von Hohenzollern."

"Yes."

"In the middle of the night, Martha Bergman switched babies. But she didn't see any of the name tags; it was too dark, she was in a hurry, she was in a panic."

"Yes."

"All right, let me get to the bottom line. We have four baby boys, and there's been a switch. We don't know who was taken, and we don't know which crib the Bergman baby was put into."

"That's right."

"So that means we have three men now, only three, since Daniel died. They were all born on the same date, in the same hospital. Three men, who really don't know who they are."

"You understand. When I decided to tell you, I was very confused. I did not know what to do with this information. Now I know I have put it into the right hands. Remember, only you and I know. I will tell no one else. Also, remember that no matter who I am, I love Israel and I love my people. I am doing this for them, for the children of Israel."

Sharef was passionate when he said this.

"Maza, I don't know how to thank you. You have done so much, sacrificed everything, and did it all for the truth."

Maza nodded. "I know we will meet again, at least I pray we will. Now we must part and go different ways. Retrace your steps and get back to the *Jagdschloss*. That is the safe way. You will be well protected."

"Where will you go?"

"I will go through the forest. No one knows me. I don't even exist."

Abruptly, Sharef turned and walked away from the lake, not following the footpath but disappearing into the forest.

CHAPTER XXXVIII

Berlin, September

MARK WEISS KNEW THE TERRITORY. HE knew Lake Grunewald and the forest. The mist, the light fog, had been an act of God. It was easy to follow the two. They never noticed. Mark was patient. That is how Sharef had trained him.

He had been too far away to hear the conversation. But he clearly saw the men's faces. He waited. The men separated, one walking back along the path toward the Jagdschloss Grunewald, the other stepping into the trees, making his way toward a pickup point where a helicopter would be waiting.

It was a short hike, no more than ten minutes. Sharef had studied the map; he knew where he was going. He felt good and relaxed. It seemed that all his burdens and responsibilities of his job had been lifted. He was trusting the right man. The man would make sure that everyone was treated equally. He would make sure the children of Israel would survive.

When he heard the sound, he stopped. He had heard it many times before. It was the sound of a pistol being cocked. And it was close. No more than ten yards. He raised his arms and turned around.

Weiss, his *katza,* was only seven steps in front of him. The Beretta was pointed at Sharef's head.

"Mark, what are you doing here?"

"I'm sorry, Maza, but I need to know your game. I killed for you. I killed one of our own because I did not know."

"Relax," Sharef said gently. "Put down the gun. Everything is working according to plan. Trust me."

Sharef took a step forward.

"Stop, Maza, please stop. I need to know. I killed Jacob. I didn't know it was him. Why didn't you tell me he was following Bergman? I should have known."

"It's all right," Sharef said. "Give me the gun."

Sharef took a step forward, his hand reaching for the gun. The bullet hit Sharef between the eyes, killing him instantly. He stumbled, then fell on his face. Weiss pulled the trigger four more times. That is how Sharef had taught him.

Peter Schneider saw it on the news. An unidentified man was found shot to death in the Grunewald. They showed pictures. It was Sharef, so there is no doubt about it. As yet unidentified, they had said. Well, he never will be, Schneider thought. The head of the Mossad does not exist; there is no such person.

Schneider leaned back in the leather chair in William von Hohenzollern's library. This had become his home. From here, he would plan and prepare for his destiny—his destiny to be president of the United States of Europe.

It would be simple to decide which baby was which. DNA analysis could confirm this without a doubt. But did he want to know? Would it make any difference? What would it change? Schneider was now the only one who knew the secret. Maybe that's the way it was meant to be. An American, a Jew, a Prussian? Did it really matter? Do we really care? After all, now they will have it, they will all have control, because I'm one of them. That, he thought, was the true path to worldwide democracy, a leader who had not one interest at heart, but many.

Finally, the world could be one. He picked up his cognac and inhaled his Padrón cigar.

"Sir," a man interrupted, "may I refill your glass?"

Peter was startled and looked up. It was Heinrich, the butler.

"Please, Heinrich," he said. "Just one more."

Then Heinrich the *Sayan, Heinrich who had also been trained in the North African desert, pulled the trigger and ended the dream—the dream of the United States of Europe, the dream of a United States of the World, the* dream of how all people on earth could live together in peace. One bullet ended it all.

"THE END"

www.ingramcontent.com/pod-product-compliance
Lightning Source LLC
Chambersburg PA
CBHW041043310726
48978CB00011BA/418